"Will you hide me in the Palace?" Tron asked.

"I can't trust my servants."

"They will search all the Temple."

"Not this one place. We have blown the death horn. They have broken down the Gate of Saba. They can't stop the Ritual now, so they will be forced to show me as the new king to the people. By then you'll be far away. You will travel with my father."

Tron's heart leaped so that his body shook with the spasm.

"It's all right," said the King. "You'll travel alive . . ."

The coffin was like a mouth, waiting to swallow Tron. He twisted himself between its jaws, feeling with his bare foot for bare wood. Something rattled as he touched it, then he found the bottom and crouched shuddering down

"All right," he whispered.

The darkness came down on him and on the Hawk without a sound . . .

"A REAL RITE OF PASSAGE!"
  —Ursula K. LeGuin

PRAISE FOR
THE BLUE HAWK

"A lovely book . . . a novel that speaks to people of many ages . . . Warfare, ritual mythology, youthful questionings about life and death all combine to make a likeable adventure tale with special appeal for the Tolkien and Richard Adams audience."
— *Publishers Weekly*

"This is a book to be devoured, then reread and savored."
— *Library Journal*

"It is tempting to dwell of the fascinating political and philosophical overtones of the book. They are of the greatest interest, but they are inseparable from the tale of adventure and the study in depth of a most subtle character."
— *Times Literary Supplement*

"Dickinson has created a very credible mythical kingdom . . . a compelling and suspenseful story in which the gods work through humans to achieve their ends . . ."
— *ALA Booklist*

THE
Blue Hawk

Peter Dickinson

DEL REY

A Del Rey Book

BALLANTINE BOOKS • NEW YORK

A Del Rey Book
Published by Ballantine Books

Copyright © 1976 by Peter Dickinson

Library of Congress Catalog Card Number: 76-1857

ISBN 0-345-25759-6

This edition published by arrangement with Little, Brown and Company in association with the Atlantic Monthly Press

Manufactured in the United States of America

First Ballantine Books Edition: August 1977

Cover art by Michael Herring

I

THE HOUSE OF O AND AA BOOMED TO THE DEEP
voices of the priests. The vast stone pillars, and the
stone Gods twenty feet high, seemed to quiver to the
sound, almost in the way that a boulder in the desert
quivers in the heat of noon.

The Hawk Throne had been carried up from storage
and set between the gold pillar of O and the black pillar
of Aa, and on it sat the King. His face was as brown as
a peasant's, his short-clipped beard black but streaked
with gray. On his head, instead of the usual plain gold
circlet with the Eye of Gdu at its center, he wore a great
hawk-shaped headdress encrusted with chips of lapis lazuli. He sat as still as one of the towering stone Gods,
but even so he looked angry and impatient.

Gold-robed behind the pillar of O and black-robed
behind the pillar of Aa stood the priests of those two
Gods, ranked and silent. It was the priests of the Hawk
God, Gdu, who caused the building to boom, standing
in front of the throne and singing the Great Hymn for
the Renewal of the King's Soul. The rest of the House
of O and Aa was filled with the priests of the other
Minor Gods, all silent. The nobles of the King's court
watched from side aisles.

Behind the throne, with his back to it, the Keeper of
the Rods stood watching a fine thread of light as it
moved across the patterned stonework of the altar. He
was waiting for the exact moment of noon, when O
would be strongest and Aa weakest, so that he could
give the signal for the sacrifice of the Blue Hawk,
whose soul would renew the King's. Already the One

1

of Aa had moved forward and was bending over the black stone basin into which the blood of the hawk would drip; his hands moved to and fro as he blessed the basin with the whispered hymns of Aa. His face was hidden by the cowl of his robe, but his hands were as pale as fine sand because sunlight had never touched his flesh since he had been chosen as a child for Aa.

The front rank of the priests of Gdu consisted of the boys who had been chosen for Gdu. Their mouths moved to the wavelike phrases of the Great Hymn, but they were only whispering the words, learning them in the way that all the hymns were learned. Great Hymns were easier than most, because they consisted mainly of stories. This one told how once, long ago, before the days of the Wise even, Gdu had been flying above the river when O in sport had loosed a gold arrow at Him. (The Gods were young then and the desert green, and Aa walked in daylight and was welcome in the houses of men.) O's arrows cannot miss, so, just as He'd intended, He had knocked the jeweled crest-feather from Gdu's head. Gdu, enraged, had soared to attack O in His gold tower, but even Gdu could not fly so high. By the time He came to search for His crest-feather He could not find it, because O had caused a wind to blow it away.

> At dusk Saba crept by the river,
> Saba, murderer, first of the Kings.
> His father's blood crusted his sword.
> He hid among reeds.
> He heard his brothers ride by, shouting for
> his death.
> Their hooves faded.
> Bright between reeds lay the crest-feather of
> Gdu,
> Large as a palm frond.
> "Saba, murderer, take me to Gdu."

Fourth from the left in the row of whispering boys was one called Tron. He was little different to look at, from any of the others—slighter and darker than most, perhaps, but there was not much to it. They all had black hair, close-cropped, and wore the coarse blue tunic proper for boys chosen for Gdu. They all kept their eyes fixed straight ahead, so that at one rim of Tron's peripheral vision he could see the hands of the One of Aa floating like pale fish above the blood basin. At the other rim the brilliant headdress of the King flashed in the pillared gloom. Directly in front of Tron, swaying on its perch, was the Blue Hawk, minutes only now from death.

At last year's Renewal Tron had stood in the second rank and farther to the right. Then this had been just another sacrifice, performed so that the King should stay alive through the ninth year of his reign; Tron's whole attention had been given to making sure he whispered the words of the hymn correctly, and he did not now remember what that Blue Hawk had looked like. This year was different.

Tron stared at the bird, seeing it with a bleak intensity. He had come to the House of O and Aa in a state of shivering excitement, sure that the Gods would speak to him. They had sent him such signs of warning—a vision, a feather, the white Goat-Stone. Tron had never been made Goat before, though other boys had found the white stone baked into their breakfast loaf three or four times. He had always promised himself that if the stone came to him he would choose a quiet moment in some ritual and then turn cartwheels all down the center aisle from the altar to the door. But now it had come on the day of Renewal, and he had seen Gdu in the night and found a feather in his bowl of offering. So he tingled and waited for the Gods to speak.

The hawk swayed at the center of his vision. It was not what he had expected. He was familiar with the little brown reed hawks that were used for teaching the boys that part of their art, and he had sometimes seen the larger hawks that the nobles carried on their wrists. So he knew the true look of a hawk's eye, that hard bright amber that seems proud enough to outstare the sun.

This hawk's eye was dull and despairing. Its slate-blue plumage seemed drab, and the sky-blue stripe across its wing lacked the brilliance of living plumage. The blue scales of its legs and the patch of blue bare cartilage around its beak had the same dull tone. Several times the bird swayed so violently that it almost tumbled from its perch. When this happened it didn't try to right itself with a wingbeat, but allowed the One of Gdu, standing beside it, to steady it upright.

> Saba, I take the blood from your sword.
> See, it is clean bronze.
> Your father walks unwounded beside a fresh-
> dug water channel.
> Your brothers are feasting.
> Go now, Saba, to the west of the river.
> I give you that land
> For you and your sons to rule for ever.
> You shall not be conquered.
> I breathe into you now the Blue Hawk's soul,
> The soul of my loved one,
> The hawk that consents to sit on no wrist,
> That cannot be tamed.

The hawk on the perch was both tamed and conquered.

It is sick, thought Tron. He stopped whispering the words of the Great Hymn and ran through in his mind the little hymn of the sicknesses of hawks. This was the first little hymn that boys chosen for Gdu had to learn, as it linked the God's two arts of hawking and healing, but now it told Tron nothing. All he knew was that the bird was sick, that it had forgotten its heritage of fierceness and wildness, which ought to have showed in an eye clear as a jewel and in plumage every feather of which lay in its place as smooth as plate armor.

They are giving a sick soul to the King, Tron thought.

Almost as if to assure himself that pride and fierceness still lived, he allowed his glance to slip sideways to the King.

The King too had been looking at the hawk. The small movement of the boy's eyeballs must have caught his attention. For an instant they stared at each other, as though their lines of sight had touched, locked together into a single shaft, true as a lance.

In the King's eyes Tron saw anger, and disgust, and a sort of weariness. In Tron's eyes the King saw—what? Suddenly the corners of the royal mouth twitched, and into the royal glance crept a curious light of mockery. If he had not been sitting so still and balancing that towering headdress on the pillar of his neck, the King might almost have shrugged.

"Little priest," his glance said, "well . . . ?"

And then he looked away.

In the talons of the hawk the King's lance.
In the eye of the hawk the King's judgment.
In the blood of the hawk the King's courage.
In the least feather of the hawk the King's soul.
In a feather the soul of a man.

The gold line of light sidled across the altar. The Keeper of the Rods made an almost invisible gesture. The black-robed priest who was called the Mouth of Silence touched the shoulder of the One of Aa, who picked up a leaf-shaped obsidian knife from beside the basin and stood straight, his face still shadowed by his cowl. The One of Gdu loosened the light thong that tied the hawk's leg to the perch. The rhythm of the Great Hymn changed, as the rhythm of waves changed when they feel the coming shore. Tron stared at the hawk, all his soul focusing into his gaze. And the Gods stared at Tron, narrowing Their mighty spirits down to the single point where he stood. They spoke in his heart.

The tingling stopped. He took the white Goat-Stone from the pouch of his tunic and hung it by its cord round his neck so that it lay in the middle of his chest.

Now he was Goat, sacred as a God for one whole day. Whatever he did during that that day he could not be touched or punished. He stepped forward. The One of Gdu glanced down, his mouth already open to hiss a furious command; then he saw the Goat-Stone and glanced away, picking up the beat of the Great Hymn as though he had never left off.

Tron took another pace, lifted the hawk firmly from its perch and settled it on his wrist. For an instant the talons dug in, raising two small drops of blood on the brown, bare skin, but priests are almost as used to small pains as they are to stillness and waiting, so Tron did not wince. He bowed to the One of O and the One of Aa, to the motionless back of the Keeper of the Rods, and last to his own master, the One of Gdu; then he turned and walked with a priest's gliding pace down the main aisle, between the chanting priests of Gdu, and then, rank on rank in their various-colored robes, the priests of the other Minor Gods—Tan of the Great River, mistress of crops, Alaan of the mountains and the underworld, Sodala the herdsman's helper, Gdaal who moves the slow dunes of the desert and guides the hunter home, Sinu lord of war, and all the rest. Last of all stood the white-robed Sons of the Wise.

Not a single pair of eyes flickered toward Tron. They might all have been as blind as the One of Sinu, who stood sightless at the front of the red-robed priests of the War God. Tron glided down the aisle between them to where the glaring rectangle of the Door of O and Aa opened onto the noon-dazzled inner courtyard of the Temple.

Behind him, at some point before he reached the door, the Keeper of the Rods made a sweeping gesture with both arms, the One of Aa mimed the sacrifice of a hawk, and the One of Gdu dipped his forefinger into the basin and drew with invisible blood the symbol of Gdu on the King's forehead. The priests sang on, continuing the ritual of Renewal as though nothing had interrupted and the symbol were plain to see on the brown skin. The nobles muttered in the darkened side aisles. The King stared down the aisle at the bird and child, black and dwindling against the bright doorway. He smiled the thin smile of defeat.

Tron carried the hawk out into the desert noon.

II

THE RAYS OF O BEAT VERTICALLY DOWN ON THE INNER Courtyard. Apart from a yard-wide strip along the bottom of the south wall, the only shade lay under the arch of the passage into the Great Courtyard. A flight of the white temple doves wheeled across the square of sky, their wings making a quick, whimpering beat. If the hawk saw them it gave no sign. It seemed to cower from the light, and almost fell from Tron's wrist. He steadied it as he walked toward the shade of the gateway.

It was strange to be pacing alone over these flagstones. It was strange to be alone at all. It was strange to be Goat, to choose to step this way rather than that. As the Gods withdrew their spirit from him Tron found himself dazed and frightened by what his own limbs and fingers had done. It was not even pleasant to be able to choose.

"Hey! What you got there, then!" said the guard lounging under the gateway. "Going to join the nobility, are you? Hey! That's the Blue Hawk!"

He lunged forward and barred Tron's way. In theory he could be lashed a thousand times for touching even a boy-priest; but the guards tended to repay their awe of the Major Priests by a careful rudeness with the boys, provided there were no witnesses. Tron sensed that the hawk settled a little in the sudden shade, so he halted and tried to soothe it still further by gentling the ruffled neck feathers.

"What's up? Where you taking it? Lord Sinu!"

"Speak more quietly. It's sick."

"Sick! Drugged, more like!"

8

"Oh . . ." Tron hadn't even considered the possibility.

"Who told you to take it? You just took it? So the King's got to die just because you took a fancy to a pretty blue bird? Lord Sinu! They'll flay you alive!"

The tone of the guard's voice dropped and became more formal, as though he could actually see the dark wing of Aa shadowing the King on his throne and the boy under the archway. Tron's own mind was so taken up with the concrete act of rescuing the hawk that there was still no room in it to consider the consequences of the act.

"I am Goat," he said.

The guard spat.

"Goat! What's Goat for? Goat's chosen to make a piddling little change in the rituals, just so they don't get too stuck in their ways, that's all. You ever seen a Goat do anything like what you've done? No? Well, I have. Thirteen—no, I'm a liar—fourteen floods ago there was this boy who took it into his head to stand up in front of all them priests and sing a hymn to O that he'd made up himself. O he was chosen for, too. They heard him through and they didn't touch him that day. But by the time he passed for priest he was a cripple, so bad they had to carry him up to his village—some potty little place in the hills. What had done that to him? I'll tell you. Punishments! Oh, not for singing his hymn, of course, but day after day for all sorts of other little . . ."

The guard stopped, stiffened and moved back to his place. Tron waited, listening to the approaching flap of sandals across the flagstones. All but the Major Priests went barefoot. He shivered in the noon heat. If only the hawk would fly away and be done with. When the sandals began to echo under the arch Tron could no longer pretend not to hear them. He turned and bowed, carefully, so as not to unbalance the hawk.

The Keeper of the Rods, having given the signal for the exact hour of noon, could leave the ritual. He was fat for a priest, brown-faced and black-bearded, dressed in a plain white tunic but carrying on the crook of his left arm a scepter with the gold sphere of O at the top and the silver sphere of Aa at the bottom; between the spheres ran a twisting lattice crusted with lapis lazuli to represent the river. Serving no particular God, the Keeper had less stylized manners and movements than those of the other Major Priests, and was thought by the boys to be friendly and kindly. But now he looked at Tron with no expression at all, then turned to the guard.

"You," he said. "Present yourelf to the Treasurer. Draw your pay. Go to your village. If now or later you say one word about having talked with this boy, Aa will take your children and Sodala blight your cattle. Come with me, boy. Hold that bird so that it cannot be seen from the Courtyard. Walk between me and the wall."

That in itself would seem strange to any guard watching from the Main Gate, or to the group of boys chosen for Tan, who were jerking their limbs to the cry of the dancemaster over in the northwest corner of the Courtyard. Normally Tron would have followed exactly four paces behind a Major Priest, but now they walked side by side along the inner wall to the Door of the Wise. The noon of O hammered on their scalps and shoulders. The hawk again almost fell from Tron's wrist. Then they were suddenly in the cool and dimness of shaded stone.

Though Tron had lived all his remembered life in the Temple, its minute-by-minute ritual had kept him to definite tracks, so he had never before passed through the dark little Door of the Wise with its strange and indecipherable symbols over the archway. Draggingly he followed the Keeper up a worn flight of shallow steps. In his mind's eye he still saw how the face of the guard had paled and broken into sweat when the Keeper had spoken to him. As Goat Tron had nothing to fear, but still he was afraid.

At the top of the steps the Keeper turned left into a long room, big as an eating hall and filling the width of the south wall of the Courtyard. On its right-hand side rose the familiar statues of the Gods; but on the left, instead of more Gods staring back at them, was a plain

wall pierced by big windows below which, along the full
length of the room, ran a sloping rack of hundreds of
colored rods. As Tron entered the room, one of the
Sons of the Wise reversed the sandglass he had been
watching, rose, crossed to the rack, muttered a line of
some hymn and moved a platelike gold object a few
inches along the sloping layer of rods. The symbol of O
was embossed deep on the gold.

The Keeper picked out a striped black-and-white rod
from beside a blue one.

"Amun!" he called.

A white-haired Son of the Wise rose from a work-
bench where he had been polishing a bright green rod,
banded with gold. His bow to the Keeper was stiff with
age, but casual.

"There is no space for another band on tomorrow's
rod," said the Keeper.

"So many Kings have died after Renewal," grumbled
Amun. "I did not know there was to be another one."

His glance flickered to the hawk on Tron's wrist. A
look of understanding came into his eyes.

"What's to be done?" said the Keeper, running the
rod between his fingers. Tron saw that all the bands
were of different widths.

"Lord," said Amun, "I will make a thinner rod, copy
these old deaths on it, then pass it through a hollow
reed on which I can paint this new death—and twenty
more, if need be."

"I knew you would think of something. Follow me,
boy."

The next room was small and square, furnished with
a mattress and a stool like any other priest's cell in the
Temple. Only the elaborate carvings on the walls made
it different. The Keeper closed and bolted the door, then
turned as if to pray to the image of Tan that filled the
far wall. But what he did was to grasp the stone head of
one of the crocodiles that twisted in a decorative pattern
all round the Goddess; it moved under his hand, inward
and upward, leaving a rectangular slot, into which he
reached. Something clicked. He leaned against the wall,

and the whole slab on which the Goddess was carved pivoted silently around.

"Go in there and wait, boy."

Being Goat, Tron could perhaps even now have turned away, refusing to cross the threshold of the trap. But at this moment the full, cold flood of fear washed over him. *I have killed the King. I have stolen his soul. The Keeper knows he must die. He told Amun to mark his death on tomorrow's rod. And now I am being shown these secrets, as if they know I shall not have to keep them long.* In a chill daze he walked forward and was only aware of having done so when the slab swung shut behind him, making a faint, deep boom as the stone lips closed.

The sound cut through the daze. He stood for an instant, shaking the fear away like a dog shaking water from its fur, then whispered, "Lord Gdu, You spoke in my heart. If I did what You asked there is nothing to make me afraid." With careful calm he settled the hawk on the back of a thronelike ebony chair and refastened its leg thongs. It closed its eyes and seemed to sleep, perhaps mistaking the dimness of the room for night. Tron looked around him.

This new place was not the prison cell he'd expected, but a large room, its walls smothered with carvings. Several more of the ebony chairs stood round a long black table. The light came mainly from a shaft in the roof, but one of the longer walls was also mottled with patches of what could only be daylight. These turned out to come from four odd-shaped openings, slanting downward and allowing Tron to see different sections of the Inner Courtyard. He was puzzled, because from the Courtyard itself the wall seemed to contain nothing but the enormous statues of the Gods, on either side of the Gate of Saba, which was opened only for the funerals of Kings and beyond which lay the Palace. But here was this hidden room, with its secret doors and spyholes, a granite trap.

There was a cupboard containing bread and a water jug, plates and a pile of coarse napkins. Tron took one of these and bandaged it carefully round his wrist, not to protect himself but to give the hawk something firmer to grip on. When he went to pick the bird up, it opened its eyes and struck with a sort of halfhearted ferocity at his hand. He didn't flinch, but stayed quite still while it swayed itself upright and stood with half-shut eyes. The eyes, in fact, seemed a little less dull.

In a soft voice Tron crooned the refrain of the long little hymn that describes the training of hawks:

> "By days of watch,
> By days of care,
> By days of patience,
> The hawk becomes the eye of the man, far-seeing,
> The hawk becomes the arm of the man, far-striking."

He sang the familiar words a dozen times before moving with deft firmness to pick the hawk up by the legs, settle it onto the napkin and grip the leg thong in his left hand. It seemed to have sunk back, after its momentary stirring, into its strange daze. He gentled the staring feathers between its shoulder blades, then, without knowing why, froze and slowly turned.

The One of Aa was in the room, watching him. A pivoted slab of stone stood open in the other wall.

Tron bowed very low and stayed with bent head. The black robes stirred and rustled and swung out of his line of vision. He heard a rattle, then saw one of the pallid hands place a coarse bronze knife on the table. *So now I go to Aa,* he thought, dreamy with the stiff trance of fear. It is a table of sacrifice. But then beside the knife appeared a plate and cup, a loaf of ordinary priest-bread and a slab of pale cheese. When the One of Aa sat down to eat, his head came in sight. With a careless movement he threw back his cowl.

There was one part of Tron's life over which the rituals had never ruled, his dreams and nightmares. He had sometimes dreamed of meeting the One of Aa, uncowled, and of seeing a face sallow and bloodless and older than the longest-lived of men. But now . . . true, his face was as pale as his hands, with a beard trimmed so close to the skin that it was little more than a mat of stubble. His lips were full, and red with life, his nose snub, his eyes bright and quick. He nodded to Tron and settled to munching as hungrily and untidily as a peasant resting from the waterwheel. Naturally he had fasted for twenty-four hours before the sacrifice.

The Keeper of the Rods returned, fetched food, and started to eat. A little later three more Major Priests came in through the opposite door. The One of O and the Mouth of Silence went to the cupboard, but the One of Gdu strode up to Tron and stared down at him, hot-eyed. Tron had never faced his Master alone. He felt his whole soul try to flinch backward from this anger, but his training held him still.

"What do you think you are?" snapped the One of Gdu.

"Lord," whispered Tron, "I am Goat. Last night . . ."

"Goat!" shouted the One of Gdu, and in his fury and contempt snatched at the white medallion on Tron's chest.

The shout and the sudden movement broke the hawk's daze. Instinctively it struck out at the darting hand, a movement far faster than a man's. With another shout, of pain this time, the One of Gdu flinched back with blood streaming from the two-branched vein that runs above the back of the wrist. He raised the hand to suck it, but it never reached his lips. The blood trickled down his forearm to his elbow while he stood staring, not at Tron but at the hawk. The glare in his eyes faded and the bunched muscles of his cheeks subsided. He licked his lips, afraid. Gdu had answered him.

"Come and eat, brother," said the flat but slightly amused voice of the Keeper. "Boy, fetch bread for your Master."

When the One of Gdu was seated and sullenly chewing, Tron took the bird to the far side of the room and began once more to try to soothe its terrified but jaded wildness. The presence of the Major Priests made it restless. Twice it cast droppings and once eased its wings, almost as if thinking of flight. At last, as the Priests finished eating, it dropped its head and began to preen feebly at its breast feathers. Tron was sure now that the guard had been right, and that it had been drugged to keep it quiet during the ritual. It was the wildest of wild creatures, untamable. Quite soon the drug would wear off and it would return to that state.

"Child," said a dry voice, "tell us now why you did what you did."

It took Tron a moment to grasp that it was the One of O who had spoken, so different was his tone from the drumlike bass that led the hymns.

"Lord," answered Tron, "Gdu spoke in my heart."

"Yes?"

"I had seen signs, Lord. In the night I saw a great Gdu—it was not a dream, Lords! I lay on my own mattress and heard the breathing of the boys on either side. I lay thus while the shadow of Aa—She was high— moved from one edge of the window slits to the other. Then I heard a noise in the dormitory, a movement at the southern end where there is no door. I was afraid. In the dormitories, Lords, there is a tall thin window slit opposite each mattress. . . ."

"We have been boys," said the Keeper.

Tron hesitated, baffled by the thought. The Priests watched him in silence, without expression. Then, even in the middle of this new fear he grasped back at last night's fear, and the picture came clear in his mind.

"Aa shone on the slits," he said. "The farthest slits were thin silver lines, but they widened as they came nearer my mattress. I saw something move across the far lines, too tall for a boy. Then I saw it was too tall for a man. Then, when it was a few slits away I could see its head. Lords, it was Gdu."

He could not tell from their expressions whether they believed him.

"I saw His beak, Lords. I saw the jewels of His crest. They glittered in Aa's light. He walked like a man, but

He was a head taller. More, I think. He made no noise. He passed all down the dormitory, pausing once. He did not come back."

"You said *signs*," said the One of O after a short silence.

"Had you drunk your sweetwater at nightfall?" interrupted the One of Gdu.

"Lord, that was a sign. The bowl had cracked in my hands as I raised it to drink, and the sweetwater spilled. I . . . I . . . I was afraid. I said nothing, but fitted the two halves together and put them on the sill of my window slit, according to the ritual. This morning, when I stood at the window for the Hymn of O, I found a feather in the bowl, lying across the crack. . . ."

"Did none of the other boys find a sign?" snapped the One of Gdu. He sounded as though he were once more working himself up into a full gale of rage against the boy who had ruined his special ritual.

"Yes, Lord. Diran found two red beans in his bowl. That's a common sign. It means the Gods are pleased with Diran. He sang a hymn of thanks, but I said nothing. I didn't know what my sign meant. Here is the feather."

With his free hand he took it from his pouch and showed it to them on his palm. It looked drab and bedraggled compared with the pure arc of silvery white he had found on the cracked clay. The One of Gdu snorted.

"And at breakfast, Lords, I was chosen for Goat. I have never been chosen before. When we went to the House of O and Aa I was sure that the Gods would speak to me. I'd always said to myself that when I was Goat I would turn cartwheels down between the minor Priests, but now . . . We sang the Great Hymn. The hawk was straight in front of me. I could see it was sick. I waited. Then I heard us singing this—

> In the least feather of the hawk the King's
> soul,
> In a feather the soul of a man.

And then Gdu spoke in my heart, saying that He had come in the night and left me the feather in a broken bowl as a sign that I should break the ritual, because it was not proper that the soul of a sick hawk should renew the King's soul, and that I had been chosen for Goat to do this. He spoke in my heart, Lords. That is why I did . . . what I did."

He looked along the line of priests. The Keeper of the Rods seemed bored, as though he had expected a more interesting story. The One of Aa was smiling and nodding. The One of O kept all expression out of his magnificently imperious face. The Mouth of Silence, who had also thrown back his cowl, looked troubled. (He was a much older man, bald and with a close-shorn gray beard. His skin was yellow and wrinkled, his eyes dull and sunken. If he had been anyone else than Aa's servant, one would have said that Aa must soon take him.) The One of Gdu could no longer master his anger.

"That's nothing but a feather from one of the doves, blown in by the night breeze. A sign, uh? We cannot have the rituals turned to nonsense every time a boy wakes in the night and sees what he shouldn't. He broke his bowl before he was Goat—he can be punished for that. It is clear that the Gods do not love him. Let Aa take him."

He spoke loudly and harshly enough to disturb the hawk again. It roused from its trance, turned its lean head, opened its beak and hissed soundlessly at him. Once more his expression changed as he shrank back into the cave of doubt and awe, like a snail withdrawing from menace.

"Lords," said Tron, "we must speak in low voices. The servant of Gdu is fretted by sudden noise."

"It is not often that a boy says 'must' to the Major Priests," said the Keeper of the Rods.

The One of Aa laughed soundlessly.

"I do not like to see the rituals broken," the Keeper went on. "We live by rules—not just the priests, but

King and nobles and peasants too. Listen. I move my rods along the Rack of Days according to rules invented by the Wise. I move the symbols of O and Aa and the planets by other rules, also invented by the Wise. Thus I know the exact hour in any season at which a particular star will rise. I know the death days of priests and kings, and the times and heights of the floods, back through thirty generations of men. I know in which year and day Aa will fight with O in broad daylight, or a darker shadow fight with Aa by night. The Keeper before me foretold the great comet. It took me half a lifetime to learn the rules from him, and will take another half lifetime to teach them to my successor. Now, during those years I have not only learnt but thought, and I have seen that if I miss one small motion prescribed by the rules, that error will do more than repeat and repeat itself year by year. It will cause other errors, which will also repeat themselves and also cause further errors, so that in a very few years the Rack of Days would lose all meaning. We would be holding the flood feast at the time when Tan was weakest and calling for the harvest tax at seedtime. This I know as well as you know your Great Hymns. And I also know that it is the same with the hymns and the rituals. You think a little change here and there will do no harm? I tell you that if anything can be changed, everything can. Very soon men would be trying to change the Gods. And who would rule in the kingdom then, do you think?"

"But Goat," said the Mouth of Silence. "There has always been Goat."

"I have wondered," said the Keeper. "That medal the boy wears is not like any other ritual object in the Temple. What else is white, of a polished stone hard enough to stand a thousand years of knocks from irresponsible boys?"

"It is right that it should be different. Wait. Hear me."

Though his function was to speak for the One of Aa and interpret his sign-language, speaking seemed to hurt the Mouth of Silence. His voice was suited to a servant of Aa, grating and slow. He gathered his strength while the others waited.

"The boy *is* Goat," he said. "It is not the medal, it is the boy. You have seen how the hawk answered our brother, twice. The servant of Gdu knows. He allows himself to be touched and carried because the boy is Goat. I too would fight to preserve the least of the rituals. But Goat is a ritual himself. The Wise decreed him. Listen, you are saying to yourselves that the boy broke his bowl by accident and did not drink his sweetwater and that everything follows from that. He did not sleep, because he had not drunk the sweetwater drug. Therefore he woke and saw our brother visit the dormitory to bless the boy Diran, wearing the mask of Gdu. Chance sent the feather to his bowl. Chance set him opposite the hawk in the House of O and Aa. Chance caused our brother to move and speak so that the hawk should seem to answer him. I am older than you all by thirty floods. I say that there is no such thing as chance. It is all the working of the Gods. I say that the Wise decreed that every day a Goat should be chosen by a stone baked into one of the boys' loaves just for this—so that there should be room in our stiff rituals for the Gods to act, when They so choose."

By the end his voice was a difficult whisper, but the Major Priests heard him with respect. Only the One of Aa sat easy, rubbing his bristly chin and seeming to take pleasure from the rasping movement in the same way that a dog takes pleasure in having its hackles teased. When the speech finished he fluttered his hands across the table in dancelike gestures.

"He asks if he should take the King," said the Mouth of Silence.

"Of course," said the One of O. "His soul was not renewed."

"He can die in his sleep," said the One of Gdu. "I will mix the powders. Has he shifted his bed? Who has been watching?"

The pale hands danced through a different message.

"He says the bed is where it was," said the Mouth of

Silence. "He asks if he should take the boy too. He proposes a knife sacrifice on the Tower, this midnight. He will not need powders for the boy."

"I should think not!" snapped the One of Gdu. "Powders are scarce as emeralds! Huh!"

His anger, twice frustrated, was still looking for a way to release itself. The One of Aa shrugged and smiled at Tron, but his eye was speculative, as if measuring the body for the Dark Altar.

"My brothers," said the One of O, "it is not a matter of how Aa shall take the boy, but whether She shall take him."

The One of Aa shrugged again, but his smile was a sulky pout now.

"We can't have him joining the other boys as if nothing had happened," said the Keeper. "Think what the next Goat might try!"

"Think what the nobles will say if he's not punished!" said the One of Gdu. "They'll spread it about that we put him up to it to get rid of the King! So . . ."

He hesitated, his eye on the hawk.

"Renewals have failed before," said the Keeper. "Tomorrow's rod is full of the deaths of Kings."

"He is Goat," said the Mouth of Silence. "If we send him to Aa, we shall ourselves have broken a ritual, and it will seem that we did so merely to silence a witness."

"You are all making strong points," said the One of O. "But I think you are not trusting the Gods enough. Let us tell the truth, and as far as we can let us follow where the Gods seem to lead. The truth is that the Gods spoke in the boy's heart, telling him to remove the hawk because it was unfitting that the Renewal should be completed; we do not know why. But let us attempt to question the Gods further, and discover why. We have a sign. The Blue Hawk cannot be tamed, but it sits at ease on the boy's wrist."

"It is drugged," said the One of Gdu.

"Not so drugged that it could not answer you, my brother. I say we have a sign. I take it to mean that the Gods will permit this boy to tame this hawk."

"It cannot be done!" said the One of Gdu. "The hymn says . . ."

"Just so," said the One of O. "He must train the hawk in secret. If he fails the failure must not be known. If he succeeds, that must also not be known until we are ready. The King dies tonight, but it is a hundred days or more—is it not, Brother Keeper?—before Tan begins to rise in flood. At the height of the flood the dead King will travel on Her breast to the land of Alaan, and only then can the live King be shown to the people. Suppose on that day, at that showing, the Blue Hawk were to fly, and kill one of our Temple doves, and return tame to its master . . ."

It was as though the Major Priests perceived, one after the other, the answer to a question that had been troubling them. No one said a word, but their eyes seemed to change as they gave small nods of agreement. The One of Aa stretched as he gave his voiceless laugh, and the frown left the forehead of the Mouth of Silence, leaving his old face smooth and saintly.

"Where will the boy do the training?" asked the Keeper of the Rods.

"The Temple of Tan," said the One of O.

"Yes, there's good open ground above that," said the One of Gdu. "If it can be done, that will do. I shall choose a discreet priest to help him."

"No," whispered the Mouth of Silence. "He must do it alone. He and none other, or why did the Gods choose him? Praise the Gods, boy, and be happy. You serve in a great business. There is no doubt that Gdu spoke in your heart."

III

~~~~~~~

TRON HAD SEEN THE ONE OF GDU TRAIN A COMMON
river hawk to complete obedience in fifteen days. But
Tron had been at the Temple of Tan thirty-seven days
before the Blue Hawk settled again onto his own wrist
and stayed there without a frenzied struggle against the
leg throng. It was another twenty before, flying on a
long, fine leash, it learned to return to a swung lure and
thence without fuss to Tron's gauntlet. He knew that he
would never have progressed even that far without the
help of the Gods.

The deserted Temple of Tan stood at the point of a
large sloping triangle of rocky desert, around which the
river curved in a vast, abrupt bend. On the far bank
spread peopled miles of fields and irrigation ditches, but
the Temple on the promontory was deserted, except for
the little scurryings of bats and lizards and the huge
presence of the Gods. Their statues watched him as he
moved across courtyards deep in blown sand, or along
corridors slimy with bird droppings and bat mess; Their
slow breathing seemed to fill the evening air; Their
voices whispered in his dreams. At times the fear of
Them so overcame him that he longed to run out into
the desert, to run and then walk and finally stagger and
fall and sink into Aa's embrace and thus be free of the
pressure of Them.

Only the hawk kept him sane. That was his work,
and the fear of the Gods concentrated him onto it.
While he was with the bird—simply sitting beside it to
accustom it to his presence, or stitching a hood, or
coaxing it to take a scrawny gobbet of meat from his

hand, the work occupied his mind and freed him from
dread. This was what the Gods had asked him to do, so
the Major Priests had said. How could there be anything to fear? Or perhaps the Gods had sent the fear to
help him understand the bird, whose terror of his presence was much the same as his own terror of the presence of the Gods, a wild and useless struggle to escape,
a blank failure to realize that he meant only good.

The nights were worst, when Aa ruled the cold desert
sky and there were no black-robed priests to weave a
web of spells over the Temple, a barrier against the
nightmare creatures of Aa. There was not even any
sweetwater to drug him so that he didn't wake and see
the staring statues of the Gods, frosted with silver and
casting shadows blacker than the cave of Aa. Sometimes the dark sky was full of a sudden whirl of bats. A
fox would bark in the desert. Something large would
rustle against the Temple wall. . . .

Then he would look at the hawk, sleeping on its
perch, indifferent, and think, *We are both servants of
Gdu. Gdu will guard us both, the hawk knows.*

Once the hawk had learned to fly readily to the lure
there came a great change. Every day it seemed to learn
new things. When he picked it up in the morning it ruffled its feathers with an eager air, as though it looked
forward to the day's training. Within ten days he had
taken the heart-stopping but inescapable risk of letting
it fly free, watching it curve away, hesitate, mount into
the sky above him while he made the falconer's wavering whistles, and then come plunging to the lure. When
it stood on his gauntlet again tearing at a bloody tidbit
Tron found that all his own veins were tingling with a
new, wild joy, something he had never felt before and
would never know again to the same degree, the estab-
lishment of a bond of trust and partnership between the
pair of them, sealed by this single, intense moment.

Four days later the hawk made its first kill. It was an
accident. They were still training to the lure and the
hawk had swung to its proper height above him when a

small gray wading bird came carelessly out of a reedbed on the riverbank. The hawk plunged. The wader made a zigzag dash for the next reedbed, but the hawk, hurling down with half-folded wings, crashed into it a yard from safety, coming with such an impact that there was an audible thud and a puff of gray down in midair. When Tron came up, the hawk was neatly plucking out the victim's thigh feathers, but raised its head and made its silent hiss at his approach. He spoke quietly to it, the usual lines from the little hymn, and it jumped to his wrist without trouble. With his free hand he finished plucking the wader's leg, cut off the drumstick and gave it to the hawk, who tore at it, full of the lust of the kill.

The training went well for eight days. Then Tron lost the Blue Hawk. Being a mountain bird, it suffered more than he did from the bludgeoning heat of noon, and even Tron was glad to rest for the hours of O's greatest anger in the shade of the massive stone of the Temple, so for both their sakes he preferred not to stray far from there. Faint breezes off Tan's surface made the riverbanks a little cooler than the still dry heat of the desert, and there was plenty of easy game along this haunted and unpeopled shoreline. Besides, though Tron was aware of the danger of hawking close to a barrier that he could not cross, he had begun unconsciously to feel and act as though the Gods would not let him fail.

Of course he avoided the areas where the reedbeds made too much cover. The fat little rust-colored bird that rose at his feet looked straightforward enough, but it must have been some kind of burrower because, just as the hawk came whistling down it flicked into a neat hole in the bare scree of the bank. The hawk rose, baffled, but before Tron could begin to swing the lure, a flight of small black duck rose scuttering from the water. At once the hawk was after them, but they were far too fast for it, moving like fish shadows above the calm surface and disappearing among reeds on the far bank. At the limit of his vision Tron saw the hawk rise to search along that bank, a tiny dot, wavering and vanishing and coming again in the hot, unsteady air. Quite soon he could not see it at all.

All afternoon he swung the lure, whistled, hooted. Loss was like cold fire burning his bones. He wasn't afraid of what the priests might do to him, or even of the anger of the Gods at his stupidity. It was the breaking of his bond with the hawk, a feeling that half his soul had been snatched from him—that was worse than any deaths. O settled in the west, making the pillars of the deserted Temple half a mile up the bank glow as if they had been taken fresh from a smithy furnace. The gold-wrinkled river blinded his eyes. Despairingly he prayed to Gdu, whistled, and swung. Then out of the glaring sky the hawk dropped to the lure. The first he knew of it was the thud of its striking. It tore eagerly at the meat tied to the lure and then at the tidbit he gave it when it was safe on his wrist, so he knew that Gdu had prevented it from catching any prey on the far bank, and perhaps had arranged for the burrowing bird and the duck to teach him not to rely too much on the goodwill of the Gods.

That night he slept little, but for the first time since he had come to the Temple of Tan he lay in the dark, unafraid. He realized that he had become a different person. He had discovered how to be alone.

The great Temple had always been full of noises, the throb of gongs, the steady pulse of hymns—either the priests singing the deep praise of some God or the shriller noise of the boys learning a fresh section of the million lines they needed to know: one of Sodala's little hymns about the cure of sheep maggots; or Tan's describing the choosing and shaping of wood for a waterwheel; or Gdu's listing the symptoms of marsh fever. Then there had been the cracking cry of the dance-masters as they led their groups through the exercises that kept limbs supple for the great rituals, and from over the Palace wall the slap of wood on leather and the shouts of young nobles learning the arts of war. And the silence of night had been concealed by the sweetwater drugs.

Except in that sleep Tron had never spent more than a few minutes at a time without the consciousness of sixty other boys all around him, eating the same bread, moving the same limbs to the cry of the dance-master, muttering the same lines of a hymn. That tide of boys was all he knew. He could remember nothing else. He had no idea—in fact, he had never asked himself before now—how he had come to the Temple. He must have been born somewhere. Aa was the sole God of birth, as She was of death; but Gdu's priests had to know many little hymns about the sicknesses and cures surrounding the process of birth, so Tron supposed he had a mother who had endured the normal human pain of bringing him into the world. But boys never asked questions; what they needed to know they were told in due time.

Now, lying in the dark, Tron saw how he had changed. A boy brought from the Temple to this loneliness would be like an ant taken far from its nest to a flat place where there are not even any hostile nests. The ant would meander about, aimlessly, or stand still for long minutes, but neither its stillness nor its dashes hither and thither would have meaning or purpose. Those things belong to the nest.

However Tron's life had meaning and purpose, in the hawk. This was not the priests' mysterious purpose, nor the Gods'. It was a purpose in itself, the contact between the soul of a man and the soul of wildness in the bird. He had placed its perch so that from where he lay on his mattress the hawk was outlined against an arched window that gave onto the moonlit courtyard. Now he whispered, as he had done so often, not only with his lips but with his movements and glances and the reaching out of his soul, the words that Gdaal had spoken to Tan when they had met in the mists of the first morning,

"I will not be your master
I will not be your servant
I will be your companion
As two horns on one antelope

Two wings on one bird
Two eyes in one head."

Perhaps the bird heard his whisper, for it stirred on
its perch and settled again. But in that moment he felt
the bird's soul reach out to meet his. They touched.
Soon after that he slept.

Next morning Tron walked a couple of miles inland,
thinking as he peered around the shapeless hummocks
of sour earth and tumbled rock and the occasional
stunted scrub that there wouldn't be much to hunt here.
But he found great sport. There was a harelike creature
that would dash at great speed for fifty yards and then
cower and become a mottled rock; he found that if he
marked the exact spot where it finished its first dash he
could put the hawk into the air above him and walk
forward to startle the hare again—if he missed it by
three feet it would not move—and then the hawk could
hurl into it from above, using its height to reach a speed
that would match the hare's. So fierce was the impact of
that dive that the only hare they killed that first day—
they missed a couple—died with a broken neck and its
fur barely marked by its blood. There was a slower yellow bird about as big as a dove, which had the ability to
sideslip almost at right angles in flight at the last instant, dodging the hawk's dive as it labored on to cover.
Then followed a swirling and jinking pursuit, which the
yellow bird usually won until the hawk taught itself a
technique of turning so rapidly out of its first dive that
it could hit the yellow bird on the upstroke. It took a
week to learn this, but after that it seldom missed.

Meanwhile, the two of them had discovered by accident the best prey of all. Walking forward to put up a
cowering hare, with the hawk poised sixty feet above
him, Tron was startled by an explosion of hitherto invisible large birds, eight of them whirring out of the rocks
around him. Instantly the hawk stooped from its height
into a whistling dive, talons foremost, hitting into the
fattest of the bunch with a smack like two fists struck

hard together. When he picked the dead bird up, Tron found that it was something like a guinea fowl, but brown and streaked with black. He knew because of its occasional appearance among the Temple paintings that it must have some ritual significance, but he didn't know what. (If he had been chosen for Gdaal, he would of course have known the names and habits of all these creatures from the little hymns, long before he ever saw a live specimen.)

The thrill of hunting this bird came from its shyness. It moved about in small coveys and seemed always to have a keen-eyed sentry at watch, for often a flock would rise and lumber away when Tron was half a mile off. Then it was a matter of putting the hawk into the air, letting it gain its full height, and walking carefully forward to the spot where he had seen them settle. The presence of the hawk in the air discouraged them from moving off again until Tron was almost among them, and if the hawk was flying too low they would not rise at all. This meant that provided Tron had marked the birds down accurately he was close enough to see the marvelous moment when a hawk plunges from a hundred and fifty feet in one clean dive into a prey twice its own size, knocking it out of the air by the speed of its onrush. It was difficult. It depended on teamwork and luck. Three times out of four Tron failed to put the birds up at all. But when it worked it was glorious.

Tron, though aware of his changing nature, did not put into words the question how a boy reared in the machinelike, minute-filling ritual of the Temple should make the leap from the ordered satisfaction of a hymn well learned or a dance well done to the vivid thrill of the moment when a hawk strikes home. But he knew that this was something true to his own nature, a nature that had found no outlet in the Temple until that moment when Gdu had whispered in his heart and he had lifted the Blue Hawk from its jeweled perch. When he woke each morning, stiff among the motionless Gods, his first thought was of the day's hunting. When he lay waiting for sleep each night his mind was full of hoarded images, the eye of a hare glazed with death and the dribble of purplish blood from its mouth, a yellow bird making the last jink to the safety of a scrub patch, the hurtle of the hawk's dive.

Except for what he needed to feed the hawk he gave the creatures they killed to the deaf-and-dumb old man who came every third day with supplies. He accepted them with slavering amazement. Otherwise Tron saw nobody while Aa veiled and unveiled her face three times, and the whole land waited for flood time.

IV

ONE MORNING A PARTICULARLY SHY COVEY OF THE large birds took Tron farther from the Temple of Tan than he had yet explored, and by the time the hawk had made its kill O was beginning to make breath scorch in the nostrils, the ground burn under the feet, and the whole landscape seem to jump and waver in the unsteady air. The heat would have been unbearable by the time they had got back to the Temple, so Tron made for a large rock outcrop in the hope of finding an overhang or gulley where they could sweat out the worst of noon.

Rounding the boulders on the northern side, he found that there were men there, on the other edge of a pebbly arena that stretched away from the rock. He saw three nobles on horseback with hawks on their wrists, two servants carrying a stretcherlike framework on which more hawks perched, several other servants erecting gaudy parasols and beginning to lay out cushions and baskets of food.

Tron froze and began to back away, but one of the nobles had already seen him. This man spoke, but stayed where he was. Another noble wheeled his pony and came trotting over, frowning—a middle-aged man, heavy-shouldered, his hair and beard curled and dyed bright orange. He reined in and stared at Tron, craning forward in his saddle as if to study him better. The Blue Hawk began to fidget at this unknown presence, so Tron slipped its hood on its head and it quietened. (He never used a hood, but he had trained the hawk to accept it because the little hymn told him to.) Despite his apparent anger, the noble thought it proper to wait until Tron had dealt with his bird.

"So priests want to be nobles now?" he snarled. "What do you hunt, priest? Men?"

Tron unslung the coarse bag he had made for carrying game and took out a hare and the covey-bird. The noble leaned forward to peer at them, so Tron held them up. The noble's expression changed. Shock struggled with anger.

"That's royal game!" he cried.

"I did not know," said Tron.

The noble called, but already the two others were trotting across. One was a tall young man with a bent nose. The second was also young, and Tron knew his face before he saw the Eye of Gdu in the center of his forehead. It was not the same King who had listened to the Great Hymn in the House of O and Aa, but it was the King—the same hawk look, the same wary but arrogant regard. Tron stiffened inside himself. More and more he had become certain that the Gods approved of all he had done, and the priests too. But what about this King, whose father had died because a certain boy had taken the Blue Hawk from its perch—and died, too, not by the direct working of the Gods, but because the priests had seen to it that he should die? Would *he* make any allowances for the will of the Gods?

"Look, Majesty," said the older man. "Priests are hunting kingfowl!"

"Hunting well, too," said the King in a cheerful voice. "A hare. Kingfowl on foot. Chancy sport."

He looked at the hooded hawk, stared, and then studied Tron's face. Not a muscle changed but a withdrawn look came into his eyes. His horse scuffed a hoof. He shrugged. His smile was thin.

"My Lords," he said, "I must talk to this priest who hunts my birds. Have them send food and shade over to that slab of rock there. And two stands."

He slipped neatly down from his pony without unsettling the large and fantastically hooded hawk on his own wrist. The younger noble took the reins and led the pony away while Tron followed the King to a flat red boulder almost like an altar slab, which shouldered out of a scree of smaller stuff. The King dusted the surface of the slab with a gauntlet and sat down. Tron stood waiting.

"How do you catch kingfowl on foot?" asked the King.

Tron explained. The King nodded.

"You must mark them down well," he said. "That needs a hunter's eye. I will see that after we've eaten. Yes, I'd like to see the Blue Hawk in flight before I go to that kind woman."

Tron blinked. He knew that the common people of the Kingdom would never pronounce the name of Aa, but always found other ways of talking about Her. He hadn't realized that even the King acknowledged the same fear. The King didn't notice his surprise, but sat brooding, then studied the hawk again.

"Will she sit on my wrist, d'you think? Is she a female, by the way?"

Tron had never considered that question. There were no females in his world, other than Aa and Tan.

"I do not know, Majesty," he said. "But they would not choose a female for . . . for . . ."

He saw where the King's question had led him.

"For the Renewal," said the King with the same bitter smile. "I thought it was that hawk. I thought you were that boy. I saw you from the side aisle when you murdered my father."

O burned on Tron's scalp and shoulders, but his stomach was cold. Chill crept outward along all his flesh.

"Don't say anything till the food's come," said the King. "Turn away now. Rohan's too shortsighted to have seen what kind of hawk it is, and Kalavin's my one friend. But servants . . ."

Tron turned away and made a slow business of adjusting the hawk's leg thongs. The bird, hooded though it was, seemed to sense his fear and stirred uneasily. When the King told him to turn again he found that a gold parasol had been set up to shade the rock and a blue one over a pair of hawk stands. The King was peering into a basket of food, but he patted the rock beside him.

"Put your bird on a stand and come and sit with me," he said. "How old are you?"

"I do not know, Majesty. I have been in the Temple twelve years."

"Thirteen, then. It doesn't matter. This is the main advantage of hunting—you can go where you like and think what you please—but I never thought I'd get the chance of cornering a priest to talk to. Come on. Sit down. What's your name?"

"Tron, Chosen for Gdu," said Tron. Shyness made him perch on the very edge of the rock, and he had to throw out a hand behind him to steady himself. Something tickled his second finger.

"Stay still!" hissed the King.

His arm moved, fast as a striking snake. His loose-held gauntlet slapped stingingly against the back of Tron's hand.

"That hurt, I'm afraid," he said. "You know how to obey orders, at least. Look. Gdu knows no cure for that one's sting."

Tron twisted his head to see. The orange scorpion was not an inch long, apart from the curling tail. The little hymn that deals with the bites of poisonous insect ends baldly:

> "Last the small scorpion,
>   Colored like a marigold.
> If a man be stung by it
>   Give him poppy for the pain
> And start the ritual
>   To send him to Aa."

"My life is yours, Majesty," Tron whispered.

"Four times over now," said the King. "Have some duck."

He held out a drumstick that reeked of rich cooking.

"I . . . I may not eat meat," stammered Tron.

"Seriously? I'd bet my best horse that your Major Priests stuff themselves with goodies when nobody's watching."

"No, Majesty. I have seen them eat. Only priest-bread and cheese. They drink water. Their chairs are bare wood. Their tunics are as coarse as mine. The riches and jewels are for the Gods."

The King started to smile, changed his glance, and nodded, as if some puzzle had been explained to him. Tron took his loaf from his pouch, broke off a corner and nibbled.

"May I try that?" said the King, stretching out a hand. "Thanks. Gnff, dry as a dust devil. Good for the jaws, I expect. Well, Tron, now we've broken bread together, so there's an Obligation between us. Tell me what they promised you if you took the hawk from the House of O and that kind woman."

"Promised me?" said Tron. "Nothing, Majesty. In fact the One of Gdu was so angry that he demanded that I should be sent at once to Aa."

"*They* wanted my father's soul renewed?"

"I don't know . . . but . . . they were not ready, I think. And that the ritual should be broken so publicly, and by a priest . . ."

"Yes, of course . . . so why did you do it?"

"Gdu spoke in my heart, Majesty."

"No arguing with that, is there? And then my father died, just like that, uh?"

"Majesty," muttered Tron, "I . . . I . . ."

"Tron," said the King, dropping his gossipy tone and speaking as formally as a priest, "you owe me your life four times. That is four High Obligations you are under. I release you from all of them. But we have broken bread together. I do not release you from that."

"A powder was mixed for the One of Aa by the One of Gdu," whispered Tron.

"All my father's food was tasted before he ate."

"They asked if the King's bed had been moved. The

One of Aa signaled that it had not. There are powders which are death to breathe . . ."

"I am watched? In my bedroom? Lord Sinu! . . . The powder could be blown through a tube into the face of a sleeping man, do you think? What might the symptoms be?"

Tron quoted from a little hymn of Gdu:

> "The lips blue, the veins
> Hump on the back of the hands,
> Blood bright behind each cheek,
> The eye's black center wide,
> No antidote."

"That's it," said the King. He sat silent, picking little yellow grapes from a tight bunch.

"Majesty," said Tron hesitantly. "My life four times? One for the scorpion, one for the King . . . but . . ."

"One for the kingfowl—didn't you know? One for myself."

"Yourself!"

"They decided not to send you to that kind woman, because they still had a use for you. What was it?"

"To train the hawk."

"Did they give you a time limit?"

"By flood rise, when the Dead King goes to Alaan. . . ."

"And the live King is shown to the people . . . and in front of those people—most of them will be priests, of course, but there'll be a few of the real people—as I stand to be proclaimed as the finder of the feather, the man with the soul of the hawk untamable, a boy-priest comes out with a Blue Hawk on his wrist, trained and tame. What does the hymn say? 'I breathe into you now the Blue Hawk's soul, the soul of my loved one, the hawk that consents to sit on no wrist, that cannot be tamed.' And then this boy flies the hawk and it returns docile to his wrist. Can you read the sign, priest?"

"The hymn cannot be wrong," said Tron slowly. "That must mean that the hawk that I fly is not truly a

Blue Hawk, though it has all the plumage of one. And this was the hawk sent by the Lord Gdu to renew your father's soul. So He sent it as a sign that your father was not truly King!"

"And therefore that I am not either, eh?"

"I suppose so. But why . . ."

"I am at war with these priests, Tron. So was my father and my grandfather. It's a war without soldiers and without battles, but no less deadly for that. In the old days the Kings ruled in partnership with the priests, working together to honor the Gods and guard the people. But the priests grew jealous of the Kings, and slowly, slowly they have taken our power from us, working always (they say) for the honor of the Gods, but in reality judging all matters according to whether they will increase or decrease the power of the priests. For three generations my family has fought against them. If they kill one, then there is another to take up the fight. But suppose they could discredit the whole branch of us . . . I have several cousins who would make good Kings in a priest-ruled land."

By the end of this speech the pride and scorn in the King's voice had darkened toward despair. Tron sat still, brooding in the stifling heat. Nothing had changed, but everything had changed. What had the Mouth of Silence whispered? "You serve in a great business." A great wickedness, more likely. Somehow until this moment Tron had accepted that the Major Priests had to do everything they did, even taking the King's life so that the ritual of Renewal should be shown to have power. But now . . .

"The Lord Gdu *did* speak in my heart," he muttered. "The hawk is truly a Blue Hawk. Those are not lies, Majesty."

"Yes . . . yes. We must hold to that. So perhaps I am the true King. What do you think?"

The King's tone was taunting, but Tron looked earnestly at his face. How would you tell a true King? By the Eye of Gdu? No. By the look of pride and fierceness and command? No. These were no more than the hawk's plumage. How could you see the soul untamable? You couldn't, but at instants you could know it was there. Just as in the House of O and Aa Tron had felt all the vague confusions of the world narrow down to the sharp certainty that he must lift the hawk from its perch, so now was suddenly sure that the brown-faced young man smiling at his side was somebody to serve and to love.

"You are the true King," he said.

"Good," said the King, relaxing. "I think so too. In fact in my soul I know it, but . . . Anyway, and we'll hold to that. And the hawk is a true hawk, and the God spoke in your heart. So if the priests intend to read the signs the way you read them just now, they'll be mistaken. That's not so bad, after all. Do they let you eat grapes?"

Tron took the bunch unnoticing.

"If the hawk doesn't fly . . ." he began.

"Oh, I can hold on for a while. But we are coming to a crisis—they just weren't ready for it when you took the hawk . . . but you aren't reading the signs, Tron. Gdu *did* speak in your heart. I *am* the true King. So the Gods are preparing for something else, which we know nothing about yet. If you don't want those grapes I'll finish them."

Gingerly Tron slid one of the little gold globes into his mouth and was almost overwhelmed by the shock of unknown sweetness. He handed the bunch back, smiling for the first time.

"I had better not spoil my taste for priest-bread," he said.

The two of them spent the afternoon hawking. The King sent his retinue away by another route and walked off alone with Tron. He chose for himself a sulky-looking black-headed kite, almost twice the size of the Blue Hawk, but they couldn't fly both birds together for fear of a fight in midair. It is far harder for two people to stalk game than one, but after one missed chance they were lucky. Tron put up, almost at his own feet, a covey that curled away toward the flank where the King was coming carefully up, so the hawk made its kill barely ten paces in front of the King and he saw at close quarters that astonishing dive and impact, the deed the hawk was shaped for.

"Lord Sinu!" he said. "She strikes home like a lancer, full tilt. I'm glad to have seen that. That's how I've always imagined a cavalry charge . . . oh, we train and train for warfare, but no war comes. You priests wouldn't care for one, would you?"

"I think priests are as brave as anyone else."

"Braver, in some ways. That wasn't what I meant. Suppose I blew the Horn of War and gathered my army and fought and won. The Gods love a conqueror, and I'd have my nobles about me, armed and eager. They fret as much against the priests as I do."

"The Horn of War?"

"Yes? They don't teach you about that? Why should they? It's a vast thing—takes four priests to carry it and a fifth to blow it with a sort of bellows . . . I don't know what kind of noise it makes. My father never heard it either."

"But if it's the priests who blow it . . ."

"Ah, Tron, you see the priests as a single mind, because that's how they teach you. One mind doing the will of the Gods. But in fact there are as many minds as there are men. Do you know the One of Sinu?"

"I have seen him. He's blind, isn't he?"

The King nodded but said nothing for a moment. Tron thought about the One of Sinu, a tall gaunt man, yellow-skinned with age and quite bald, leading his red-robed followers through the processions and rituals of his angry God, sightless but knowing every step and every position because the rituals never changed and he had performed them since he was Tron's age.

"Yes, he's blind," said the King suddenly. "That helps to cut him off from the others. I see quite a bit of him, at initiations of cadets into military orders and things like that. He's a proud man, and angry—angry that the other Major Priests are slowly making less and less of his order as part of the process of whittling away at my power. If my Obligations called me to fight, he'd blow the Horn of War, and once that was done the others couldn't stop me from mustering my army."

"But who is there to fight?"

The King snorted.

"You don't imagine we're the only nation in the world?" he said. "Why, I could reel you off a dozen High Obligations I have to other Kings, beyond the deserts and mountains and marshes. It's the priests who've closed the Kingdom, though they say it's the will of the Gods—but the Obligations are still there . . . supposing the other Kings remember them. . . . You'd better pick up your bird before she's gorged herself too stupid to fly."

The King's voice was harsh with frustrated energies; even if he had kept it quiet and steady his mere presence would have fretted the Blue Hawk. As it was it took Tron some time to coax the bird onto his gauntlet and slip its hood into place; and then it didn't settle into its normal stillness but fidgeted with its talons and made half-movements with its wings as though longing, blind though it was, to soar away from his wrist.

"My hawk will never fly in the Temple," he said slowly. "Not in front of all the people. Even one stranger . . ."

"Yes," said the King. "I thought of that some time ago. I was bothered about whether I oughtn't to tell you. Perhaps I would have. But I have to fight with what weapons I've got, you see. What will they do when you fail?"

"Send me to Aa."

"Hm. Yes. The One of Gdu must know it can't be done, surely."

"Yes—but he was so angry, I think he'd prefer me to fail. I must run away."

"Not easy. Every village has its priest. Every face is known, because every man is bound to one village.

There are no vagabonds in my country . . . if I could get you to the far south, to Kalavin's house near the Jaws of Alaan. His father . . . hm . . ."

When the King thought, his face became unreadable. During the hunt he had lived, as it were, entirely on the surface of his being, taking all his pleasure in the minute of action. Now he seemed to turn inward and explore his own depths. Tron waited until he laughed and returned to the moment.

"I've an idea," he said. "Tell you later, when I've worked it out. Mustn't waste good hawking time. My turn now."

He led the way southwest at a steady march, far too fast for serious hawking. Once he put up a hare but was slow in loosing his hawk, which turned out to fly in a quite different style from the Blue Hawk. It hunted level, and very fast, but the hare escaped it by a sudden break to the right; the hawk's pace carried it far too wide on the turn, and by the time it was ready to pick up the line the hare was still, a rock with the other rocks. At a cry from the King the hawk lolled back to his wrist without a lure, as though it were used to missing its prey.

"She's lazy with hares," said the King. "I'd like you to see her after kingfowl someday. My method is brisker than yours, at least, and a lot more dangerous. When we spot a covey we simply ride them down. They rise and rise again, but if we go hard enough we get among them. We yell and tootle our horns to keep them on the move, too. It's rough riding, half a dozen of us, hawk on one wrist, horn in the other hand, reins loose on the pony's neck—you've got to have a pony who knows the game and can pick its own line, but it's up to you to keep him going flat out, come rough come smooth. I've seen plenty of bones broken, including some necks, but the risk of that is part of the fun. And yet . . . it's only a game compared to your way. Your way is the real thing. You use as little as you need, but use it to the utmost. If ever I fight a war, it will be like that."

He gave up all pretense at hunting and walked beside Tron, asking questions about the life of priests.

"Where will you sleep tonight?" he asked suddenly.

"At the Temple of Tan."

"Whew! I told you that priests were braver than us in some ways. We don't go near it. It's not just that it's priest-ground, but . . . you know, I'm a servant of the Gods, just as much as you. But I don't think the Gods are altogether what the priests say they are . . . at least, I'm certain that the priests try to use the Gods, in the same way that they try to use you and me. . . . Now, here. I wanted to show you this."

For the last half mile they had been striding through thorny scrub land, hopeless for hawking, so it was startling to come out into an open place from which it was possible to see for a hundred miles. The King had led Tron to the southern edge of the rock plateau. O was halfway down the sky to their right and His slant beams lit the enormous tract of land that the river had smoothed out in her passage toward the Jaws of Alaan. They stood not two hundred feet above the plain, but in that dry air eyesight seemed to reach on forever. Far to the left in a gray and yellow line lay the beginnings of the dunes of the true desert. Even farther to the south Tron could see a line of blueness bluer than the sky and separated from it by a faint, erratic, glistening thread that was the snow that lay all year long upon the impassable Peaks of Alaan. To the west the plain was dimmer, veiled in sun glare. The river flashed like steel where it rounded the Temple of Tan at the point of the plateau, then became a black snake wriggling endlessly toward the mountains.

"Look there," said the King. "What do you make of that?"

He pointed almost at the foot of the ridge on which they stood, then gestured along to the left. The plateau didn't immediately give way to the silted plain. Instead a lower line of hills came curving out of the southeast and almost joined the main mass, leaving only a tongue of flatland half a mile wide. As it reached eastward this tongue widened into a broad, empty plain of extraordinary whiteness over which ran a series of strange lines, almost like veins, branching into lesser lines or sometimes widening into regular-shaped flats. It was hard to see from above whether the lines or flats were above or below the main level. They did not look natural, and certainly the earth rampart that blocked the narrowest part of the tongue seemed man-made.

"What is it?" said Tron. "Why is it so white?"

"The white is salt, priest. In my great-grandfather's time that was a fertile valley. Those lines are water channels. It was good earth and grew huge crops. Then the yield diminished. We deepened the channels. The soil turned sour. Cakes of salt began to form on the surface. It was the King's land, so armies of peasants were gathered to carry the salt away. More water was poured on the land, but the soil died. My grandfather built that rampart so that a high flood couldn't reach into the valley and carry the salt out to other fields."

"Perhaps the Gods . . ."

"If the Gods were angry with my fathers, who served them well, then they're angry with the whole kingdom. The same thing is beginning to happen everywhere, always on the best land. We can dig new channels to cultivate poorer land, but that is no answer. We've been building up a sickness in the soil, too slowly for a man to see in one lifetime. But soon it'll be too late and the soil will die, except for two narrow strips along the riverbanks where Tan brings down fresh silt each year. So we must change the way we farm."

"Change?"

The King laughed at Tron's astonished tone.

"That's the priest in you. All knowledge is in the hymns. The hymns never change. Only the priests know the hymns. Who teaches the herdsman's son the management of cattle? His father? No, the priest of Sodala. Who teaches the noble's son to fly a hawk? An austringer? No, a priest of Gdu—though, mark you, old Tandal, who taught me, was a lord of his art and fun to

hunt with too, not like this One you've got now. Huh!
Think, Tron. Must I live in comfort and do nothing but
hawk and feast and practice warfare while my kingdom
is dying, dying because nothing can change, dying because every year the One of Tan measures the flood
level and from that moment the hymns decree exactly
how much water must be lifted by how many turns of
each wheel into which channels, and what seeds are to
be sown in every yard of my land? Are you surprised
that I enjoy hunting? Gdaal knows where the hare
crouches, but the One of Gdaal doesn't!"

Tron stared in dismay at the glaring valley.

"Is it because of the salt that we left the Temple of
Tan?" he asked.

"It was empty long before my great-grandfather's
time. My guess is that the priests withdrew into the desert partly to increase their mystery and partly so that
they could not see with their own eyes what they were
doing to the fields. But you, Tron—you've tamed a
Blue Hawk, so you've changed the hymns. Will you
help me change more?"

"I . . . I owe you my life four times, but I . . . I am
a priest."

"I released you from those Obligations. Besides, I
owe you one back. I shall find a reason to sleep in another room, one with plain walls. That's nothing. But
because of the bread we've broken . . . Listen, Tron.
Do you know how you came to the Temple?"

Tron shook his head.

"I guessed they wouldn't tell you. You were the
thirty-third child born in some village since the last
priest was taken. If you'd been a girl you'd have been
sacrificed, still wet with the birth-fluid, to the God of
your village—Gdaal, I should think in your case—a lot
of those desert hunters have your dark skin, and you
seem to have the knack of stalking, and there's one or
two other things you can't have learned from the hymns
. . . never mind. You were a boy baby, so they let you
live. Your mother suckled you for a year, then the

priest paid your father five bronzes and sent you away to the Temple. Your father paid the priest five bronzes to make beer for a village feast, so the money came back to the priests."

"I didn't know."

"That's what I thought. I've heard that sometimes a mother will mark her boy—cut off the top joint of his little toe or something like that—so that she can tell him if ever she meets him. But the priests of that kind woman, who look after the babies in their first years, inspect them when they are brought to the Temple and give to Her any who've been marked. They do everything they can to separate the priests from the people . . . somewhere, Tron, you have a village, and brothers and sisters, and a mother who fed you at the roundness of her brown breast."

"And a father who sold me."

"What else could he do? Kalavin's elder brother is now a priest, and he was the firstborn son of the General of the Southern Levies. Only the priests know which priest he is. His father doesn't. But Tron, you and he . . . in spite of everything they can do, you are still part of my people. Has your blood changed, which your mother gave you?"

"Perhaps, Majesty. The Gods . . ."

"The Gods are powerful, but They left you the step of a hunter. Tron, you've spent twelve years in the Temple and three months in the desert. What will you feel when you go back to the Temple?"

Tron stood silent, gazing at the unreachable snow line of Alaan. Never to walk alone again, with a hawk on his gauntlet, every sense sharp, and a whole long day before him!

"It's hard for you," said the King. "That's another thing. Your whole training is mapped out so that you never have to make a single decision for yourself. Everything is laid down. That's why, in the end, priests are bound to make bad rulers—they've never learned to decide."

"Majesty, you talk as though they did not serve the

Gods, as if all they were interested in was keeping themselves in power. But they do, they do."

"Oh, yes, they do. A lot of people serve me, in my place and in my kingdom, but not all of them serve me well. Will you serve me, Tron?"

Tron hesitated. He didn't know what to say or do, or what he wanted, or how to fend off the onslaught of the King's appeal.

"I can serve only my Lord Gdu," he muttered.

He wanted to turn away but the King's eyes held his, eyes like his murdered father's, a look of defeat, fierce and sad. Nobody had ever trusted Tron before. They had given him orders and known he would obey, but that was not trust. Nobody had befriended him; he had companions living with him under the same rules of fear, but that was not friendship. Now the King offered him trust and friendship but . . .

He wrenched his eyes away and stared at the glaring valley. Out of its whiteness a shape seemed to swim, a hawk, a Blue Hawk, his own hawk, sick and bedraggled as when he'd first seen it. He had broken the ritual to take it out of the House of O and Aa. Now it came to him again as a sign.

"I'll try to help you," he said. "I cannot serve you, but I'll try to help you."

"Good," said the King, unsmiling. "In fact, better. I saw your face change, Tron. What did you see?"

"He sent me a sign," said Tron with a vague gesture at the salt-flats below.

The King nodded, accepting it as a fact.

"I come here often," he said. "Whenever I feel I can't fight them anymore. That place is a sign to me. It isn't only that the fields are dying, Tron. That's true, but the Kingdom is sick in a quite different way. It's sick like a caged hawk. We've been cramped into these plains for too long, between Alaan and the marshes and the desert. D'you know, in my Obligations there are a dozen trade routes that I'm supposed to keep open, and they're all closed. There are wells in the desert too that I ought to guard, but I can't because whoever drinks their water falls sick and dies. When I look at those dead fields it seems to me that we must either burst out of this trap or die. Do you understand?"

"Yes, I think so. The Temple's like that, in a way. You don't realize it while you're inside it, but now I've learned to be free. . . . What do you want me to do?"

"Nothing yet. But . . . is the Temple of Tan built at all like the Great Temple?"

"Well, there's no Palace, and there doesn't seem to be a Room of Days and Years. But other bits are exactly like."

"So there might be hidden doors and passages in it? Will you look? I'll come there at noon in three days' time. We haven't got very long. The embalmers finished my father's body nine days ago. It's less than twenty before the flood begins and he must go on his journey. . . . Listen! that's Kalavin's horn! I'd like you out of sight before they come, in case one of them recognized you. Then they'll think I took you off alone so that I could kill you and bury you somewhere back there. Hurry! Noon in three days' time!"

Trained to obedience, Tron moved quietly away down the ridge, crouching until he was hidden by a belt of sprawling cacti. *Killed me? Buried me?* He began to reason it through. A King is suddenly confronted with a boy who helped to murder his father and is now a threat to himself and his whole dynasty. What does he do? Seems friendly, breaks bread as a sign of trust, finds a reason to go alone with the boy into a tract of wilderness, and there, unwitnessed, the murder is avenged, the threat broken, and the boy vanishes. This King, though—perhaps he had considered it, and then had taken the greater risk of offering trust and friendship— not just for the sake of having a spy among the enemy, but because it was his nature to be direct and open, wherever he dared. He had the soul of the hawk in him.

Tron picked his way westward until at last the ridge tilted abruptly down toward the river. Now O lay almost on the horizon so that the whole sky was aflame with His going. Beneath it the irrigated plain stretched endlessly away, a monotonous dun expanse that looked as if it were covered with ashes, not dying but already dead. Nearer, the gold sky glowed again, reflected in Tan's curve round the promontory, and against this fiery arc the pillars of Her Temple stood black as the priests of Aa.

V

THE THREE DAYS PASSED AT A DREARY PACE. EVEN hawking seemed curiously savorless. Tron was watching under the shade of the archway into the Great Court-yard when the King came down the slope to one side of the ancient road, striding from rock to rock. Before he reached the sand-strewn paving he sat down and took off his sandals.

"I'm bound to leave footprints," he said, grinning. "Bare feet will look like yours, or the slave's who brings you your food. Phew! I'd forgotten how hot sand could get. How does your hawk stand this heat? Blue hawks are mountain birds, you know—it's cooler up there."

"I try to hunt near dawn and dusk, Majesty, and rest when O is high. The hawk's asleep in my cell now. The stonework is thick enough to keep it cool."

"Is it thick enough to hide secrets, Tron? Have you found anything?"

"A door, Majesty, but . . ."

"Good! Let's see."

Tron led him to a long, low room, which must have been one of the eating halls, and turned to a deep-carved relief of Gdaal, fox-headed and carrying the sacred bow. Around the God ran a dance or procession of wild animals, hares and lions and desert asses and antelopes. Tron gripped the horns of one of the antelopes and twisted inward and up, sliding that small section of the frieze along hidden grooves into the cavity behind.

"The catch is like that of an ordinary door," he said. "This one was so corroded that I had to break it. There are three doors I can't move at all. I think the sand must have clogged under them."

The King grunted, then fiddled with the secret section, trying its movement along the grooves. He looked at the floor.

"You swept the sand clear here?"

"I had to. There was sand on the other side too, but I rocked the door to and fro till I could squeeze through. It moves quite easily now. Look."

The slab swung silently under his weight and he led the way into a bare little chamber lit from above by a shaft. River owls nested here and had covered the floor with their mutes and droppings. The King grunted again.

"You won't be able to hide the fact that this door's been opened," he said. "Not on the inside, anyway. But when we've finished you'd better sweep the sand back on the outside. Where now?"

"I . . . I haven't explored very far, Majesty. I . . . I was afraid."

"No wonder," said the King, looking at the two narrow slits of darkness that led out of the chamber. "Let's try this one. I'll go first."

The slit was so narrow that Tron had to edge sideways along it. Even when it was still faintly lit by the light from the chamber they had left Tron felt that the massive walls were poised to move in and press him into nothingness, like a midge between a man's fingers. He crept along, tense to snatch himself back from any touch or rustle.

"Hello!" said the King's voice some distance ahead. "Steps, going up. Light at the top . . . twelve steps, Tron. Ah. Come and look at this."

The light was only a faint grayness, but Tron yearned toward it as though it were safety and sanity. When he reached it he found the King gazing through an irregular shaped opening, two inches across at its widest.

"Know where we are?" said the King, giving way.

The spyhole funneled down and gave on a patch of

sandy floor, mottled to a regular pattern. The taloned feet of a colossal statue of Gdu showed at the upper rim of vision.

"That is a side aisle in the House of Tan," said Tron.

"What made those marks on the floor?"

"I did, Majesty. I do my dances to my Lord Gdu morning and evening."

"Yes, of course. And that's where the King would sit during the Rituals. One would think this hole was big enough to spot from down there. What's on this wall of the aisle?"

"I think we are looking out of the ear of Sodala, Majesty."

"Hm. I wonder how far these tunnels lead."

They seemed endless. For an hour the two of them crept like spiders along the crannies between the Temple walls, and still Tron trembled with the horror of the darkness and closeness of these secret ways. They were never wholly lost, because of the frequent spyholes which gave onto every major room or courtyard in the Temple.

"Are there any hymns of Temple building?" said the King suddenly.

"No, Majesty. That knowledge was lost with the Wise."

"I just wanted to know whether these passages were built on purpose for spying, or whether they would have built the walls hollow anyway, and just took advantage of the fact to make this network. I think that must be it. There're places so narrow even you can't get along, and other passages that don't lead anywhere. Now, I want to try something else. Stand still. Listen."

Tron shut his eyes and waited, straining for sounds. Nothing stirred. Then, against all his training, he cried out with shock as a hand touched his face, and the cry was muffled into silence by a hard palm over his mouth. The King laughed and let go.

"I'm sorry," he said. "I wanted to practice. It looks as though there'll be passages like this in the Great Temple—yes, even in the walls of my own palace. So

I'll have to explore them and that'll take some delicate stalking. You didn't hear me coming?"

"No, Majesty . . . but the boys chosen for Aa learn a dance called Flying Shadows. The steps are done blindfold, swiftly and in silence, with a knife of sacrifice in the hand."

"Hm. . . . Are you afraid of this place, Tron?"

"Yes, Majesty."

"So am I. It's going to be heart-stopping work. Let's leave now. I don't think there are any more secrets to be found here—it's just the same secret, repeated and repeated."

The King was wrong. In the narrowness of a dark crevasse he disturbed a roost of bats. Tron, following some paces behind, felt them whirl past like a sudden soft wind, musty and rustling. He stood rigid, locked in fright and revulsion, and when they had gone reached out to pat the solid wall, to reassure himself with the reality of stone. His hand, however, touched nothing.

He moved it about, and found a rectangular opening containing a bronze latch.

"Majesty," he called. "Here is another door!"

A tug, and the latch clicked up. The door swung easily.

"Lord Sinu! What is this?" said the King blinking in the blaze of light.

"It's a Room of Days and Years," whispered Tron. "But . . . but . . ."

"You said there wasn't one. Look, that door's been bricked up."

He stepped inquisitively down into the drifted sand on the floor, but Tron stood where he was, staring in dismay. The room was a desolation. Its windows looked west across the river, but as the wall ran sheer to the water they could only have been seen from a boat or the far bank. Beneath them ran the proper sloping rack, but heaped with dust and bird-mess and tumbled bits of nests. Even from the door Tron could see that beneath the mess the rack was all disordered. In the Great Temple he had been awed by the ranked mystery of the rods, the sense of their counting away the generations, themselves unchanging. Here they seemed to lie all hugger-mugger. When he overcame his shock and stepped down into the room his foot scuffed up a rod from the floor, and brushing the mess off the rack he found places where twenty or thirty rods lay side by side, quite neatly, but then there would come a gap, a rod lying sideways, and then a stack of rods trying to fill a single place. The medallion of O lay in an empty space; the medallion of Aa he found leaning against one of the stacks, as though the Goddess Herself had begun to hold back the orderly march of days.

For all his pleasure in his own new freedom Tron still felt a rooted reverence for the order and discipline of the Temple, for the pattern of life that brought two thousand priests each exact to his place, each to chant the same line of the same hymn as their predecessors had chanted in that place a thousand flood-times ago. Though the Lord Gdu had chosen to set Tron free from this pattern for a while, and though he would have liked to continue that freedom, he still knew that his own happiness was nothing compared to the continuing life of the Temple. He had promised to help the King, and the King was fighting to break the power of the priests, but until this moment he had not understood how little might be left when the fight was over. If it should end like this!

"Lord Gdu," he whispered. "How can I choose? Send me a sign."

Leaning on the bar that ran along the bottom of the rack he stared out of a window to where the vast flatness of the irrigated plain lay shimmering under the noon of O. Out there, invisible, were peasant villages—but now he saw one, a circle of huts each with its pointed reed roof like the helmet of a Temple Guard. The huts seemed to float toward him. There was the Headman's eldest daughter feeding the communal fire with dried cow-dung, as was her right and duty according to the hymns. There was a green-robed priest performing a prayer-dance before Tan's square mud shrine. There were the men talking over their priest-brewed beer, and the women hoeing between the half-grown beans. And now he could hear the steady, heavy knock of the village water-lift as it raised its allowed gallons into the irrigation ditches. The vision came and went as if half-veiled by the heat haze. Now the women were bending between the stunted bean-plants, picking up irregular scales of gleaming white stuff and throwing them into baskets. The village men fell silent as two priests glided out from behind the shrine, one in green and the other black-robed, black-cowled, black-gloved. The priests paced slowly toward the hut where a woman lay in labor, about to give birth to the thirty-third child in the village since last the Gods demanded their due. . . .

The vision was broken by a sigh. Tron took a moment to realize that it had come from his own lips.

"What's the matter?" said the King gently.

"The fields are dying. The people are sick."

"Yes, I told you. That's one of the things you and I are going to change."

"But if it ends like this!" said Tron, turning with a gesture that swept the abandoned room.

"I don't understand about this," said the King. "The Room of Days and Years is a priests' mystery. Kings aren't shown it or told about it."

"I've seen the one at the Great Temple," said Tron. "It was all in careful order. And later the Keeper of the Rods told us that if he made one mistake in how he moved the rods, that mistake would repeat itself again and again, and each time it would cause other mistakes, which would repeat themselves too, and cause more mistakes, until he couldn't tell from the rack whether Aa was full-faced or veiled, and whether it was flood-time or harvest-time."

He picked up a white rod banded with one black ring and one brown.

"Look," he said. "I don't know what this means—up at the Great Temple they paint a black ring onto the rod of the day on which a King dies. Perhaps the One of Sodala died that day in another year. It probably told a lot more, in itself and combined with the rods around it. The Keeper of the Rods could have read it then. Now it says nothing."

The King leaned across the rack and blew the dust off the medallion of Aa, but when he realized what it was he drew sharply back and cupped his hands to make the good luck sign.

"Yes, I see," he said. "And that's what happened here? You'd think they'd have sent up to the Great Temple, when things started to go wrong, and copied the position of the rods up there. In fact the Wise must have meant there to be two racks, so that one could check the other. . . . That's it! Look Tron—there *were* always two racks, for that reason. But when this one began to get disordered the priests at the Great Temple refused to allow it to be corrected by their rack."

"But why . . ."

"Priests! They were jealous. Or perhaps this Temple supported the King . . . in fact, it would be much easier to be King in a country where there are two factions of priests to set against each other, and that would be reason enough for the priests at the Great Temple to try to close this Temple down. They could say that the disorder of the rack was proof of the Gods' displeasure. When I'm truly King I'll bring the priests back here, and set this rack in order again. It's madness to rely on one rack only. Do you think that's why the Gods caused us to meet, Tron—why They have sent you such signs?"

Tron turned again to stare out of the window, but no vision came, no word whispered out the distances. Even so he shook his head.

"No," he said. "I think this room is a sort of sign, like your salt valley, Majesty. They let us find it, but when I felt I couldn't help you if it was all to end like this, They sent me a vision of the land dying. I don't know what it means."

"Good," grunted the King. "No doubt it's a great thing to restore a Temple to the service of the Gods, but

I feel . . . have you ever seen the river at the very start
of the flood, Tron? It takes a fisherman's eye to notice
that there's anything different at all; the ripples hump
against the reeds, there are smooth patches like
stretched silk between the wavelets, then the lungfish
begin to croak . . . everything that's happened so far to
us, even my father's murder, feels like that—little signs
that tell of a huge change coming. The Gods don't send
me visions, but I'll tell you how I read this room. It's a
sign like the salt in the fields. It says that a country
cannot be ruled without system and order, just as the
Gods cannot be worshipped without rituals. But if the
order and rituals are so stiff and unchanging that they
cannot alter, ever, then when a time of change comes
they become like this. They die."

Tron shook his head again, knowing that even if
change was what the Gods desired, he was afraid of it.
Not for him the King's excitement at the prospect of
riding the flood wave. He understood very well how
strong was the priests' desire to hold the Kingdom to its
ancient, rigid ways. But for the Goat-Stone and the Blue
Hawk, he could well have grown to be a priest of that
very kind. He sighed once more.

"Who are you to be afraid of change, Tron?" said the
King mockingly. "You began it all. In fact it's like what
you told me about these rods—each change causes further changes. Because of what you did at the Renewal
the priests themselves are planning to change the ritual
of my Showing to the People, by letting you fly your
hawk then. And because of that . . . you know, you're
like a child who takes one pebble out of a great cairn of
stones and brings the whole pile rumbling down."

Tron didn't answer, and was glad to leave the ruined
room and to close at last the door into the secret ways.
Though he said nothing more about it, the King seemed
aware of his need for assurance. They shared a meal of
priest-bread by the river and spent the heat of the afternoon lazily trying to snare the young bream that loi-
tered beneath the undercut mud banks. Tron fell in, and
the King jumped after him to help, though he was in no

danger. After that they lay on a bank of almost burning gravel to dry their clothes in O's rays.

In the heavy, steamy silence, where no life seemed to stir, something gave a sharp and rasping bark. Another bark echoed it before the silence closed in again.

"What was that?" said Tron.

"Lungfish waking," said the King somberly. "I told you it was a sign. The flood is coming sooner than I thought. The priests will send for you in a very few days, Tron. I must get back to the Temple and try to find out what they're planning."

VI

THE PRIEST-LITTER SWAYED TO THE TRUDGING STEP of the slaves. Tron had never ridden in one before, and sat awkwardly in it with the Blue Hawk on the pole beside him hooded and still. He was near the end of the procession. First came a detachment of Temple guards, each with his own slave marching beside him to carry the spindling parasol that kept the sun off the soldier, then the three litters—Tron's last—and finally a smaller party of guards. They moved in a rigidly straight line across the desert, constrained by the causeway that the Wise had built. Already the Great Temple rose lumpish on the horizon, looking like a natural outcrop of sandstone. Even the Tower might have been a pillar of windcarved rock.

As the distance slowly closed, fear came and went in waves, and Tron was glad when a guard came to draw the litter curtains so that nobody should see him, leaving him alone with his hawk in a stifling, swaying, cloth-walled box. He closed his eyes and tried to drive the fear away by remembering the details of the morning's strange hawking.

Five days after the King's visit to the Temple of Tan a young priest of O had brought him a message to be ready. Late next morning the three litters had been carried into the Great Courtyard, one empty, the others containing the Mouth of Silence and the One of Gdu. Guards and slaves had been sent out of sight, and then the One of Gdu had put his hand into the closed basket he carried.

"Now let us see what your hawk can do," he had

snapped, tossing the dove into the air. Tron had hooded the hawk so that it shouldn't be flustered by the strangers; his fingers were awkward with nervousness; it was several seconds before he was ready, and by then the dove was spiraling upward, so white that it glinted like metal against the even blueness of the sky. The hawk had missed its morning's hunting and rose eagerly, apparently without yet seeing the dove. But the dove's wingbeat quickened as though it were trying to escape by climbing into the sky itself. The hawk rose slowly up the tower of air to seek its natural height to hover and search. The three watchers in the courtyard craned upward, their necks aching with the angle. The Mouth of Silence shaded his face with a black-gloved hand.

Suddenly it was almost as though the dove's nerve had cracked. It broke from its spiral and headed east, diving for extra speed. Now there was no hope of the hawk catching it. A wild dove can outfly any hawk, and even a Temple dove with that advantage of height had nothing to fear. The hawk for another full circle took no notice, simply continuing to climb, while the dove fled toward the desert. Tron began to pull the lure out of his pouch.

But the dove was a Temple dove. Its home was among pillars and crannied statues, not the featureless wild. When it was almost out of sight it turned, seeking the familiar safety of buildings. It was halfway back when the hawk flung itself out of its circle, arrowing down. The dove twisted aside, but was now too low to gain speed by a dive of its own. The hawk hurled down, fast as a flung stone. The lines of flight converged, vanishing behind the Temple wall, but before the watchers could stir or comment they saw, framed under the brilliant arch of the main gateway, the terrible moment of impact signaled by a puff of white down.

"You gave the boy no time, brother," began the Mouth of Silence. "I have heard of hawks lost."

Tron was already running for the gateway and didn't hear the answer. Beyond the gate he slowed, so as to move calmly up to the kill. He found the hawk perched on its prey, and, as usual, delicately plucking away the thigh-feathers. When it gave its customary silent hiss of warning at his approach, Tron paused in his stride.

For an instant he saw the two birds, living and dead, with different eyes. It was as though time had loosed its hold on this little orb of matter, so that everything in it would endure for ever. The slate feathers and the white became untarnishable metal; the clear, fierce eye was a topaz; the ball of blood at the joint of the dove's closed beak was a ruby. Tron knew that a God was using his human eyes to look at these things.

The instant itself was timeless. The priests at the gate probably didn't notice his hesitation before he moved in and whistled the hawk to his gauntlet. He slipped the hood on, then cut the dove's leg free at the joint. The hawk was tearing at this morsel as he carried it back to the gate.

The One of Gdu looked sulky still. The Mouth of Silence was saying, "There is a suitable passage in the Hymn of the Birth of Sinu, I think. After the fight with Ktimmu O speaks thus . . ."

The One of Gdu had been barely listening. Though his head was attentively bowed, he had stared at boy and hawk with bright-eyed fury.

Now, in the swaying litter, Tron worked out meanings. The One of Gdu had come hoping for failure, and had done his best to see that it happened, but Gdu had turned the dove back toward the Temple and the hawk had made its kill. So the failure would take place in front of King and people, with great loss of prestige to the priesthood of Gdu. That was certain. Both the One of Gdu and Tron knew that the Blue Hawk, trained to the presence of a single quiet-footed boy, would revert to wildness if they tried to fly it before three thousand priests, nobles, and people in the humming crush of the Great Temple Courtyard.

The Mouth of Silence, meanwhile, was considering how the priests could justify this change in the Ritual. If they were to use the flight of the Blue Hawk to break the King's dynasty, they must be able to prove that they had not done this for their own purposes, but because it was something they could not avoid, something they were ordered to do by the unquestionable hymns.

Both those things were clear. But what was the meaning of the vision? Tron was sure that Gdu had sent him another sign, but he couldn't yet read it. Was it a warning that the King (the Blue Hawk) would after all destroy the Temple (the dove)? A promise that what Tron and the King had begun would come to its wished-for end? There was no telling. The hawk gaped on its pole, distressed by the airless heat. Faintly through the muffling curtains Tron heard the wavelike pulse of the Farewell to O, sung from the Tower by the choir of gold-robed priests. This sound had marked the rapid fading of daylight since he could remember, with a mixture of comfort and dread—dread at the approach of Aa, comfort at the protection of the Rituals. Now all comfort was gone from it. Succeed or fail, he guessed that the Major Priests would have no further use for him once the Live King had been shown to the people. The Temple would be his tomb.

Only the King had a plan. Just as the hawk seemed to have lost the dove that morning, so Tron felt he had lost all contact with the King. But Gdu had turned the dove back.

Once again he drank sweetwater. He and the hawk were alone in a small, north-facing room. It was already too dark for him to look for spyholes without being seen to do so. The King and his plans seemed far away—in fact he was not sure that the King would even know about his return to the Temple. So for the moment it seemed safest to act in everything as though he were the priests' obedient tool.

The water was sweeter than he'd remembered, or perhaps they'd mixed it stronger for him. He carried his bowl of offering to the sill with the drug already dragging at his mind. As he whispered his night hymn he found himself thinking, *I shall not leave here alive. It would be better if I died.* He did not remember lying on

his mattress. Next instant, it seemed, he was waking to
the old clear note of welcome from the Tower as the
rim of O's disc broke the desert horizon.

The drop from his window was thirty feet sheer. The
room had its own latrine, an arrangement that Tron
knew of nowhere else in the Temple. He guessed this
must be a prison cell—not one of the "tombs," of
course, those cramped cubes of darkness below the
Tower in which erring priests crouched the hours away,
but a place to keep a prisoner safe without seeming to
punish him. So it would be well watched. The inner wall
was covered with an intricate carving which told the
story of Tan's imprisonment in the Country of Alaan.
Tron looked at all the pictures with interest, as was natural, and found two spyholes and a place that he was
sure must hide the catch of a secret door, though he
didn't dare try it.

The breadboy who brought him food and water
wouldn't meet his glance, a bad sign. The breadboys
had a strange knack of knowing what was happening in
the Temple. No one else came, but Tron occupied the
lonely hours with the slow and difficult job of splicing a
new end into a broken tail-feather, an operation that the
hawk bore with great patience. He moved its stand to
the window, and sometimes it stirred and ruffled as a
flight of doves swung past. He decided to let it fast for a
day. For his own reasons he was anxious that it should
be eager to fly.

That dusk, knowing where the spyholes were, he decided it was safe to stand at the window and merely
pretend to drink his sweetwater. When he tilted the
bowl, the slight slope of the sill carried the water outward and let it trickle down the Temple wall without a
sound. In the middle dark he woke to a stir of air and a
faint rustle. A blackness blocked the lower half of the
window. His heart thudded. Had they come to inspect
the sill for traces of the spilt drug? Would its smell taint
the night air? The figure vanished and the air stirred
again as the stone slab closed. Tron took a long time to
sleep again.

Next morning he found two red beans in his bowl of offering. He smiled, taking it for a God-sent sign, though the priest who had brought them had been only plotting to keep him content. That day they sent him out into the desert in a curtained priest-litter to show the Keeper of the Rods and the One of O what the hawk could do. This time he set the hawk up into the air before they loosed the doves. It killed two almost perfunctorily among the sullen dunes. The Major Priests looked pleased.

"The flood begins to rise," said the One of O. "In two days Tan must carry the Dead King on his journey, and that evening the Live King will be shown to the people. You will have your hawk ready?"

"If it takes a full crop now it can fast tomorrow," said Tron.

"Like a priest, eh?" said the Keeper of the Rods, jolly and friendly. He glanced at the hooded bird, then at Tron, then away, much as the breadboy had done. Tron shivered.

No sign came that night. If anyone slipped into the room Tron slept through their visit. Next day was stillness and loneliness. As the last notes of the Farewell to O sucked the light out of the sky a new noise filled the dark, a deep, windy, repeated groaning. It was so eerie and inhuman that for a moment Tron felt that some vast creature of Aa had stirred from its lair below the dunes and was lurching, slow as a toad, toward the Temple. Then human voices answered, thin and high, and then the unmistakable bass chant of priests singing one monotonous phrase again and again. A fourth sound joined in, more rhythmic even than the priests, a heavy and repeated thud that seemed to jar the bones of the Temple. Then Tron understood. The huge painted coffin in which lay the embalmed body of the Dead King had been carried down to the Palace courtyard. The groaning noise came from some enormous funeral horn. The King's wives were wailing their farewell, and the Priests chanting their welcome, while one heavy beam was swung and swung again to break down the wall that blocked the Gate of Saba so that the coffin could be carried through and lie all night alone in the House of O and Aa. Tomorrow, when the Live King had been shown to the people, he would be carried back through the Gate of Saba on a litter gay with the symbols of the blessings of all the Gods, and then the Gate would be walled up once more, not to be opened until he too went on his journey.

The thought of the King filled Tron with fears and imaginings which bustled around in his skull, swelling and shrinking and then repeating themselves as though they were quite new fears when they were old, old. He dared not even sigh for sleep in case some watcher saw that he had not drunk his sweetwater. Once more his priest's training, the habit of stillness, helped. In the end, without his noticing the moment, fears became dreams.

A touch woke him. He opened his eyes but did not stir. A warm breath in his ear whispered his name.

"Majesty?" he answered.

"I could not risk coming before."

"We are watched! Spyholes!"

"That kind woman has that watcher. It is the One of Gdu. He mixed a powder for you to breathe, but I caused him to breathe it himself. Now you must hide."

"I planned to let the hawk loose at dawn and then throw myself from this window and go to Aa myself."

"I'd have grieved, Tron. Truly. Now, put your hand on my shoulder and follow me."

"Will you hide me in the Palace?"

"I can't trust my servants."

"They will search all the Temple."

"Not this one place. We have blown the death horn. They have broken down the Gate of Saba. They can't stop the Ritual now, so they will be forced to show me to the people. By then you'll be far away. You will travel with my father."

Tron's heart leaped so that his body shook with the spasm.

"It's all right," said the King. "You'll travel alive."

The walls of the Great Temple had been built thicker than those of the Temple of Tan, so the tunnels in their heart were wider. Still, creeping from dark to dark with his right hand on the King's shoulder and his left carrying the drowsy hawk, Tron sensed all around him the fearful pressure of stone. They moved with many pauses and listenings. From time to time a slot of silver would appear where a spyhole opened into moonlight. Once a trick of sound brought the muttered chant of the Priests of Aa so clearly through one of these that Tron sensed a huge, pale mouth grumbling just behind the stonework. At last the King reached back and pulled him close.

"There's a niche two steps to your left," he whispered. "Wait there."

Tron waited in a dark as intense as that in the Cave of Aa from which O first stole the pot of clay to mold the world. He could even hear the minute movement of the breath of the hawk. After a long time a voice whispered, "Tron." He managed to suppress the jerk of fright.

"No watchers," whispered the King. "Eight short paces. Turn left. One pace. Nineteen steps twisting down to the left."

The moon-streaked House of O and Aa semed vaster than by day. They had emerged from a hidden door to the left of the altar. The King led the way, keeping in the blackest patches, to the center of the main aisle where the coffin lay. By daylight Tron would have seen a round-topped chest, four feet high and wide and ten feet long, brilliantly painted, lying on a framework from which protruded a dozen carrying-bars. What he saw in the moon shadow was like another altar, a black slab of sacrifice.

"The lid is bound down with linen bands," whispered the King. "I sealed them—that's part of the Ritual—but I did it so that I could unseal them. There's an inner coffin at that end. This end is full of offerings to go with my Father on his journey. I saw to it that there's plenty of bread and wine and water. At the foot of the inner coffin there's a gold box. It's got a couple of ebony wedges in it, and a jade slab you can use as a hammer. When you are clear of the quay you can wedge the lid up enough to cut the bands with my Father's dagger. I've seen that it's sharp. There's a basket with two doves, alive. They've got their own grain and water. You can give the hawk fresh meat. You'll come to Kalavin's father's house some time on the second day. I must tell you, I've had no answer from Kalavin, but there has not been much time, and it's hard to find a messenger one can trust. We must pray to the Gods. Ready?"

He worked at something in the dark near either end of the coffin, then with a faint grunt heaved upward.

"Be quick," he whispered. "The space is right against the end."

The coffin was like a mouth now, waiting to swallow Tron. He twisted himself between its jaws, feeling with his bare foot for bare wood. Something rattled as he touched it, then he found the bottom and crouched shuddering down.

"All right," he whispered.

The darkness came down on him without a sound.

VII

THE STRANGE THING ABOUT THE DARK BOX WHERE Tron crouched at the feet of the Dead King was that he found it comforting. The doves shuffled their plumes, destroying silence, and the air was thick with smells of life, fresh bread, spices, herbs, rich meats. Now that he was faced with the actuality of this ghostly journey Tron was no longer afraid. It was as though he had used up in the last few days all the fear that was in him. He whispered his night hymn again, settled the hawk to perch on what felt like a jeweled casket, laid his forehead on his updrawn knees, and fell asleep.

He slept through the dawn hymn on the Tower, and woke with a jerk when the doors of the House of O and Aa crashed open and the horns marched groaning in. The sound of them came gradually nearer. He could envisage the slow procession led by the King's trumpeters with their high-curling instruments passing within arm's reach on either side of him. At last the groaning ended, but there was no pause before the voices of the priests of Aa swelled out of the echoes.

> Mistress of dark,
> Mother of Gods,
> Aa never born,
> Ruler of birth,
> Aa never dying,
> Ruler of death,
> A man's life, yes, a King's life,
> It is birth, it is dying,
> Coming from Aa,

> Going to Aa,
> Between them is nothing,
> Beyond them is nothing,
> And over that nothing
> Aa rules also.

Between each of the many verses the horns sounded
a long note that began strongly and ended in a barely
audible stirring of air. Tron could picture the priests of
the other Gods still filing in, and the benches of the
nobles filling, and the Inner Courtyard thronged with
lesser nobles and the headmen of a thousand villages,
all summoned to see the Dead King go and the Live
King ruling. Then the pulse of the hymn changed and it
began as most Great Hymns did, to tell a story. The
coffin stirred, but so slightly that it took Tron time to
realize that twelve nobles had gripped the carrying-bars
and lifted it. The rhythm of the hymn set their pace as
they carried it slowly down the aisle. Sudden as a knife-
thrust a bright gold thread shot down the blackness
above him and he knew that they had come out into the
Courtyard and O was blazing down onto an unsealed
crack between two boards of the coffin lid. The light
was welcome, but Tron found it odd and shocking that
the coffin should have been so carelessly made, as if for
a one-day show, rather than a noble vessel to carry the
Dead King safely on his long journey to the land of the
Gods.

> Saba, said the woman
> Speaking from darkness,
> How shall I judge you?
> I had in my cave
> From one moon to the next
> A ghost who howled
> Like a jackal for vengeance
> On his son who killed him.
>   "My sword is bloodless."
> He drew the blade slowly.
> See the bright bronze.

See the blood on the bronze
Glistening like the streams
From the throat of a victim
On Aa's dark altar.
See, see, as dew fades
At O's first coming,
The blood dwindles, vanishes,
And the bronze is bright.

The coffin-bearers marched at a pace so slow that
Tron could not sense the movement across the Inner
Courtyard. The gold thread vanished and returned as
they passed under the connecting arch, and again under
the main gateway. Meanwhile in the hymn Saba
threaded his perilous way through the tests set by the
Goddess, ate the dark bread and not the white, sat on
the ebony stool and not the ivory throne, chose for his
journey the black goat and not the white pony.

A faint jar marked the moment when the coffin settled on the sledge that waited on the Great Causeway.
Whips cracked. The headmen of a hundred villages,
lined along the paving, strained against the thongs and
lugged the greased runners of the sledge into motion.
Every unevenness of the paving jarred through the coffin with unpredictable thuds and scrapings, so that Tron
seemed to be crouching inside a drum beaten by a
crazed giant. Each new blow boomed in his ears and
sent a shock wave along his bones. The hawk flung itself about in flapping panic, which, but for the noise of
the runners, must have given them away to the priests
pacing beside the sledge. Desperately Tron felt about,
found a wing, gripped it and with his other hand
grabbed the scaly legs. Rough though his touch was, it
seemed to quieten the bird, and in a few minutes he was
able to still it completely. Then for mile after mile he
knelt in hot, stale, strange-scented air gentling the bird's
feathers, cushioning it from the impacts of the paving,
and whispering comfort. Three times the sledge halted,
and while the teams on the thongs were changed, the

hymn, which had been an endless background to the jar and grate of the runners, rose clear. Then the whips cracked and the torture began again.

All the while O beat down on the coffin and the air inside became more stifling. Tron took water from the jug and sprinkled the bird with it, then splashed his own head and neck and found a few minutes' relief. But soon after the third change at the thongs the jug was empty and he knew that unless they soon reached shade hawk and boy would travel dead with the Dead King, to Alaan. Despite the risk of its betraying him by some wild movement he slid the hood off the hawk's head and held it close to the crack in the hope that it might find better air. By that faint light he saw that it was in a miserable state, almost in coma and gaping continuously. Even if he were somehow to lever up the lid and set it free, it would not fly now. There was nothing to do but endure and pray with swollen lips to Gdu.

They halted again. New voices joined the hymn, the priests of Tan welcoming the coffin to the care of their Goddess. The coffin grated slightly as it was lifted from the sledge, and then there was the rustle and creak of slings being slid around it and tightened. It swayed, but in silence, as it was hoisted through the air. The gold slit in the lid vanished. Men gave brief, whispered commands, close by. Water sucked and gurgled. Another rustle as the slings were drawn free. Then

> Son of Saba
> Servant of the Gods
> Go now to Aa
> In whose palace
> The just are happy.
> Tan shall take you
> Gdu shall guard you
> O watch over you
> Alaan guide you
> Aa receive you.
> Go.

At the last enormous note wood scraped on wood, the voices of rivermen rose in a work-chant, feet moved on stone, the coffin lurched with the heavy movement of the barge below it, and the light slap of waves grew louder and firmer. Six thousand throats shouted all together, horns growled, gongs boomed, cymbals crashed. For a mile up and down the river birds rose shrieking and squawking.

As the uproar of farewell faded in Tron's ears he felt at the foot of the inner coffin and found a box whose lid rasped with jewels. Setting the hawk down, he opened it and took out the tools the King had prepared for him. The ebony wedges were so close-grained that they felt like metal, and the heavy jade brick fitted his grasp as if it had been made to hammer with. At first the wedge tried to bounce out of the crack between the lid and the coffin, but he managed to tap it firm and then hammer with greater force. All at once a streak of light showed, which each blow widened until it was as broad as his little finger; there the wedge stuck, having driven the linen band taut. He put his mouth to the crack and gulped river air, as cool in that heat as a draft of midnight, then lifted the hawk to do the same. While he held it there he peered through the crack.

He saw a tumbled mess of brown water, frothy and thick with the silt of unknown mountains. Beyond this a riverbank swung suddenly into view as the barge twirled on the torrent like a leaf on a stream. The reedbeds raced past, and then he was looking back up the river to where, already half a mile distant, lay the thronged quay from which the barge had been launched into the floodstream. Sunlight twinkled off armor and instruments, and the gaudy parasols of the nobles looked like tiny flowers, but the people—priests of O and Aa, Gdu and Tan, the nobles, the headmen, the guards—were all merged by distance into common humanity.

The hawk seemed refreshed, so Tron let it perch on the end of the inner coffin while he wedged the other end of the lid open. By the light from the slit he had made he could now see that the jade slab he was using as a hammer was the clearest pale green, unflawed, carved with pictures of warriors on horseback, each no bigger than a pea. It must have been worth the harvest of a hundred villages. Wriggling back, he discovered another water jug, from which he drank. One of the doves was dead with heat and the other very feeble, but it revived with startling speed when he held it up to breathe the fresh air. Having failed to persuade the hawk to drink (hawks seldom do so), he settled into his space among the spice caskets and nibbled a little bread.

Some time later, a new noise began to rise above the ripple and cluck of the river, a steady hoot mingled with a patterned thud and clatter. He rose and peered nervously through the slit, wondering if he ought to knock the wedges out. The river seemed very wide here, and the barge, though twisting more rapidly, appeared to be traveling less fast. It was difficult to estimate. The reeds and mud walls of the far bank slid out of sight and he was looking back up the churning waters, all mottled with yellowish froth. Then he gasped as the other bank hove in sight, a mud wall pocked with the tunnels of river creatures, not twenty yards away. No wonder the river had seemed wide. He was almost aground.

The strange noise rose louder. A human voice boomed through it. A hut came into sight, then another, then . . . just as he thought he was about to gaze all down the curve of the near bank he saw a barricade across the river, a series of spindly stilts, carrying a platform with men waiting, some of them holding long forked poles. On the bank was the village orchestra of drums and flutes, and the Headman's son standing to one side and swinging round his head, like a hawk-lure, a cord that ended in a block of hollowed wood through which the air thrummed and hooted. The platform was clearly makeshift. The brown flood-waters frothed angrily round the swaying stilts, and as soon as they rose another few feet would whisk it away. The barrier didn't run clear across the river. At its outer end stood a green-robed priest of Tan, arms raised in welcome, singing with all the strength of his old lungs. Tron dared not knock the wedges away now. He was too close. He crouched, trembling, and waited to be discovered.

Sluggishly the barge settled against the jetty, but with the betraying slit below the lid facing upriver. The rivermen's poles rattled on the thwarts. The racket from the orchestra rose to a crazy, shapeless mess of sound. The villagers yelled at the top of their lungs, calling on the Dead King to ask the Gods, when he reached Their land, for blessings on crops and cattle. The barge lurched and began to trundle faster and faster, cutting sideways through the streaming waves. The platform creaked and crackled. The priest boomed his farewell.

Now the barge twirled in the opposite direction, so Tron was forty yards clear before he saw the platform again. A few twists later he saw the river foaming and eddying over a mudbank on which he would certainly have been stranded but for the villagers' help. He wondered how many generations of Kings had swept this way before, and been thus passed on. No doubt that priest knew a local little hymn which told exactly how and where the platform should be built.

Next time, warned by the distant din, Tron knocked his wedges out in time, and waited in darkness while the barge was coaxed past ancient obstacles. So he did not see the men of three villages roped together in gangs and working up to their knees in tearing water to pass him out along a great sickle-shaped sandspit. Nor, near O's going, did he see the faces of another village change as the barge swept past ten yards beyond the end of their jetty, not needing their help. There, behind the back of the impassively chanting priest, each man glanced at his neighbor, wondering what offering the Gods would demand to avert the effects of this bad sign. Which cattle? Whose child?

Despite the slit, the coffin was dark enough for the hawk to sleep unhooded all afternoon. It was heat-bedraggled still and would be unfit to hunt for a week, but Tron was no longer afraid for it. He sat among the treasures quietly chanting as many of the common hymns to Tan as he could remember.

He had never thought much about Tan. Unlike the other male Gods, Gdu had taken no lovers, either among the Gods or the Daughters of the Wise. He was like a priest among the Gods, whereas the love story of Gdaal and Tan and the jealousy of Sinu ran through a hundred hymns. But now Tan carried Tron in Her care and seemed to be protecting him from discovery, so it was proper to be grateful. As he sang the soft words he wondered a little about his own brothers and sisters and his own mother, and what it might be like to live in a village, to love and be loved—never, in fact, to have been chosen. He found it impossible to imagine, and Tan sent him no vision.

Through the slit he watched O's going redden the brassy sky until the God seemed to stand on the dusky level strip of the western bank. The barge was now right in the middle of the river, so he cut the linen bands and raised the heavy lid inch by inch, propping it open with the jeweled offerings to the Dead King until it was wide enough for Tron to wriggle through. He fetched the food, the hawk, and the dove out but was able to lower the lid only by leaving outside the last two treasure boxes he had used to prop it open. With the King's dagger he poked the cut ends of linen into the slit below the lid so that they looked complete.

The prow of the barge curved up into a slender arc, like the antenna of a grasshopper; behind this on a gilded perch rode a jeweled and enameled image of the Blue Hawk; the perch stood on a small deck from which an embroidered curtain hung to the main deck planks, screening off a little triangular cave, which, Tron found, held nothing but a coil of mooring rope. There was just room for him to curl up on the rope, with the birds, caskets, and food tucked into the corners.

As soon as his mind was free of the business of making these small arrangements, fear came seeping back.

Aa, he calculated, was now moving toward the night of Her Most Darkness and would not rise for several hours. But when She did . . . That glaring eye would look down on the desert and the fields and the shining river and inspect everything that man had done during the day. It would see the barge, see the slit bands, see through deck and curtain to a boy who had broken the Ritual of the King's Going and now lay huddled and helpless on a coil of rope. . . . The fear closed around him. It was like a pool of darkness in which he was drowning. He was suddenly certain that the only safe place for him was back in the coffin—the birds and the other things could stay where they were. He pulled the curtain aside and scrambled out onto the deck.

There, in the last of dusk, he saw the spread arch of the canopy, which had shielded the coffin from the sun all day, painted above and below with the image of Gdu in flight, still dimly visible. He whispered his hymns to the God, and then a late farewell to O. While he was doing this he noticed that Tan was beginning to make a mist on Her surface and knew that by the time Aa rose the barge would be veiled from Her seeing. Then distantly through the dark he heard the chant and clatter of yet another village waiting to help the King on his journey. Feeling he was doubly protected by kind Gods, he crept back and hid in the curtained cave.

This time the scene was lit by flaring bundles of dried reed soaked in wax, and the villagers were protected from the dark by a priest of Aa, to sanctify their presence in the night. Tron, peeping through the curtain, shrank back when he saw that cowled figure as black as a midnight shadow amid the glitter and glare. It was said that Aa gave Her servants power to see in the dark. Tron was suddenly certain that the eyes hidden in the shadow of the black cowl would notice that there was something wrong with the linen bands, or even pierce through the curtain and see him crouching there. But the priest made no sign, the villagers did their age-old duty to the Dead King, and at last the clatter and flame dwindled back into the night.

An hour later, on the other bank, another village passed the barge on in much the same way. Then it became very dark as the mist hid the stars. Tron slept.

A heavy thud woke him. He was just thinking that the barge must have drifted into an unexpected sandbank when a voice swore, fiercely but softly. He lay rigid. Something scraped. Another voice whispered. "No harm done. I'm aboard. All fast this end."

Kalavin, thought Tron. *He must have brave servants to come and look for me in the utter dark of Aa.* He was just about to call out when the man spoke aloud, his voice sharp with anger and surprise.

"Gdaal's arrow! Someone's been! This band's cut!"

A different voice told him to keep his mouth shut, then cried out with equal anger that the other band was cut too. With extreme care Tron twisted and peeped through the curtain. By starlight he could just make out the bulk of the coffin and the curve of the canopy over it. Outlines changed as the lid heaved open.

"In you go, Kintali," whispered a voice. "Feel about. They may have missed something."

"I'm frightened," said a child in a whimpering voice.

"Gdaal gave you the right, boy. I robbed the King's coffin when I was no older than you. How can you teach your son if you don't do it yourself?"

After a long, shuffling pause the boy's voice said, "But there's a lot of things here!"

"Hand them out one at a time. Got it. Hnff! That's spices. Tip 'em over the side, Anagdaal—we can't have the priest sniffing out myrrh under the floor of your hut. Right, Kintali. Got it. Got it. What in Gdaal's name is this? A dead bird! That's new. Better put it back. Got it. No, Kintali, that's his sword. That stays. We never take the weapons. That all? Sure? There's usually a couple more boxes and some food."

"The other thieves must ha' took 'em," said the second man.

"Why didn't they take it all, then?"

"Not time. They'd have to get it done in that reach between Tan's elbow and Para-para."

"Perhaps they took some and left some so that we should be satisfied, and not cause trouble," said a softer voice.

"It's never happened before," said the leader angrily.

The soft voice chuckled at him. Tron heard them lower the lid, refasten the bands, cast off, and ripple into the dark. He lay still at first, locked in shock at the callous blasphemy. But slowly, like warmth after chill, a sort of exhilaration crept through him at the discovery that there were people in the riverland living a secret life, unknown to the priests, and had been living it for generations. And yet they too believed in the Gods. The man had said that Gdaal approved of this hunting, and the woman had been named for that God. . . .

The woman. The softer voice! The chuckle in the dark! Tron had known that when he was eventually confirmed into the service of Gdu he would most probably be sent to be the household priest of some noble family, blessing their hawks and healing their serfs, and that there he was bound to meet with women. He had never dreamed that his first encounter with that half of his own species would come as he crouched in hiding and listened to the talk of a family of hereditary coffin-robbers.

The chill of dawn on the river caused Tron to wake thinking he was still in the Temple of Tan, and then to realize that quite early on the previous afternoon he must have drifted past that house of ghostly Gods without seeing it. When he edged his curtain aside he found both banks of the river hidden in mist, so it seemed safe to explore the barge again and check that the robbers had set all to rights. They had done better despite the dark, he discovered, than he had managed by daylight, except that they had left the dead dove lying against the foot of the coffin. He picked it up and took it back to his hiding place, where he cut its leg off and gave the drumstick to the hawk to tear at. The thigh he dropped all bloody into the pouch of his tunic, having already acquired the hawker's absentminded habit of carrying odd gobbets of raw meat around.

He merely whispered his morning hymns, in case he was close enough to either unseen bank to be heard. While he ate breakfast he looked at the paintings with which the coffin was covered; they told the story of the wanderings of Saba in the land of Aa, and showed him riding a wicked-looking black goat from adventure to adventure. On the barge too, every inch of wood above the water was covered with garish pictures. The canopy over the coffin was bright blue, and the winged Gdu that had appeared black in the previous dusk turned out by daylight to be a blaze of blue and gold. The barge rode on the sludgy torrent like a brilliant-scaled beetle on a ditch.

Soon O sucked the mist off the river and Tron found himself being swept across an enormous flatness. Yesterday, though the flood had raised the river by twice the height of a man, it had still channeled between steep banks. Here, over a thousand floods, it had lifted its own banks above the level of the plain by building up ramparts of silt on either side. Though these embankments were the work of Tan, men had adapted them to their own needs, leveling and strengthening them and then cutting wide notches through which they allowed the flood waters to flow in a controlled surge to fill the hundreds of miles of canals and ditches that covered the plain. At every notch a swarming gang of peasants toiled with balks of timber, sheaves of reed, and thousands of earth-filled sacks to raise the floor of the notch to keep pace with the rising waters. All these materials must have been made ready since the last flood in accordance with exact instructions in the hymns. The banks were still too high to see over, but through each opening Tron could watch the whole vast plain swing by, apparently limitless rich earth pimpled with the huts of ten thousand villages.

Crouched at the gunwale, keeping to the west of the barge so that the small round of his head should be in-

visible against the glare of O's rising, Tron stared hypnotized. As the barge surged past in midstream the peasants would straighten their backs and cry out for
blessings, then bend at once again to their work. Tron
was appalled by the hugeness and richness of the land,
and the enormous system invented by the Wise and still
organized from the Temple, which saw to it that the
plain neither dried out into desert nor flooded into one
ruinous vast lake. It was terrifying to think of meddling
with a system like this, which worked as it had worked
through O and Aa knew how many generations. If the
system broke down there would follow ruin, chaos,
deaths in tens of thousands.

And yet the land was dying. The King said so, and
the vision had confirmed it. Dying despite the clever-
ness of the Wise and the labor of the people. The King
was like a priest of Gdu who held his knife poised over
the abdomen of a patient. If the priest made his cut in
exactly the right place, and continued so, he might
come to the cause of sickness and remove it, and the
patient might live. If his knife slipped either way by the
thickness of a fingernail, the patient was sure to die.
Though Tron's part in the operation was no more than
that of the boy who holds the lamp, he was afraid.

The fear broke the spell. He tore his eyes from the
plain and gazed forward along the line where the river
drove south, almost as straight as a canal, toward the
Peaks of Alaan. They were much nearer. The snow line
was no longer an unsupported twinkle above the southern horizon. Now the crags were there, dark blue with
distance, seeming steep as the walls of the Temple,
streaked with ravines. Unused to guessing distances,
Tron thought they might be twenty miles away, a day's
march. The arid air deceived him. The plain ended not
in foothills but in a sudden tableland, which climbed
abruptly for a few hundred feet, then tilted impercepti-
bly toward the mountains. It was from this tableland
that they rose sheer, more than a hundred miles to the
south.

All morning the barge plunged down the middle cur-

rent; O rose steadily; the banks and the laboring peasants seemed hardly to vary. Tron started to fret with the
idleness and the heat. How was he to know when he
neared Kalavin's house? How was Kalavin to reach
him, among so many watchers? From time to time he
raised his head and peered forward from where he lay
beside the hawk and the coffin in the shade of the canopy, and when he did so he began to see the end of the
plain approaching, a wall of hill, smooth and rounded
like the muscles of an arm, lion-colored. The river
surged straight onward, though there seemed to be no
way past the barrier; the surface of the water changed
from a steady, driving current full of eddies to knotted,
hummocky waves and patches of foam. The barge
rocked and staggered as the river swung in a vast plunging curve and headed eastward. In three miles it fell
from ten feet above the plain to twenty feet below. On
the north side the embankment was punctuated with
elaborate stairs of waterwheels, but the south bank was
now a series of pale cliffs carved out from the rim of the
tableland. The current ran strongly under the cliffs,
driving the barge faster than it had so far traveled and
bringing it closer and closer to the rock surface. Tron
hid in his cave, because from each of these cliffs dangled a crude platform manned by peasants with forked
poles who fended the barge away from the rocks and
sent it undamaged on its journey. Not all the platforms
were needed, but for mile after mile Tron had to crouch
in hiding, alarmed by the new sense of hurry in the waters, the feeling that they were racing forward to a final
destination.

It was lucky that he stayed in hiding, for the roar and
grumble of the river along the rock face almost
drowned the clamor of the next group waiting for the
barge. A long stone quay lined the bank and curved out
into the river, making an artificial bay of calmer waters,
into which the barge drifted stern-first. Through the slit
in the curtain Tron could see the whole scene. First he
slid past a group of shepherds led by a brown-robed
priest of Sodala. The men were blowing reed pipes and

the women rattling tambourines; all wore coarse sheep-skin jackets and wide straw hats. Next, after a small gap, came a typical group of peasant cultivators standing behind their green-robed priest of Tan, with their drums and flutes and bull-roarer, the priest singing a different hymn from the priest of Sodala and the band thumping out a different rhythm. Beyond them stood a small tribe of Gdaal's people, half-naked, wearing tangled hair to their waists, howling like jackals round their yellow-robed priest. Soldiers in armor were ranked behind the red-robed priest of Sinu on the curve of the quay; their brass trumpets blared, and they shouted and stamped in unison to their priest's hymn. The quay itself was thronged with the brilliant-liveried household of a great noble, including an orchestra of harps and oboes that twittered quite inaudibly behind the uproar of the lesser people; the noble himself, a small gray-bearded man dressed in green and yellow, sat on a brown horse at the very end of the quay. Beside him, as was proper, stood his priest of Gdu in the blue robe.

Tron stared at the crowd in panic. This must be Kalavin's house. The man on the horse must be his father, General of the King's Southern Levies. This must be the end of the King's river journey, the destination to which the river had been racing. From here on he must journey by land to Alaan. But how was Kalavin to rescue Tron, unseen by all these people and five separate priests?

As Tron crouched there, biting his lip, six rivermen stepped forward from between Tan's people and Gdaal's. They wore the General's livery (dark green skirts and yellow sleeveless jackets) and carried poles, with which they cunningly twisted the barge on its axis and then propelled it steadily along beside the stonework. Once they were round the curve they leaned with all their strength against the poles, straining to shoot the barge as fast as possible out into the main current. The shouts of the people rose. The barge reeled with the shock of surging out of stillness into the turbulence of the racing waters that boiled round the point of the quay. Tron stared back with ice in his stomach. The hawk, perched on an emerald-crusted box, flapped for balance.

Now most of the crowd was hidden, but the priest of Gdu was still clear, chanting, arms raised. The General sat on his horse as still as a hooded hawk. On the downstream side of him, hitherto hidden by the horse, stood a tall young man with a bent nose. Tron knew him at once, though he had only seen him briefly in the shadow of the rock outcrop above the Temple of Tan.

Kalavin's face was working with distress. He laid a hand on his father's knee, but his father turned his head away and gently removed the hand. Kalavin snatched a glance over his shoulder, checked that he was unwatched, raised his arms as if to dive into the furious river and then, still poised on the brink, made swimming motions with his arms until the General dropped a warning hand on his shoulder.

The barge began to turn again on the current. A slow revolution carried the whole scene out of sight.

"Swim," Tron muttered aloud. "I was not chosen for Tan. I cannot swim."

Kalavin had spoken to his father, but his father had forbidden him to act and insisted that Tron must ride on with the Dead King. Kalavin had failed.

VIII

~~~

THE BARGE BUCKED AND HEAVED ON THE HURRYING
waves. Its turning was no longer a steady, stately revolution but an erratic twisting. It was like a lizard wriggling in the grip of a hand. As soon as a spur of the
southern hill hid the crowd on the quay Tron slid out of
his cave and looked around. The land had closed in on
the northern side now, too, and there was nothing to be
seen but brown, featureless slopes, except where the rub
of the river had scoured out bare rock and made a cliff.
There were also occasional ravines carved into the
south side, contributing little trickles of water to the
brown flood.

At first when the current carried him toward one
bank or the other Tron craned over the gunwale,
searching the water for shallows where he might hope to
survive. But he soon found that the current took the
boat always through the deepest places, so he settled
down in the bows and ate a little of the strange, soft
court-bread. O was past noon, but far less fierce than in
the desert. The dun hills stumbled backward, unpeopled.

At last, in the early afternoon, there came another
change, a stretch of boiling and clashing water in which
the barge hesitated and circled where a fair-sized river
foamed down white rapids from the east and the mingled waters turned south and ran straight into the hills.
For a while Tron was certain the barge would founder
in this turmoil, but it rode it out, shipped very little water, and finally staggered into the gorge. On either side
now, cliffs rose sheer. The black rocks hissed and driz-

zled. The surface of the water was roaring foam, and wild eddies, and patches of greasy smoothness that came and went. The barge lurched toward the far cliff, then plunged away again, but in that instant of panic Tron could see that the drenched rock offered no footholds if he had summoned up the nerve to leap for it. And they were now traveling so fast that to jump would have been like being thrown from a height against the cliff.

He staggered back to his cave, took the live dove from its basket and flung it in the air. It rose, terrified. He watched as if it were an omen.

Out of the strip of harsh blue sky between the clifftops a dark shape hurtled, striking the dove with that familiar impact that loosed the little puff of white down. Four wings battled as, locked together, a white and a slate body fell. Then, less than a man's height above the torrent, there was a Blue Hawk climbing steadily away with the dead dove clasped in its talons.

"You are here also, Lord Gdu," said Tron in a croaking voice. "I praise Your name."

He fetched his own hawk from the jeweled box and undid its leg thongs, so that it could fly in its regained freedom with no danger of tangling the leather around some branch and there starving. Its plumage, bedraggled yesterday by the heat of the coffin, had been preened smooth but had not yet recovered the armored gloss of real health. He held it up to fly but it clung to his gauntlet, looking about it with the air of an old priest who has just remembered a hymn forgotten since childhood.

In the bewildering chaos, with the barge twisting and dodging on the breakneck foam, it was hard to know even which way the river was taking them. The gorge was a crooked crack in the tableland and often seemed to end in a sheer black wall, which turned out a minute later to be a place where the river raged round a zigzag corner. In one such place they touched a hidden rock. The barge groaned through all its planks, staggered and tilted, then rode on with an inch of water slopping to and fro around the gaudy coffin. At the next bend the sky, which a moment before had been an intense, jagged strip between the dark cliff edges, paled to pearly white. All shadows vanished. Tron and the hawk were drenched as if by one of those freak desert thunderstorms he had experienced only once in his life. The gorge ahead seemed filled with smoke, and above the rush and racket of the river there rose a deep, growling bellow.

As they plunged toward the smoke, this sound drowned all others, so that Tron felt that he would not even have heard a scream close to his ear. The surface of the river lost its foam and tumble and became glassy, boiling in places but stretched taut, as though it were being hauled by a God into the smoke.

All at once, without thinking, Tron knew what caused the smoke.

"Lord Gdu! Save me!" he yelled, flinging the hawk with all his force into the air and rushing across the deck toward the nearest cliffs.

The sheer rock raced past, hopelessly out of reach. But then the barge twisted suddenly in toward it. Tron tensed for the impact, but the swing of the barge continued until they were actually moving against the main current, upstream, quite slowly, about ten feet from the glistening wet stone. The curve of their course continued out into the main current again, and once more they were rushing with stately smoothness toward the smoke. This time Tron saw against the whiteness the long, wrinkled rim of water that seemed almost motionless as it strained over the edge and flung itself down in foam.

But again the big eddy carried the barge in toward the cliff and now he saw what was causing it. Right against the cliff, jutting out several yards along the rim of the fall, ran a sort of wall, sheer-sided and square-ended as if it had been dressed stone. Its top was a horizontal line about eight feet above the surface of the water. It formed a stubby barrier, forcing the current outward around its edge but at the same time trapping some of the water to turn in this dizzying circle.

Now they were moving toward the cliff again, with the upcurving prow of the barge actually scraping the smooth wall. Tron stood still, hypnotized by noise and fear. Then, as if an invisible hand pushed him on the shoulder to break the spell, he darted forward, grasped the prow with one hand, trod unhesitatingly on the gunwale, flexed his legs, and flung himself upward. His hands clutched at the rim of stone, his arms convulsed as he swung his body sideways and up. A knee and elbow hugged the cold surface, then dragged his body up to lie on the flat stone, gasping in the steady downpour.

The barge held his gaze. More brilliant than ever with wetness, it nuzzled its way along the wall and then moved slowly up the cliff, probing here and there against the rock like a huge insect searching for a cranny. Because it was close in to the cliff the eddy took it farther upstream than before and then farther out into the current. The rush of water caught it and carried it clear. In three heartbeats it was at the rim of the fall, poised on the brink, tilting, gone.

Crawling to the other side of the barrier on which he lay, Tron gazed down. He was very tired. The unimaginable weight of water foamed endlessly down, seeming to move slowly like something in a dream, following set paths and patterns. It dragged at his mind. The face down which it fell was not sheer, but curved outward, not much but in a strange, smooth arc. The foam smothered most of the curve, but the wall on which he was lying protected the part immediately below him, and he could see hundreds of feet down, though not to the bottom. At the limit of his vision the rock face had ceased to be a cliff and become a very steep slope.

So this was the end to which the King—countless Kings—had traveled. This fall into nothingness was the gateway to the country of the Gods. He stared and stared, appalled.

His own sneeze shook him aware. He was drenched

and icy cold. *I must leave this place,* he thought. *Lord Gdu, I am part of Your purpose. You saved me from the falls so that I might continue to serve You. Your hawks know this place. Lord Gdu, save me again.*

He rose to hands and knees and, not daring to walk so close to that beckoning drop, crawled along the wall to the cliff. There he found that the rock face was a smooth surface—so smooth that man must have made it so—but that to his left a flight of steps climbed into the smoke. Up these, dizzy with the bellow of the falls, he made his way. Everything streamed with water. In places the folds of the cliff gathered the falling drops into rivulets and little cataracts, which drizzled around him. Thirty steps up he looked back and could no longer see the surface of the river or the rampart that had saved him. His teeth chattered and his body shuddered in fierce spasms. He was terrified of climbing alone into this icy blankness.

"But Gdu is here," he said, unable to hear his own voice through the boom of falling water. The smoke thickened as he climbed on, and soon he came to a place where a larger rivulet had washed six steps away, leaving only the stubs of them sticking out from the cliff. Spreadeagled on the rock he forced his body through the numbing stream and knelt gasping on the far side of the gap.

When he had strength he climbed again, and found quite soon that the steps turned back on themselves so that he was now directly above the flights he had just climbed. The smoke thinned. The streams on the rock face dwindled. His own limbs gained a faint warmth from the effort of climbing, but he was still colder than he'd ever been when the smoke turned gold and he climbed out into sunlight—sunlight veiled and feeble, but enough to cast a shadow. Ahead of him the line of steps snaked up the cliff. Below and slightly behind, the boiling waters plunged over the fall.

He climbed slowly on up the endless steps until the mist thinned enough for O's caress to warm him fully.

Here he found a small platform from which the next flight zigzagged back into the smoke, so he rested and looked down into the gorge. Slowly his awe of the falls changed to amazement—amazement at their enormous boom, and the smokelike pillar of spume that towered a mile above the cliffs on either side, and the strange, clean beauty of the moment the water went over the edge. From this height the rim of the fall seemed not to be moving at all, despite the turmoil on either side of it. It lay across the gorge in a single sweep like hard glass, following a line as exact as Gdaal's half-drawn bow in a Temple painting. It seemed impossible that nature had cut so perfect an arc, or that man—even the Wise— had performed so stupendous a work, though man had clearly made the rampart that had saved him and the steps on which he now stood. But the falls could only be the work of a God. Quickly he whispered the incantation that must be used when one stumbles by accident on a secret ritual:

> "If I have seen
> What the Gods had hidden
> If I have walked
> Where the Gods forbade
> Undo my deed
> Lords of all life
> Take back the minute
> Lords of all time."

As he spoke the last line the gorge altered. O in His westward journey had been slanting directly between the cliffs, but now, as if sending a sign, He moved beyond the rim, and the chill shadow of the rock swept across the platform. Tron praised Gdu again, then climbed on.

Almost at once Gdu seemed to fail him. Some two hundred steps above the platform the stair vanished at a point where it had once leaped across a thirty-foot cleft on a climbing bridge. Tron could see the jagged supports of that old arch on either side of the gap, and looking up he could also see where the same thing had happened again as the steps swung back out of the mist. There seemed to be a few holds and crannies in the rock, but not enough, and even if he were to edge across that hideous traverse and climb on into the smoke he would have the same crossing to make again a hundred feet higher.

For the moment he couldn't face it. He sighed and started despairingly down the steps in the faint hope that in his absorption with the falls he had failed to notice some other way up from the platform. When he was about halfway back he was startled by a sudden whimper in the air and a blur of slate-blue plumes hovering at his side. Habit raised his left arm chest-high and thrust slightly forward. The Blue Hawk settled, ruffled and sulky. Habit again made Tron feel in his pouch and find the thigh of the dove that had died in the King's coffin. The hawk accepted it with no grace at all, but gripped savagely at his arm while it tore at the tough sinews.

The pain pierced Tron's tiredness and numbness like a trumpeter's alarm piercing to the brains of sleeping soldiers. Gdu had sent him this signal by His servant the hawk, saying "Here! It is here!"

He looked about him. Below the falls boomed on, unpitying. But above him the cliff was split by a jagged, sloping fissure, which vanished over a jut of rock. Carefully he eased the hawk from his bleeding wrist and settled it onto one of the fallen stones that lay in places on the stairs, where it continued to rend at its meat with absorbed gusto. He reached into the crevice with a hand and a foot, found holds, and pulled himself clear of the steps.

The dances of the Temple, precise but strenuous, do not teach how to climb raw rock. But they do make the body strong and supple, give it true sense of balance, and most of all teach the limbs to move exactly to the demands of the will, so that if a movement is physically possible the body can perform it. Tron didn't consider

this. Wherever he rested and hung panting he praised
Gdu for still continuing to lead and guard him.

Beyond the jut of rock the crevice widened and deepened, then tilted from the vertical so that for a long way
he was able to crawl inside it up a very steep slope with
plenty of jags and roughness to cling to. When it closed
and forced him out onto the cliff face again, he found a
narrow ledge running upward toward the smoke, and
this in turn reached an area of broken cliff where there
was a crisscross pattern of fissures to use as holds.
Nothing was as difficult as the start, and even where he
was clinging to a cranny above some plummeting drop,
Tron wasn't afraid. He knew that Gdu was showing him
the way and would give him strength to reach the top.

He climbed continually to his left, so reached the upper stair just at the edge of the cleft from which the
bridges had dropped away. The remains of the man-
made supports gave him the footholds he needed to
wriggle up onto the first unbroken step. Here he rested,
in case Gdu should be moved to send him the hawk
once more; either as a sign or a companion, though he
had no lure and it was useless to cry or whistle against
the monotonous roar of the falls. As he waited, lonely
above that deadly drop, he became more and more
piercingly aware of how much of himself had gone
when he had flung the hawk into freedom. But it is
Gdu's servant, not mine, he thought as he turned once
more to the stairs.

They seemed to climb on for ever, but ended abruptly
where a fall of earth and boulders had filled a
narrow ravine. Out of the earth grew tussocks and
shrubs, lush with the ceaseless spray, and clinging to
these he climbed on without much difficulty, coming at
last to the top almost unaware. From below it had
seemed to be just another grassy ridge, which he clam-
bered onto with elbow and knee; but then he looked up
and found himself staring into the setting sun across an
upland of close-cropped grass, a huge, rising wold dotted with sheep. Between him and them sat the shepherd,
facing away from the falls and dressed in a shapeless

smock of undyed wool. He hesitated, then walked forward, raised his right hand, and began to speak the common blessing.

The shepherd looked around. It was a child, a girl about ten years old. Her brown face went pale. As she leaped to her feet her scream was a clear, harsh note, piercing the steady boom from the falls.

IX

~~~~~~~~~~

Exhausted though he was, Tron smiled at the strangeness of it. The first woman he had heard had been a coffin-robber in the dark. The first he spoke to screamed at the sight of him.

"O watches us. Aa sleeps. What do you fear?" he said, automatically falling into the half-singing speech which he had been taught to use to peasants, but pitching it loud enough to be heard through the drumbeat of falling waters.

"I . . . I thought you were a ghost . . . Revered Lord. I thought you'd crept out from the Jaws of Alaan. It's full of ghosts down there."

She had a sharp, perky little face, on which curiosity sat more naturally than fear.

"The Jaws of Alaan!" he exclaimed, awe and astonishment piercing the priest-trained calm.

"Down there. Didn't the Revered Lord know? That's His voice, roaring. That's His breath you can see."

The Jaws of Alaan! How many of the hymns spoke of that chasm of mystery and fear, that home of ghosts, not to be visited by living men! *But I have set foot there. I have seen Gdaal's bow curving across the rim of the falls, where He was forced to leave it when He rescued Tan from the lightless kingdom. I have walked among spirits, under the wing of Gdu.*

"I was on the river in a boat," he said. "Tan swept us between cliffs. Then a mist came down and I slept. And in my dream my Lord Gdu carried me to the clifftop, and there I woke."

"What it is to be a priest!" she answered. If Tron had

91

ever lived among villagers he would have recognized
this as an everyday remark picked up from the child's
elders, half sneer and half acceptance of a fact of exis-
tence. He turned his back on her, raised his arms and
praised Gdu, Alaan, and Tan. His knowledge of where
he had been filled him with deep awe and made his
voice as solemn as a Major Priest's. When he had finished
he saw that the child was watching him with almost
absurd respect.

"May I milk an ewe for the Revered Lord to drink?"
she said.

"I drink water," he answered. "Have you any bread?"

"A . . . a little, Revered Lord. And there is a
stream of good water over the rise there, by the cave."

A cave, a stream. Bread. Gdu guided him still.

"Child," he said solemnly. "I do not know why my
Lord Gdu brought me to this place, but I do know that
it is dangerous even for priests to interfere with the
plans of the Gods. So until my Lord Gdu has spoken to
me and shown me His will you must tell nobody that
you have seen me, not even your own priest."

"Oh, we hardly ever see our priest in Upper Kalakal," she said. "He lives in Lower Kalakal, and he's a
cripple, so when we want him to bless a hut or something he has to be carried up. Curil—that's our headman, brews his own beer, but of course he doesn't tell
anyone. Oh!"

"And I will not tell anyone," said Tron, "just as you
will not tell anyone about me. I will take the bread from
you as a sign."

She opened a sheepskin satchel and took out a
strange, flat loaf, very dark. Tron broke it in two and
gave half of it back to her, at which she seemed surprised. As she was replacing her half in the satchel, he
saw a roll of stout cord there.

"I will take that cord also for a day and a night," he
said. "Will you need it?"

"Oh no, that's only for training lambs that won't follow my clatterer. The Revered Lord can . . . that's
meat! Priests don't eat meat!"

"It is for my companion," said Tron, hacking away a corner of tough mutton. When he rose he saw that she had gone pale again, and was glancing round her with her eyes while trying not to move her head.

"He will do you no harm," said Tron. "He is quite small."

"I must go, Revered Lord."

"There is nothing to fear."

"No. Look. It is time."

She pointed back over his shoulder and he turned. O's beams now lay flat across the grassland. Tron's shadow reached almost to the cliff edge. To the right, where the last of the falling spray drifted across the hill, a gold arch began to rise, made out of nothing. It was vast, though there was no more of it than the start of a curving column, which now gathered colors to it and stood there glowing.

"Lord Gdu!" said Tron. "What is it?"

"Don't you . . . doesn't the Revered Lord know? That's O's answer."

"I know the hymn," said Tron stiffly. "I had not seen the thing."

"It means I must take my flock home before Her time."

"Go then," said Tron. "This cave and stream are easy to find?"

"Just beyond that ridge, Revered Lord," she said. She picked up from beside her satchel two slabs of shaped wood and clacked them together, making a rapid rhythmic rattle, which pierced the boom of the falls. At once all the sheep raised their heads and started to drift toward her.

"They won't come if the Revered Lord stands too close," she said.

"I will go," said Tron. "Will you bring me more bread tomorrow, and a little raw meat?"

Her eyes widened, but she seemed relieved and pleased when he gave her the common blessing. He walked wearily away, but looked back from the ridge of the hill to see her moving slowly across the slope, followed by an obedient line of brown backs. He blessed her again in his mind.

The stream was formed in a cup of land that gathered the spray from the falls but sloped away from the gorge. The cave was a dark little hollow where a wall of stones and turfs had been piled beside a big sloping boulder to provide shelter from the endlessly falling droplets.

Tron was very stiff as he did his dances, and for the first time for many years his tongue muddled the hymns. He found it difficult to eat more than a little of the tough, salty bread, and difficult too to stop drinking from the stream. He slept uneasily, drifting in and out of muttering dreams, and woke feeling sore in all his joints, thirsty, and dizzy.

When he had drunk from the stream he chose from its bed a suitable stone, then walked through the drenched grass back to the gorge. At the rim he paused. O had barely risen, and all the depths below him were dusky with the trapped remains of night. The roaring gulf made him dizzier still, seeming to call to him, to suck at his will, as if there was a voice below the roaring which said, "Down. Down. Drown. Drown." If he hadn't been carried on by the impetus of the plan he'd made last night he would simply have stood on the brink shivering with fever and irresolution.

But he backed away, knelt, and carefully cut the torn hem free from his tunic. With his hawking knife he pricked his forearm in the place that the hymns prescribe, and as he squeezed out the first drops of sacrifice he sang.

> "Brother of Gods,
> Son of Great Aa,
> I give you my blood,
> Answer my asking."

His voice, shivering off the note, was drowned by the boom of waters from below.

He squeezed more blood from his arm and mopped it with the length of hem, then bound stone and cloth and meat together with the end of the cord. Standing up, he swung the whole contraption round his head, letting the cord run out through his fingers until the cloth-wrapped stone was flying round him, fluttering, blue and scarlet, a wounded bird. He began the shrill, quavering whistle of the austringer, but found it difficult to maintain as his lips were strangely numb and puffy. The hurling lure made him dizzier still. He staggered about, whistling and calling, and conscious in his darkening mind that he too was being called. Down. Down. Drown. Drown. Twice he almost fell over the edge, the second time coming so near that the gulp of panic cleared his mind and let him move back and sit on the soft turf with the lure loose beside him.

As he rested there trying to swallow away the rasping soreness in his throat he heard a hiss and a thud, and there, flung down out of nowhere, was the Blue Hawk binding to the lure.

By an effort of will he forced the fever out of his brain long enough to coax the bird onto his gauntlet and retie the thongs to its legs while it pulled disgustedly at the cooked meat. As his gloved fingers closed at last round the other end of the thongs his stupidity and feebleness came surging back. He rose and began to stagger back toward his cave. Suddenly, without warning, the hawk flung itself into a frenzy. He whispered to it, but it would not be still. A voice seemed to be calling to him again, but pitched above the water-thunder.

"Revered Lord!"

The shepherd girl was floating toward him, only a few feet away now. He turned his back on her and tried to hood the terrified hawk. There seemed to be two hoods, two curved beaks, two seats of shaking fingers. He shut his eyes, and with the Lord Gdu guiding his hand he did the job by feel. Then he opened his eyes to the swaying landscape and turned to face the girl.

"O's blessings," she called cheerfully. "What's that?

It's a blue hawk! Oh! I've never seen one so close. Didn't you . . . didn't the Revered Lord know they can't be tamed? May I touch him?"

"Gently," muttered Tron. "Not used to . . . to . . . I'm sick. Fever. The cold and the wet. The cold and the wet. The cold . . ."

He stood there mumbling the words over and over.

"It's funny Lord Gdu should carry you out of the Jaws of Alaan and then give you a fever," she said.

"Yes. . . ." Half-lines of little hymns began to run through his mind. Fever. Fever-bark. They won't have it. He grasped at another little patch of memory.

> Three days, three nights
> Let the body sweat.
> Let the man drink often
> But eat no food.
> The God will heal him
> In warmth and sleep.

"Why don't you go down to the priest in Lower Ka-lakal?" said the girl. "He'll keep you warm and say hymns for you too."

"I must stay in the cave," muttered Tron. Though his mind was muddled with fever he still knew he must not seek help from a priest.

"All right," said the girl. "I'll go back and fetch you a sheepskin and two blankets. Everybody's gone down to Lower Kalakal to bale the wool to take north, so no one will see. You watch the sheep."

He remembered her trotting away. After that there was a clear little scene of his own hands pegging the hawk's leg thongs down so that it could perch on a turf in a half-dark opening. Then there was nothing but the rank, warm sheepskins, the blankets that smelt of greasy cooking, and the dreams. They seemed like dreams even when he woke and saw the hawk perched motion-less at the cave entrance, or when he crawled to the stream to drink again.

He went down a dark tunnel with rock-hewn walls.

There was nothing behind him, but he was afraid of the stone itself. Then he came out into a wide open place, a vast white plain on which the statues of the Gods stood in separate places, each as tall as the Tower of the Great Temple. He knew he was in the land of the Gods, and that he must seek out the Lord Gdu to tell him the message. But all the statues were wrong, many of Gods whom he did not know and some turning into pillars of raw rock at his approach. At last, far off, he saw the unmistakable winged shape and trudged toward it. The plain became darker. He could not remember the message. He raised his arms to sing to the great statue, but instantly it crumbled into a small heap of sand with the Blue Hawk lying dead on the slope of it. Ants crawled among the bright feathers. The boom of the falls brought him back to the land where the hawk still lived, and the boom followed him into his next dream.

On the third evening he woke from a different sort of sleep, still and dreamless, and saw the hawk silhouetted as usual against the light in the cave mouth. Slowly behind it the sky changed, glowed, became fiery, bore bright colors on either side of the fire, until the whole triangle was filled with the blaze of O's answer with the Blue Hawk perched in the middle of it, eyes closed, glistening all round its outline where the brightness caught the sheen of its plumage.

So Gdu is my friend still, he whispered. I am punished for telling the girl untrue things about the Gods, trying to use Them for my own purpose. Alaan called me to pay with my life, but Gdu befriended me, and I pay now only with a little sickness. He let himself slide again into the good sleep and woke next morning weak but sensible.

As he walked across the hillside to meet the girl, he remembered his first meeting with the King, that openness and trust and sense of shared humanity. He compared this with his own behavior to the girl, his imitation of the Major Priests to impress her, the distancing from her that his training imposed on him.

She had brought bread for him, which he made her share, and meat for the hawk. He sat on the ground beside her and told her his story, trying to free himself from the formal language of the priests and to talk in the common tongue. There was a lot she couldn't understand—it was impossible for her to imagine the life of the Great Temple, or indeed anything much more than her own village and hillside—but she listened with great excitement.

"Revered Lord. . ." she began when he'd finished.

"My name is Tron," he said.

"Oh, is it? I didn't know priests *had* names. Tron. My name's Taleel. What are you going to do next, Tron? You can't stay in the cave for ever, can you?"

"Tell me about your priest. Is he an old man?"

"Oh no. His hair's still black. He came to us the year my elder sister was born and she's two years older than me."

(. . . *they didn't touch him that day. But by the time he passed for priest he was a cripple, so bad they had to carry him up to his village—some potty little place in the hills. . . .*)

"And he serves O?" asked Tron.

"I didn't tell you that," she said, suddenly suspicious.

He beat back the natural urge to pretend to strange knowledge.

"Very few priests leave the Temple crippled," he said. "He's the only one I've ever heard of, and I've heard of him before. Look, I'll go and see him tonight and try and persuade him to help me. Perhaps I'll come back and stay in Upper Kalakal for a bit. You'll have to pretend not to recognize me. Will I be able to find my way to Lower Kalakal in the dark?"

"In the dark! You're not . . . Oh, I suppose it's all right for you. What it is to be a priest! I'm sorry. I didn't mean that. Yes, if you follow the stream by the cave—there's a marshy bit just below Mangan's Patch—you'll have to work around that but it's not deep, only smelly, if you do fall in. . . ."

She chattered on while Tron ate hungrily of the bread—though not so hungrily as the hawk did of the chicken neck and strips of raw mutton she'd smuggled out of her mother's hut. Neither of them had eaten for three days. After that he watched the sheep with her and told her the story of the King of the Wise who by magic trapped Sodala in the body of a jackal and wouldn't let the God free until he had been taken to the Land of the Gods and allowed to drink from the desert pool that contains the water of everlasting life, and as the King rose with his face dripping from that water, his reflection cleared and he found himself gazing at the rippled image of a jackal, who now lives for ever and howls in the desert night for his release.

That evening as O's answer began to glow in the mist she stood with bowed head while he blessed her and her flock with the Great Blessing.

"You are a Revered Lord, then," she whispered when he'd finished.

"I don't know," muttered Tron. He paused. His mouth seemed to speak without his willing it.

"The only Lords are the Gods," he said clearly.

She nodded, not at all surprised, then started her clatterers and led the flock away.

Tron stood still, ears pricked. Above the western horizon Aa showed only a thin arc of silver. So this must be the night of Her Most Darkness, when Her creatures roam most freely and sniff most fiercely for those who have dishonored the Gods. Behind him the changeless column of smoke from the falls hid a huge patch of stars, and those he could see seemed smaller than they were when he had gazed at them from the desert. The hawk stirred on his gauntlet. The stream he had been following hissed through the grass. He could smell cooking and see the glowing remains of a village fire. A dog yelled. He froze.

In the lumpish mass around the fire a spark of yellow light glowed, then began to move through the night with a curious, slow jerky rhythm. The creature that carried it was a hunched shape, bulky but no taller than a child. It moved out of the village on Tron's right. With a thumping heart he stole around to intercept it.

A hundred yards from the huts a low mound rose, twice the height of a man and hollowed at the top into a shallow basin in whose center lay a flat slab of undressed rock. Aa's altar was the same in all villages. Crouched outside the rim of the mound, Tron watched the thing with the light make its painful way up the slope and vanish into the hollow. It was a man, dressed in a gold robe, moving his twisted body with the gait of a maimed beast. The lantern dangled from one of his crutches and from the other a closed basket, which contained, Tron was certain, a black cockerel, a little flask of oil, and a miniature loaf of priest-bread. Tron shivered on the slope. He dared climb no farther. To listen to the ritual on the night of Aa's Most Darkness was dangerous enough. But to watch!

The priest's voice rose from the hollow, very soft but the true voice of O, golden at dawn and sunset.

> "Mistress of dark,
> Mother of Gods,
> Giver of terrible birth,
> Giver of kindly death,
> I bring the ancient gifts,
> Which are yours before I give them.
> You have taken the gold from the oil,
> You have taken the white from the bread,
> The red from the comb of the cock,
> And made them part of your dark."

There was a pause, though the priest must be too crippled to perform the dance. A current of excitement now ran through Tron's fear. Because most of the boys in the Temple would one day be solitary priests in villages or the households of noblemen, they had to know the major rituals of Gods other than the one for whom they had been chosen. Tron had learned long ago the hymn of sacrifice on the night of Aa's Most Darkness, but apart from the first two lines he had never heard these words or this chant.

The crippled priest sang on, sometimes using familiar verses and sometimes strange ones. His voice became stronger, filling the night. He poured out the oil, crumbled the bread, killed the cock. Tron grew stiff with waiting and began to be afraid that his fever would come back. The hawk, disturbed by the night movement, griped and fidgeted. At last the rite ended and the lantern glow rose out of the hollow and came at its agonized gait down the slope.

"Servant of O," whispered Tron.

The priest stood stock still.

"Servant of O, you have changed the ritual."

The lantern shook. Basket and one crutch clattered to the ground. The priest's hand dived to his pouch and came out with a knife, still glistening with the blood of the cock. The arm rose to strike, not at the voice in the dark but at the priest's own heart.

"No!" cried Tron. "I've been Goat too!"

By the weak light of the lantern he saw the blade hesitate and drop.

"Let me see you," whispered the cripple.

Tron straightened and stepped forward, but having seen how deft the priest's arms were he stopped while he was still clear of a sudden slash with the other crutch. Bulbous eyes peered at him from under hairless brows. The hurt back forced the man to carry his head so that it craned up from the neck, like a tortoise head. He wore no beard.

"A child?" he said. "Who is with you?"

His speaking voice was high and smooth, as though he were on the edge of song still.

"My Lord Gdu is with me," said Tron. "I was chosen for Him, but at the Ritual of Renewal I was Goat. He spoke in my heart to take the Blue Hawk and carry it out of the Temple. Since then . . . since then He has guided me secretly here. I did not know I would find you here. Will you help me?"

"Is that the same hawk? Tame?"

Tron held it forward but it turned its head away and shut its eyes from the light and the stranger.

"My Lord Gdu showed me," he said.

The priest coughed and nodded, thinking.

"What do you want?"

"I have had a fever. May I sleep in your hut?"

The priest coughed again, then sighed.

"It would be good to hear news from the Temple again," he said.

Tron picked up the fallen crutch and took the basket. As they made their slow way toward the village he heard a sudden growl behind them in the night, where two of Aa's creatures fought over the remains of the sacrifice.

X

CURIL, HEADMAN OF UPPER KALAKAL, HAD AN EXTRA-
ordinary wiry gray beard that stuck out all around his
weather-beaten face like the ruff of an owl. His angry
black eyes stared at Tron as he leaned on his crook.

"We've never had two priests in Kalakal," he said.

"We're not that rich," said one of his sons, standing
by his shoulder.

"Not that stupid, you mean," said the other.

"No priest-dues will be taken," said Tron in the proper half-chant. "The King's Hawk fell ill. It is thought it
may recover its health among the cliffs where it was
born. The priest at Lower Kalakal can confirm the order. Send and ask him."

"There's no priest-hut," snapped Curil. "We're too
busy to build one."

"I can build a hut," said Tron in an ordinary voice.
"I can also bless the beer you've been brewing. Or curse
it."

Their faces changed.

"It's not our fault," said Curil more angry than ever
with fright. "They send us a priest who's too crippled to
get up here and brew us a spot of beer. I don't like
drinking unblessed beer, no more than anyone else, but
what do they expect us to do?"

"Welcome a priest who offers to bless it for you,"
said Tron.

"That's right," said one of the sons.

"You mean what you said, no priest-dues?" said the
other.

"Only bread for me. When the hawk is well we will

hunt, and if we catch game you shall have it. I eat no meat."

"Priests!" jeered Curil automatically. "Well, that hut at the end's empty since my father's sister died. She's been haunting it, so we've kept clear, but I dare say a priest won't mind."

"You'll know her if you see her," said one son. "She could talk rocks to bits."

"Let's get that beer blessed," said the other. "Last two lots went sour."

The Kalakals formed an island of pasture in the vast, savage upland below the Peaks of Alaan. The spray from the falls kept them green and deep ravines defended them all around from the wild. They were thirty miles from the nearest other village. Upper Kalakal was a crescent of nine huts built on a natural platform on the side of the hill, sheltered by a ridge from the faint spray which even in apparently bright sunshine drifted over all the area. It was a peaceful life. Night and day the Jaws of Alaan thundered. Every evening O's answer remade itself. ("You've got to wait a hundred years to see that, down in the plain," said Taleel's mother. "We see it every day.")

The men sat about most of the time drinking beer and gambling next season's lambs on a complicated game that involved throwing three knucklebones into a pattern of squares scraped in the ashes of the village fire. The women did all the work and most of the talk, cooking, and weaving blankets to one ancient, elaborate pattern. The children minded the sheep.

They all watched with curiosity and enjoyment as Tron dismantled the dead woman's hut and did the silent dances that would help her nagging ghost to free itself from the place and travel to the Kingdom of Aa. The ghost's son's wife gave him a bright new blanket for this service without being asked. No doubt she had borne the brunt of the nagging.

Unbuilding the hut and rebuilding it in a new place took Tron four days. Most of the time he found himself thinking about the crippled priest, whose name was Odah. They had passed a strange night together. Pain gave Odah little sleep, and he seemed to have spent most of his life at Kalakal lying in his hut and discovering new hymns and rituals. Despite his hideous appearance he had a character full of calm and sweetness and reverence for the Gods and the Temple.

"But if it is in me to find new ways to praise the Gods how shall I not do so?" he said. "I cannot deny Their gift."

Some time before dawn he had sung a Great Hymn which Tron had never heard before, telling how Sinu went mad in his longing for Tan and tried to destroy all life, and how Sodala and Gdaal had gathered the animals of the world two by two into a secret valley and defended the place with magic and trickery against their mighty brother. This had seemed to Tron instantly right and true—as true as all the other Great Hymns—and yet it was new.

"Tell me, brother and father," he had said. "You have changed hymns and I have broken rituals. Gdu spoke in my heart and led me. Aa did not take me though I traveled in the Dead King's coffin. I have been in the Jaws of Alaan. I have seen Gdaal's bow. But . . . is it allowed for everybody to discover new hymns and change rituals and pry into secrets?"

"If the Gods wish it They will bring it about."

"But if two people—I suppose they need not be priests—disagree about what the Gods wish . . . or if somebody says, 'The Gods have spoken in my heart,' when They have not . . . he might be mistaken, or just seeking his own ends. . . ."

"I do not know how to argue with such a person. But I do know what I would do in such a case. I would look in my heart, and if the Gods spoke there also I would say so. But if They did not I would not change the ritual simply because another man said he had been spoken to. I have made hymns, lying here, of which I was proud and glad. And then after some days I saw that I had made them only for my own pleasure, so I forced my mind to forget them."

"Three nights ago I dreamed the Gods were dead," Tron had whispered.

"Aa sends that dream. I have seen it many times, in many forms. Listen. If the dream has a meaning, the meaning must have come from somewhere. The dream must have been sent. By whom? A God. If the dream has no meaning, then it is just froth on the mind, and there is no need to try to read it."

So Tron did the dances to free the ghost and rebuilt the hut and sang the hymn to bless the roof exactly according to ritual, not varying by one step or syllable from the teachings of the Temple, though the Gods stayed silent in his heart and he could not tell whether They were pleased, or angry, or indifferent.

Next day he said to Curil, "I must take the King's hawk hunting, and I'm afraid to fly it near the Jaws of Alaan or I may lose it. How do I cross the ravines?"

"There's leopards out there. Lions and snakes, too. Ghosts. Daytime ghosts."

Curil shook his head. Now that he'd overcome his suspicion he was thoroughly pleased with the new arrangement as it cost him almost nothing and raised the status of Upper Kalakal to that of a full village, with its own priest, instead of a mere appendage of Lower Kalakal. But he walked with Tron across the stream, up the slope, and over the brow. The green, sheep-nibbled pastures sloped away south, ending in the hard, dark line of the ravine, beyond which began the wilderness, mottled and dun and ragged with rocky outcrops, stretching through pale bands of distance to the feet of the mountains.

"We're the last people in the Kingdom," said Curil proudly. "Nothing south of here. General of the Southern Levies—he's our Overlord—he came here three years back. Hadn't been for eight years before that. That's how far south we are."

"I expect you visit him, though," said Tron.

"Got to, to pay our taxes, haven't we? And there's the wool and the blankets to sell. We're better off than a lot of villages farther north, I can tell you. Ragged lot, some of them. I've got a silver cup to drink out of, feast days. We cook our mutton with spices come from O knows how far. Now, here you are. Sure you want to go?"

Curil appeared to have led Tron to a thorn thicket growing on the lip of the ravine, but as they came close to it Tron saw that it consisted of a number of large bundles of thorn piled with the spiky ends facing outward and the other ends tied to stout stakes to prevent the pile slipping or being pulled over the cliff. Curil heaved several of these bundles aside, making a gap, which opened onto a steep track running sideways down the cliff face.

"I'll put these back but I won't lash 'em down," he said. "What you do is take that pole with you and leave it on the other side. Then you can use it to hummock the thorn out of the way when you come back. Supposing you do come back. You thought of that, Revered? What'll the King say to me? What'll he *do* to me?"

"If I don't come back, send to Kalavin, the General's son. He'll tell the King what happened. The King's lost hawks before. He'll pay for my keep. He won't be angry."

As he crossed the ravine Tron saw that there were sometimes floods here too which shoveled the boulders about, scoured the cliff walls, and drove the bed a little deeper below the upland each time. The bed was dry now; he stopped on a water-smoothed rock and spoke a quiet hymn to Alaan. The path up the far wall was little more than a sloping ledge and led to a forbidding area of dry scrub, a place where it would be possible to get lost in a very few strides. He looked over his shoulder and checked on the tower of smoke above the falls—he would have to journey many miles before that ceased to be a landmark.

It was bad hawking country, full of dense cover into which game could dive at the flip of a wing; a place, too, where it would be easy to lose a hawk. Tron had never belled his bird because he hadn't expected to fly it in a place where he couldn't see for half a mile, but now he wished he had. There was plenty of game in the place, spoor everywhere and sudden rustles in the bushes as he passed, but it was all very shy as though it were used to being hunted. He risked only two short flights. The first was blank and the second made a kill of a strange sort. Tron had loosed the hawk at a fat little gray bird that he saw flopping across a small clearing, but this prey turned out to be as fleet as a dove when it wanted and slid into a thicket on the clearing's edge. While the hawk hovered overhead Tron picked up a dead branch, worked his way around to the other side of the thicket, and thrashed against the twigs, in the faint hope of driving the gray bird out across the clearing again. Almost at once the hawk launched itself into its dive. Tron heard the thud of impact as he edged back around the bush and was astonished to find the hawk struggling with something more than twice its size in the middle of the clearing; there was a flurry of dark wings and long gray legs, but by the time he reached the fight it was over, with the hawk perched on its victim's body and gripping with the talons of one foot a writhing, snakelike neck. As usual the hawk watched his approach with a fierce eye, hissed and almost struck at his hand, but allowed itself to be taken up and given a gristly tidbit for reward.

This prey was a bird, brown-feathered, bald-headed, with absurd useless wings and huge thighs made for running. Later Tron saw another dashing with incredible speed down a path, but he had already decided not to risk another flight until he found more open country, so he circled back to the ravine, restacked and lashed the thorn barrier at the top of the steep path, and trudged up the hill to Kalakal.

"What it is to be a priest!" said Curil's elder son, eyeing the running bird.

"What it is not to be one!" said Tron, laughing as he gave it to him. Curil's daughter hung it outside her hut for a week until one could smell it from several yards away; then she cooked it with twenty different herbs. Taleel said that this was a famous dish, but rare, and even the smallest children would get a mouthful, but Tron was glad he was not a meat-eater.

A month passed, but time at Kalakal was strangely different from time in the Temple, though the days seemed almost as unvarying. It was not a sleepy place— even the idling men seemed lively and glad—but it was a place full of a steady, deep content. Tron thanked Gdu daily for his new happiness. It seemed to him that the God was rewarding him for having endured so many fears and dangers in order to further a mysterious purpose, in which his own part was now finished. He would have liked to send news to the King and to get news back, but he remembered the unyielding face of the General of the Southern Levies, Curil's Overlord, and the five priests on the quayside. Any message to the court would have to go through the General's household, and probably need the General's permission. Tron was afraid to take the risk. *If my Lord Gdu wants me to stir again,* he thought, *He will send me a sign. I am happy here. Praise Him.*

Meanwhile he explored the scrubland. It turned out to be crisscrossed with sudden ravines, so that from above it must have looked like an enormous mudbank, dried by the sun into an endless pattern of cracks and flats. It sometimes took him half a day to find a way past one of these obstacles. Some had small pools in the bottom but most were dry. The hawking was never very good, but the hawk usually killed at least once.

Climbing down into one of the ravines, Tron almost trod on a leopard. He was poised for a jump onto the speckled rock below when it moved, a fanged mouth yawned, and two brilliant eyes gazed into his for one of those instants which strike through the surface clutter of the mind and embed themselves in a layer of deep memory. The leopard twisted from its perch and flowed down the cliff in one lithe rush, then streaked along the floor of the ravine too fast for him to pick out the movement of individual limbs.

That had happened too suddenly for fear. Tron felt the prickle of nervousness, though, whenever he came across the imprint of a huge cat-pad on bare earth, but he saw no more leopards and no lions. The most frightening moment came when he flew the hawk near a big rock pillar that turned out to be the home of a flock of bright blue starlings, which rose screaming to mob the menace. The hawk fled, bewildered. Tron swung the lure and whistled and suddenly it dropped to his wrist, but still the starlings mobbed bird and boy as he ran. He suffered only a few unimportant pecks, but he was terrified by the screaming, unescapable whirl of blue all around him. They left him quite suddenly and he stood panting. It was as though he had strayed by accident into a sacred place and didn't know what furious God to appease.

He saw snakes, too, and a big black eagle that preyed on them. There were small herds of fleet-footed deer with horns like curved swords. There were scorpions, huge spiders, centipedes as long as his foot, brilliant lizards, birds of fifty shapes and hues, and an unseen world of burrowing creatures. By the time Aa had reached Her Most Dark again, Tron had explored a fair tract of land, and had decided that the place was very ancient. He thought that the ravines had been made over thousands of years by sudden meltings of the snow on the peaks of Alaan, and that once, perhaps, the soil had been fertile, but now the water level had sunk too far below the roots, so that only wizened and enduring thorn or cactus could survive.

Always looking for more open country, he explored steadily farther to the west until one day he came to a ravine that was larger and deeper than most. For a while he worked his way south, looking for somewhere to cross, until he was forced away from the cliff edge by an impenetrable thicket of thorn. He had moved a few yards along this barrier when something rustled in the middle of it and he stooped to peer in, hoping that it might be one of the running birds, which could be driven out for the hawk to fly at. The noise came only from a yellow lizard, but as it flicked farther into the bush Tron noticed something else, a patch of loose earth under the thorn that bore the imprint of a human heel. Looking round him he saw that his own footprints showed in what had seemed to be wind-grooved sand—but there had been no wind all day. He moved the hawk to his right hand and with his gauntleted left reached into the thicket and tugged. A whole section of bush moved.

Carefully he pulled it free, walked through the gap and closed it behind him, then resettled the hawk on the gauntlet and slipped its hood into place. A narrow but well-worn path led to the cliff edge and then down, slanting from ledge to ledge and in places reinforced with branches and flat boulders. There was water under the stones in the bed of the ravine, and occasionally a clear but shallow pool. The path seemed to lead close under the cliff. He whispered a hymn to Gdu, asking for protection, and stole along with a priest's silent step. A faint odor of wood smoke and burned meat came and went. He heard the low mutter of voices, and hesitated by a jut of cliff.

It would have been possible to inch forward and peek round the rock at whoever it was—a troop of Gdaal's people, no doubt. But it went against all Tron's training to be seen by peasants while acting in an undignified, unpriestly fashion, so he continued his solemn glide round the corner and stopped only when he was a foot or two past it.

The corner was the end of a space where flood-water had cut hard into a curve of cliff, making a wide but shallow cave, in which a group of about twenty people were moving or sitting. It took Tron a long stare to be sure that they were not some kind of ape. They were naked, yellow-skinned, and no taller than himself. Their buttocks stuck out below their spines in a fashion that made it look as though their hips were differently hinged from other people's. Some of the men carried spears. Two babies rocked about on the cave floor tugging at either end of a piece of purple cloth. Over the almost smokeless fire a woman was turning a spit that skewered a green lizard as big as a dog. Beyond the fire another man, very pale-skinned, sat leaning against a boulder with his head lolling on his shoulder and his eyes shut. His clothes were of no fashion Tron had ever seen.

A head turned. A voice spoke. The mutter instantly became silence. Then five men were on their feet rushing at Tron with spears held high. Their faces were contorted, as if they were yelling war cries, but they swept forward in total silence, daytime ghosts.

Another part of a priest's training is to learn not to flinch from an expected blow, not to let an eyelid quiver, a muscle flick. Those painful lessons kept Tron still. He forced his lungs to breathe slowly and shallowly so that all his body should seem motionless as a statue.

Five feet away from him the tumbling rush halted. Spears drew back for throwing, but wavered. Tron stared straight forward, not into any one pair of bulging eyes, seeing the men in the blur of his peripheral vision, where their contorted faces looked like those of demons. Thus they all stayed for five heartbeats. The group convulsed as a man strode through them from behind, shoving the others to left and right.

He was old, his hair and tight-curled beard yellow-white. The fold of flesh above his left collarbone had been pierced and a bird's thighbone pushed through as an ornament. His eyes, which were level with Tron's chin, were bloodshot. The huge, flabby bulge of his chest and stomach was painted with stripes of white and gray mud. He carried a black club decorated with shells.

Once through the crowd, he stood looking at Tron's soiled blue tunic, at his face, and then at the hawk on his wrist. The others jostled to see what would happen. The old man's knees bent. He put his club on the ground beside him, then folded himself over his immense stomach until he could beat his grizzled forehead on the path in front of Tron's feet.

Tron raised his right hand and sang the hunter's blessing:

> "Gdaal send the bird to your net,
> Gdaal lead the buck to your bow,
> Gdaal mark the trail of the hare,
> Gdaal bring you safe to your camp."

As he stopped the chant the men clicked their spearheads together and made a light, continuous rattling that echoed off the far cliff. The old man rose to his feet, smiling with enormous pleasure. Tron bowed sedately, keeping his face stiff as a mask.

"Agdaal mbring," said the old man, dragging the words out of some strange pocket of memory. Gaining confidence, he pointed at the hawk.

"Agoods," he said. "Mbird agoods. Agoods."

"Yes," said Tron clearly. "The bird is good. It is Gdu's bird."

"Agdu, Agdu mbird," agreed the old man, grinning. He swept an arm around to gesture at the cave.

"Agdaal us agod," he said, miming the drawing of the bow and puckering his lips to the arrow's hiss.

"You are Gdaal's people," said Tron. This must be so, though they clearly had no sort of kinship with the hunters of the Kingdom.

"Who is that man?" he asked, pointing at the figure beyond the fire. The men moved aside from his gesture as though lightning might suddenly flash from his fingertip; their movement let him see that the man was bound by leather thongs to the boulder against which he lay. The old chief frowned and pouted.

"Mbads," he said. "Man mbads. Man ngdie, uh?"

He looked consoled by this final notion.

Still keeping his face masklike, Tron glided between the hunters at his ghostly pace. As they moved aside for him he heard them whispering, but the words were not those of the language of the Kingdom. The babies on the floor stopped their tug-of-war to stare at him. The women put their hands over their eyes and turned away. Tron paid no attention to any of them as he settled the hawk on the boulder, then knelt and felt for the man's pulse, moving all the time with the slow rhythm of a dance. At his touch the man opened his eyes and muttered. It took him some seconds even to notice Tron, but when he did so he frowned, shook his head as if trying to clear it, and gasped, "Durr Kaing? Durr Kaing?"

He said the words several times, varying the sound as though he wasn't sure that he was pronouncing it right. Tron suddenly made sense of the two syllables.

"The King?" he said.

The man nodded, ran a swollen tongue across dry lips and gazed with bright-eyed eagerness into Tron's face. Then his glance slid away and his expression changed to despair as he saw the watching hunters. Tron rose and turned to them.

"Give the man water," he said, cutting each word clear of the next. "Untie the man. The man goes to the King."

The hunters hesitated. The old chief frowned.

"Water," said Tron, pointing at a brimming half-gourd by the cave wall. "Do I say to Gdaal that you are bad men?"

He spoke the last sentence in full chant, all on a single note which echoed around the cave. The chief smiled ingratiatingly and said something to one of the women, who uncovered her face, picked up the gourd and carried it to the prisoner's lips. One of the younger men undid the thongs. The prisoner seemed not to realize that his limbs were free at first, but when he did he pushed away the gourd and tried to rise. He had got no farther than a half-crouch when his legs gave way and he collapsed on the floor. The women laughed, a tinkling, happy sound.

The man rolled himself onto his knees and crawled painfully across the cave to a leather saddlebag that was propped against the cave wall. The chief frowned and muttered until Tron held up an arm for silence. With shaking hands the man undid the straps of the bag and pulled out of the side pocket a flat, rectangular red brick, which he studied for a while before crawling back and handing it to Tron.

A picture of the Great Temple, unmistakable, was cut into the clay. Beside it was a figure of a King, wearing the Hawk Crown. Below this were several ranks of meaningless little shapes made by pressing a sharp triangular object into the clay. On the other side of the tablet was a strange arrangement of lines, which at first seemed almost accidental, but suddenly, without altering their position, became a picture of the Kingdom, seen from above, with Tan running down the center to the Peaks of Alaan at the bottom. Tron nodded and returned the tablet, but the man, his strength now clearly seeping back, staggered to his feet and thrust the tablet under Tron's face. Pointing with one finger to the triangular marks, he said, "Bah ahnshent tretty ahn bah durr Rehd Shpear ah carl durr Kaing tuh ayerd oos."

The third time he said it a few words stuck out of the jumble of sound.

"The King. The Red Spear?" said Tron.

The man pointed. Leaning against the cave wall by the saddlebag was an object like a long but feeble bow, with two strings wound round with red ribbon and at the top end a bunch of scarlet feathers from which a fine bronze spike protruded. The man began to say the sounds again. At last they made sense.

"By ancient treaty and by the Red Spear I call the King to aid us."

When Tron repeated the words the man nodded eagerly and made as if to stagger out of the cave, but suddenly remembered his spear and gear and turned to pick them up. The hunters cried out angrily. In a flash Tron saw what had been happening. Once when O had been wandering in a wild place disguised as a man, He had been captured by ghosts, who had tied Him to a tree and waited for Him to die so that they could take His possessions without the guilt of killing Him, because

they didn't want so strong a ghost stalking that place as
their enemy. O, of course, had not died, and the ghosts
had grown so thin with waiting that they turned into
centipedes, and then O had burned His bonds and returned to His heaven. Just so the hunters had been
waiting for their prisoner to die, so that they could take
his belongings without his returning to haunt them. Now
they were afraid that they would get nothing after all
their trouble.

Tron tried to make the stranger understand by signs
that he must pay some kind of a ransom, and even undid the saddlebag himself, took out a soft leather belt
with a gold clasp, put it into the stranger's hands and
pushed him toward the chief. The stranger looked furious for a minute, then shrugged and undid the black
belt he was wearing. He passed this, dagger and all, to
the chief, who laughed aloud and buckled it round his
stomach. The fat bulged grossly over the leather.

With solemn dignity the stranger undressed down to
a pale linen shift; another of the hunters got his leather
jacket with its bronze shoulder plates, another his brilliantly patterned shirt, and so on. The babies even returned the piece of purple cloth so that he could give it
back to them. Then, still as solemnly as if he were taking a part in a ritual, the man dressed in the clothes
from the saddlebag. They were strange gear to take into
the wilds—curl-toed gold slippers, green pantaloons, a
long yellow robe of incredibly fine weave, a jeweled
belt, a soft blue cap with a ruby in it, and last of all a
gold chest-medal the size of a man's spread palm. When
he put out his hand and grasped the Red Spear, the
hunters sighed and drew back. Once more the chief
bowed to the ground and knocked his head on the floor.
When he rose he seemed deathly afraid, and fumbled
with the buckle of his stolen belt as if eager to give it
back; but the stranger pushed out his hand, palm foremost, as a sign that the chief must keep the gift.

Suddenly the chief laughed and the tension broke. In
no time Tron found himself sitting cross-legged on the
floor of the cave beside the chief amid the clamor and

guzzling of a hunter's feast. The stranger, whose name seemed to be Onu Ovalaku, sat on the chief's other side and accepted with dignified little bows the tidbits of roast lizard which the chief kept offering him. The hunters seemed to know somehow that Tron would not eat meat, and one of the women sat just behind him, cracking sweet little nuts for him between two stones. The men danced and boasted in their many-syllabled language, the women sang wailing songs, and the children ran hither and thither, treating the bodies of the seated adults as boulders to clamber over or play hide-and-seek among.

The pillar of smoke was gold with O's going, though O's answer was hidden behind the ridge, when Tron helped Onu Ovalaku up the last stretch of path, through the thorn barrier, and into the pastures. As they trudged up the slope, Onu Ovalaku, who seemed now a little delirious, kept saying anxiously, "Durr Kaing? Durr Kaing?"

"Yes," said Tron again and again. "We will go to-morrow."

He himself was very tired with the weight of Onu Ovalaku's arm around his shoulders, and now he was overwhelmed by a great flood of sadness at the idea of leaving Kalakal. He loved these gold pastures, and the freedom, and the sense of being part of a contented community, and he was appalled and frightened at the idea of returning into the Kingdom. There was no need for that, surely. Curil could take Onu Ovalaku to the house of Kalavin's father, who would know his Obligations and send the ambassador on to the King. What part had Tron to play in any of this? Hadn't he done all that the Gods could require?

No, said Gdu in his heart. No. Go.

XI

~~~~~~~~~~~

*Between the hills and the desert, between the realm of
the Gods and the Kingdom of Men. Scenes from that
journey.*

THE TWINKLY SHADE OF A SPARSE GROVE OF EUCALYP-
TUS. At its far edge Curil and Onu Ovalaku halt, outlined against the hammering glare of O. Tron, leg-weary
and footsore from the endless and undifferentiated track
across the hills, stops a few feet behind them, to take
full advantage of the spice-smelling shade and to keep
the Blue Hawk clear of the fret of their presence, which
it seems to sense even through its hood.

But when Curil points ahead and Onu Ovalaku claps
him lightly on the shoulder to show pleasure, Tron
strolls forward to join them and finds that they have
come to the edge of the plateau.

Four miles ahead and several hundred feet below
them, Tan drives toward the east; beyond Her the
brown hills shoulder up, like the ridged backs of gigantic
cattle, but over to the left and incredibly blue and green
after the barren upland, a vast flatness stretches away.
Onu Ovalaku lets out his breath in a slow gasp and for
want of language makes an absurd gesture with his arms
as though he could hold all that vastness in his embrace.

"Durr Kaingland?" he says.

"Yes," says Tron somberly, "that's the Kingdom."

Night. Firelight. Onu Ovalaku cross-legged on the
earth by the fire, wearing the livery of an upper servant
in the household of Kalavin's father, the General of the

118

Southern Levies. The General on a stool beside him.
The light casts masklike shadows on their contrasting
faces, Onu Ovalaku's round, smooth, solemn and eager,
the General's arrogant and impatient. Tron is still puzzled by the General. The old man seems so ready to
break into a furious outburst at the slightest deviation
from accepted behavior—a tiny mistake in dress or
speech or even food can throw him into a passion—and
yet at the same time he is prepared to break all rules
and rituals, however important, in order to fulfill his
Obligation to convey Onu Ovalaku and the Red Spear
safe to the King. Now he cranes forward to watch while
once more his guest attempts to explain his mission.

Onu Ovalaku smooths out a patch of mingled ash
and dust, dampens it and smooths it again. Deftly on
this surface he draws pictures with the point of his dagger—horsemen, naked, with great dogs leaping beside
them.

"Mohirrim," he says drily.

He adds a group of armored men fighting against the
horsemen.

"Falathi," he says, then repeats the word, tapping
himself on the chest.

He wipes the picture out and draws again. This time
the naked horsemen are burning a house. One of them
has speared a woman, and a dog is leaping at a child.
Onu Ovalaku destroys that picture and draws another
and another, and another. Each time there are the same
horsemen and dogs, fighting, killing, destroying; and
each time he draws them he says the same word, "Mohirrim."

Tron, dizzy from the first day's jolting chariot ride,
half-hypnotized by the tranced monotony of the passing
plain, the waterways and the banked fields and the
placid villages, endlessly repeated, sits a little back from
the other two, understanding that the country beyond
the peaks has been attacked by a horde of savage horsemen and that Onu Ovalaku has come to ask for help,
but not much caring. This is the King's affair, and the
General's and Onu Ovalaku's.

But Tron, when he shuts his eyes and draws into himself, can sense, even here in the General's way-house, that he is part of some other purpose. He is being watched, but not by human eyes. It is as if he were some desert creature crossing a wide, bare tract—this journey—under the gold-eyed stare of a leopard crouched invisible on a rock that he must pass: the tip of the hunter's tail may twitch as it watches the coming prey, but its instinct tells it, "Wait. Not yet. Not yet."

Crossing the river. The stench of mud and the sweet-ness of sappy new growth. The big-muscled ferrymen lean against the sweeps, singing to set the rhythm a slow and gurgling chant about a frog who had two wives on opposite banks of the river and wore himself out trying to keep them both happy. On the bank the ferry has left a green-robed priest of Tan angrily blesses the crossing. It has taken three hours of argument and a thumping bribe to the village headman to get the ferry to move at all. The priest has taken omens and declared that the Goddess was in no mood to carry chariots that day; but the headman, rheumatic and wily, has coaxed him into rereading the signs. Now the General lolls by the steers-man's side, smiling to himself, and teasing the stiff curls of his beard. Tron understands quite well what has hap-pened: the priest has seen the General come storming north, with only a few of his household and only four chariots; no village priest can question so great a noble about his comings and goings, but he can delay him for a day, send word ahead, arrange for further delays, and thus give the Major Priests time to prepare themselves for whatever this strange journey may mean. The Gen-eral is smiling because he has outmaneuvered the priest. Tron smiles too, thin-lipped and sad. As if the Gods cared about any of this!

Desert soon after dawn. The jolt and bucket of the chariot, the clatter of wheels and hooves, a tiny mess of movement on the causeway corrupting that huge si-lence. Outwardly Tron seems to be part of the judder

and noise; his body is braced against the chariot's side-
bar, his feet firm in the cloglike footholds fixed to the
chariot's floor; he is wearing the same gaudy livery as
the General's servants. But inwardly, as he whispers the
hymn of how Gdaal made the desert, he is part of the
stillness.

Above the clatter rises a sudden shout of warning
and a yell of surprise; a horse screams. A wheel floats
into Tron's vision, spinning along the causeway so close
that he could touch it if he were not trapped in the slow
daze of his trance. Tron's charioteer is hauling on the
reins; the next chariot is a wreck of wicker and wood,
but Tron himself is hypnotized by the turning wheel as
it curves with strange slowness off the paving and
strikes with perfect aim into a small granite pillar,
carved with the figure of Alaan and set there to mark
the miles. It seems to burst quite silently and still with
the same unearthly slowness, losing its shape like a
storm-stripped flower. Five spokes twirl upward, dark
against the dawn glare, floating as though they meant to
soar off into the blue.

Then, in an instant, time asserts its grip. The spokes
flop back into the sand. The wheel lies broken. Tron
climbs down from the stopped chariot and goes around
to hold the horses' heads while the charioteer runs back
to help with the wreck behind. A man is sitting by the
road with his head in his hands, but nobody else seems
hurt and both horses are on their feet. An argument
breaks out about whether the smash was caused by a
charioteer's carelessness or by a priest at last night's
way-house tampering with an axle pin. The General
stamps about on the causeway, furious at the prospect
of arriving at the Temple with a train of only three
chariots, as if he were a common second-level lordling.
But Tron stands in silence by the quivering horses, absorbed in the sign of the bursting wheel, though he cannot yet read its meaning. Several times he relives its
slow instants before he shakes himself and looks around
him.

At once he is aware that the desert has changed, becoming mere heaps of sand. The Gods have withdrawn. Gone too is the sense he had of being watched, as if by a leopard in ambush. So it is They who have been watching him during the journey north, and have now shown him this strange sign as They left. Though he still cannot read it, he is aware that he has come to a point where time pivots over like the heavy beam of a water-lift when it has emptied its load into an upper channel. He realizes that ever since he took the Blue Hawk from the House of O and Aa he has been somehow a focus, a central point in the Gods' attention to the world. Now, with the Temple a bare eight hours away, They have departed on Their own affairs. Whatever happens next will be achieved by men in a world of men.

XII

~~~~~~

IT WAS STRANGE TO STAND AT THE GREAT GATE OF the Temple and watch the little procession move through it to the steady throb of a gong and the clear note of a priest of O singing the Hymn of Welcome to Strangers. One priest of O and one of Aa led the procession; then came Onu Ovalaku in his outlandish ambassadorial robes, holding the Red Spear high before him; then the General, frowning and stiff; and then two Temple guards, snapped out of their lounging arrogance by the presence of these great people.

Tron watched them go and turned away to walk behind the chariots. He found himself swallowing with nerves, though there seemed little to be afraid of; his part of the adventure seemed over, he was under the protection of a great noble and the King himself, and there wasn't even much danger of his being recognized, in livery, with his hair a two-month mat and his already dark skin almost black from living all day under the glare of O. But he was still afraid. The Lord Gdu had left him, and he felt naked and companionless.

The path round to the palace passed beneath the enormous statues of the Gods, lining the Temple wall, patched with sharp angular shadows by the slant rays of O. At the foot of each was a priest of that God, standing by a stone bowl. Tron saw the charioteers ahead pause at the feet of lion-headed Sinu, throw a small coin into the bowl, and receive a blessing from the red-robed priest. But Tron as part of his disguise carried on his wrist the General's pretty little crested sparrowhawk— his own Blue Hawk was hidden in one of the chariots,

123

in a basket which it hated and feared—so it was natural
for him to make his small sacrifice to Gdu. The bowl
held a mound of mixed coins, and as Tron's tinkled
among them a blue-robed priest paced forward out of
the shadow of the taloned feet to chant

> "For this service,
> 　O Lord Gdu,
> 　　Take the pain
> 　　　And clear the eye.
> 　For this service
> 　　Smooth the skin,
> 　　　Heal the sickness,
> 　　　　O Lord Gdu."

For a moment Tron stared at the priest, who stared
back until he suddenly realized that he had made a mistake. All day he'd been trotting out the same blessing to
visitors who had journeyed across the desert to consult
the God about some illness, and now he'd automatically
chanted it once more, when he should have blessed this
boy's lord's hawking. He grunted and turned away, ob-
viously not prepared to produce two blessings for one
small coin.

A month before, Tron would have been appalled, but
now he began to smile to himself as he walked on. The
statue was empty, the God was not there, to heal or
bless. But Tron found, whispering the words to himself,
that he began to feel a little less afraid. Fear, after all, is
a kind of sickness of the soul.

It seemed a long way round the huge-slabbed, win-
dowless walls to the Palace Gate. When he had lived in
the Temple it had seemed to Tron to be a whole world;
during his travels it had shrunk in his mind to something no more than a big group of buildings, a place
where a lot of priests happen to live; now once more he
discovered how vast it was, and how the huge mass of
its stones seemed to weigh the desert down, in much the
same manner that the centuries of priest rule seemed to

weigh down the Kingdom. O's light lay level across the dunes as he followed the chariots into the Palace Courtyard.

This was built as a mirror image of the Great Courtyard in the Temple, but was a whole world different in feel. At its center, round a stone-rimmed pool, rose a small grove of date palms, and in their shade a group of young nobles, fresh from some war game, were laughing and drinking; elsewhere men and women lounged or bustled, all at their own pace, doing what had to be done or what pleased them. A group of young men were singing at the foot of a wall; above their heads was a screen of fretted stone through which small hands emerged, opened, and showered petals down on the singers. The arrival of three chariots and a dozen servants were hardly noticed in this bustle, but suddenly one of the singers broke out of the group and came striding across.

"Atholin!" he called. "What in Sinu's name are you doing here?"

"The General has come north, My Lord," said the head charioteer. "He brought a stranger with him. This boy knows more than I do."

The young man swung round, frowning and pulling at his broken nose. Tron knew him for the King's friend, Lord Kalavin, the General's son, but he stared at Tron in humorous bewilderment.

"You're not one of our people," he said. "Why are you wearing our livery?"

"My Lord the General gave me that honor," said Tron carefully.

"Well, what's all this about?"

Tron felt a need to be cautious. The General had not talked in front of any of his own servants about the reasons for his sudden dash north.

"My Lord," he said. "Do you remember a day, hawking above the Temple of Tan, when kingfowl were caught by a stranger?"

Kalavin's mouth fell open. He cut short a snort of

surprise, stared again, nodded and turned to the charioteer.

"All right, Atholin," he said. "Put the horses away.
Our quarters are going to be pretty cramped if my father's here. Make the best arrangements you can. Come
with me, boy."

Tron needed almost to run to keep up with Kalavin's
eager stride. He'd expected simply to be taken aside to
explain the General's arrival in privacy, but Kalavin
was evidently going somewhere, and talked excitedly as
he walked.

"Sinu, but I'm glad to see you! The king . . . he
wouldn't understand how I failed to get you out of that
barge."

"You couldn't have done anything, My Lord. I saw
that."

"Exactly! Well, I hope you'll tell him! I've tried to
explain but he won't listen. It's as though I'd broken an
Obligation to him—I suppose in a way I did, but it
wasn't like that. And he's been behaving since then—
not just to me, either—oh, I don't know—as though
he'd never be lucky again. This way."

Corridors, courtyards, arcades. Walls that in the
Temple would have been bare were hung with deep-
colored carpets; strange, heavy scents seemed to float
out of certain doors they passed. At some entrances ele-
gant young men, courtier-sentries, stopped them, more
to break the boredom of their guard duty by chatting
with Kalavin than to question his right to pass; but behind the chat Tron sensed a tension and wariness, a
sour echo to Kalavin's eager optimism. At last they
reached a round-arched passage where five men sat on
stools, whispering over a game of dice. One of them, a
black-bearded official wearing a long blue-and-gold
robe, looked up at Kalavin's step, frowned and shook
his head.

"Wait here, boy," said Kalavin.

The official rose as he strode forward. A discussion
began, but in whispers so low that Tron could hear a
woman's voice singing somewhere beyond the group.

Kalavin became stiff and angry, gesturing once or twice toward Tron. The dice-players rose and joined in the argument. Tron could see Kalavin's problem—if he was out of favor with the King, these courtiers would be reluctant to let him through, and there was no question of explaining who Tron really was, or how he had traveled in the Dead King's coffin. At length the blue-robed official beckoned. As Tron walked forward he heard this man saying, ". . . on your head be it, Kalavin."

"On my head be it, My Lord. And let everyone witness that if the King rebukes My Lord, I will forfeit to him the stewardship of Bastaan Canals. You'd better go alone, boy. I'll take that hawk."

Tron had almost forgotten the crested sparrowhawk he was carrying. Nervous and bewildered, he passed it to Kalavin, then walked through the arch at the end of the passage into a small arcaded courtyard. A slow fountain trickled at its center; gummy-scented flowers dangled from baskets hung between the pillars, and under the arcade itself dusk was already halfway to dark. He walked toward the sound of the singing, which seemed to float in among the fret-carved stone and then drift away upward to the darkening sky. More nervous than ever, he stole along the marble tiles and round the corner of the arcade.

The King was lolling on a mound of cushions in the next corner, his left hand idly stroking the black hair of the singer who sat cross-legged at his side and with pale fingers caressed a small harp, making a sound so soft that only the two of them could have discerned the faint, rainy notes behind her voice. But there was something about his pose at odds with the mood of idleness and luxury, and the moment Tron's movement caught his eye he jerked himself up, his face harsh with fury and amazement, but also a sort of eagerness, as though he welcomed the chance to pour out his frustration on this intruder. Then the fury died, leaving only the amazement, and he came striding forward with outstretched arms, his whole being seeming to pulse with pleasure in the living instant.

"I was afraid you would not know me, Majesty," said Tron in a low voice.

"I would know you in the cave of that kind woman," said the King, speaking even lower. "Come and sit with me. Don't say anything for the moment. No spyholes cover this corner, but voices carry among stonework. Namuthaa will make us a screen of sound."

He turned and called to the singer "Ah, my love, any more music like that will melt me into a pool of honey. Sing something a bit more bracing—it's a long time since I heard *Dana and Tribathu*."

He settled back onto the cushions; Tron knelt beside him; the woman, pouting slightly, slipped onto her right hand a silk glove with fingernails of bone and began to pluck at the wires, drawing out a wild and clashingly metallic cataract of music. The King smiled at her. She threw back her head and began on a long and wailing note.

> "Ohay, Tribathu! Ohay, Tribathu!
>   The soldiers of Dana creep out of the
>   marsh.
> They take the cows from your pasture,
>   Tribathu.
> They take your daughter who watched
>   them, Tribathu.
>   Away through the twisting tracks of the
>   marsh."

"Ah, it's good to see you!" whispered the King. "When Kalavin told me what had happened I felt . . . oh, it's difficult to say . . . like that emptiness when you lose a favorite hawk . . . but worse, far worse. I thought I'd never see you again until I made my journey to that kind woman, and suddenly you walk under the archways. It's like meeting somebody in a dream. Tell me where you've been."

"In the far south, Majesty. But when I was there I found a man who'd crossed the Peaks of Alaan. He'd come from a country called Falathi. He'd come to see

you. He was carrying something he called a Red
Spear. . . ."

The King's hand shot out and gripped Tron fiercely
by the wrist.

"An Ambassador from Falathi invoking the Red
Spear Treaty! Where is he now?"

"The General of the Southern Levies took him into
the Temple to make offerings."

"How long ago?"

"O was almost setting."

"Well . . . there's time to hear the song out. Tell
me what you know."

The woman's voice echoed off the darkening masonry as she sang the tragedy of Tribathu's daughter,
trapped between her love for a swampland outlaw and
her duty to show her father the paths through the
marshes. Under this screen of sound Tron whispered his
story, while the king listened calm-faced but nodding
occasionally where a detail confirmed his own knowledge.

"Falathi's in the Obligations," he said when Tron had
finished. "So are your tribesmen in the ravines. But
these Mohirrim are new to me. . . . Where's the Lord
General? He should have been here by now. . . . Go
quietly along to the entrance. Fetch Kalavin and my
Chamberlain—the one in blue and gold—bring them
round by this side of the arcade. . . ."

Tron crept away and returned with the two nobles,
Kalavin almost singing with happiness at his return to
favor, the Chamberlain frowning. Tron himself felt puzzled and disturbed. After the first shock of gladness at
the King's greeting, which had lasted while he told his
story, he now began to feel once more the menace of
coming events. Unconsciously he had supposed that
once he had reached the King he would be safe under
his protection, but he'd found the King himself having
to hide and creep. Were even the Gods afraid of this
place? Was that why They had come no farther on the
journey? At any rate, They were not here. Men had
taken over these halls and corridors just as lizards and

bats had taken over the Temple of Tan, and just like lizards and bats, men scurried around in these crannies and tunnels, working in the dark their own mean little purposes. . . . And now Tron was going to have to hide and scurry with the rest. *Nothing ever ends,* he thought. *I finish one task and find it's only the beginning of another. No, nothing ends until we go to Aa, and perhaps that will be just another beginning.*

At a sign the nobles knelt by the King. In the ballad Tribathu's daughter led her father's men toward the ambush Dana had prepared.

"My lords," whispered the King, "I have discovered that I am watched in most parts of the Palace. We can't be seen here, but our voices may be heard. Your father, Kalavin, has brought an Ambassador from Falathi, to invoke the Red Spear Treaty—that's in your Obligations, isn't it?—and my guess is the priests are delaying them in the Temple, and if they spend the night there they won't live to see the dawn. I want you two to stay here, talk, laugh, listen to Namuthaa's singing as if I were with you, after a while begin to behave as though I were growing impatient, send to the gate for news of the General and the Ambassador, let any listeners know that we are aware of their coming. . . . Kalavin, here is my shoulder buckle. Lord Chamberlain, you are witness that by this gift I appoint the Lord Kalavin to be my regent to fulfill my Obligation to Falathi under the Red Spear Treaty, supposing I don't get back. In that case the first thing you've got to do is demand to see the One of Sinu—he'll tell you what to do after that—Tron, come with me. I feel in my bones we must hurry."

It was now almost dark. As Tron followed the King through the shadowed archways he heard behind him the harpstrings weeping the tears of Tribathu's daughter for her dead father and her dead lover. The King chose a tortuous route. Tron guessed that he was avoiding not only spyholes but also places where there were likely to be courtiers on duty. Often there were not even torches flaring in the walls, and they climbed a stair or strode down a corridor in total darkness. At last they came to a long hall whose roof was supported by a grove of delicate pillars. It was unlit, but the last of dusk seeped in through the tall windows.

"Now," whispered the King, "this is what we've got to do. . . ."

"Aren't we watched, Majesty? This feels like the sort of place . . ."

The King gave a muffled snort of amusement.

"You're right," he said. "But they don't come here, and they've blocked up the spyholes. This room is used for the Dance of Tan, which my wives do—thin, gauzy clothes and long floating veils in and out among the pillars. I'm the only man allowed to see it. Very pretty, very disturbing for a priest to watch, even through a spyhole. So they blocked them up. Now, listen. I must go to that room above the Gate of Saba, the one where they took you when you'd removed the Blue Hawk at the Renewal of my father's soul. That's where they always hold their secret councils. I've got to know what they're planning. That means you've got to go and tell the One of Sinu what's happening."

"Alone!"

"It's not as bad as it sounds. I've discovered that very few priests know the secret ways. Of those the Major Priests will be at the Council, and at least one more will be watching the courtyard where he thinks I still am. They can move very silently but they don't usually bother—they're too confident. If they meet another priest in the secret ways they don't chatter, they just exchange a password. One of them says, 'She rules the moon,' and the other one answers, 'But She is not the moon.' Got it?"

"Yes."

"You understand about the One of Sinu? Once he's got reason to believe that a cause of war may have arisen he's got an absolute right to go where he wants and make any inquiries he wants. He'll jump at the chance. I told you how the order of Sinu was being downgraded by the other orders. He knows—they all know—that if he proves a cause of war then he can order the Horn of

War to be blown, and after that the hymns of Sinu take precedence over everything, and nothing can stop me raising my levies. The Red Spear is a cause of war, in itself. . . ."

"But it's come. There's no need . . ."

"Give them a night to work in and they'll somehow make it not have come. I don't know how. Now, listen. . . ."

Tron had spent half his life learning how to coil away in his mind long and detailed sets of instructions. The King had only to repeat his directions twice—numbers of paces, turnings, stairs—and Tron knew them. He nodded. The King turned to a bas-relief of Tan dancing with the river as her veil, carved into the wall behind the black and silver throne at the end of the room. He seized the tail of one of the sturgeon that danced around her, twisted it inward and up, and swung the slab round. Without hesitation he stepped into the slit of sheer blackness beyond, waited for Tron to follow, and soundlessly closed the stone.

"She rules the moon," he whispered.

"But She is not the moon," answered Tron with a hammering heart.

The King grunted and was gone, while Tron stood shuddering in the blackness. He felt that if he stirred a foot he would stumble into a plummeting hole, if he reached out a hand it would touch some clinging web at whose center lurked . . . he didn't make a picture of the horror that hung there, but it took him all his willpower to stretch out a hand and feel nothing but dry air and then clean stone. It was no use praying. The Gods were elsewhere. This was something he had to do without help, because the King had asked him. But just as if it were a hymn he began to repeat the set of directions the King had given him. Fourteen paces . . . It was eighteen, so timid were his steps, but there was the slit opening to the left. Five paces (bolder now). Stairs. He went up them on hands and knees. At the top dim light floated, where a spyhole opened on some courtyard. The black beyond seemed like wall, which he had to

force himself into. Turnings, steps, ramps, and at last a
vast reach of faint-lit passage. Now he was nearly there.

By his gropings and creepings Tron had reached the
upper story of the west side of the Great Courtyard.
This was a long barrack of a building leaning on a central spine of masonry which stretched its whole length.
Down the center of this spine ran the hidden corridor.
In the series of rooms on either side of it lived and slept
the priests of several orders, each order totally separate
from the next. Thus no doors pierced the spine, and the
hidden corridor could run level and straight. Normally
it would have been as dark in here as it had been in the
black windings through which Tron had crept, but at
this moment Aa was following O down into the west,
and Her light, shining horizontal across the dunes,
pierced through the windows of the dormitories that
faced the desert and then into the series of spyholes that
made sure that no priest could even sleep unwatched.

Knowing this light would not last, Tron moved
swiftly down the corridor, instinctively ducking below
each bar of light so that even Aa should not see him
pass. Halfway down he found a spyhole that was in
shadow, so he paused to check his progress. He peered
through it into a boys' dormitory, with its line of tall slit
windows opposite the row of huddled rectangles where
the boys slept on their mattresses; the pure curve of a
bowl of offering was silhouetted on each sill; at the center of the room the pale beams glittered off the jewels
on the statue of a hawk-headed God. Suddenly it was as
if Tron had been looped back in time. This was his own
dormitory where, on just such a night, he had woken on
one particular mattress, heard a shuffle of cloth in the
stillness, and seen the first slit of silver blank out. The
boys, already deep in their sweetwater dreams, slept un-
stirring. But something moved. A shuffle of cloth.

All Tron's senses, tense with darkness, reached for
the sound. It was not in the dormitory but in the tunnel
behind him, a faint movement of robes, steadily approaching. Crouching below the bars of light, Tron hurried on, hoping that the priest's own movements would

cover any sound he might make. Was this man simply
patrolling the secret ways? Had he come to watch the
One of Sinu, to prevent any attempt to reach him? Yes.
Then what could Tron do? Nothing for the moment, except race on, in silence and darkness, keeping ahead.

With a thump in his chest he realized that the rus-
tlings had stopped. He froze, sure he had been heard,
and that the man had halted to listen. Then, looking
back, he saw a new light glimmer, a tall slit that widened, vanished, returned, narrowed, and stayed. A secret door, which the priest had passed through and left
ajar. Tron scuttled back and peeped through a spyhole.
He saw a dormitory. Straight in front of him the lion-
headed statuette of the War-God Sinu stood black
against Aa's silver. Blacker even than that, a robed
shape slid past the slit windows.

Tron raced to the door and peered through. Few
boys were chosen for Sinu these days, so the priest stole
past empty places to the end where (if arrangements
were the same here as they had been in the order of
Gdu) would be first the cell of the One of Sinu, then
cells of three or four senior priests of the order, then the
dormitory of the ordinary confirmed priests. A passage
ran between the inner wall and the cells, joining the two
dormitories. The priest paused here, almost invisible,
but Tron saw the faint gleam of his face as he peered
back down the dormitory, perhaps checking that none
of the boys had stirred. Then he vanished.

Tron slid through the door and crept across the dormitory, his bare feet silent on the stone. Peeping round
the door of the first cell, he saw the priest kneeling by
the side of a low bed, reaching over it toward the sleep-
er's face. For an instant he stood, helpless. There was
no hope of his fighting a priest of Aa, armed with a
sacrificial knife and expert in the deadly dance called
Flying Shadows. He must get help.

As he crept into the next cell the man on the bed sat
suddenly bolt upright. He must have been already
awake.

"Who's there?" he snapped.

"A priest of Aa has come to take the One of Sinu in his sleep," whispered Tron. "He's there now."

The man thrashed out of his cot in a bound and rushed into the passage. He paused for an instant at the door into his master's cell, then shouted "Wake, Sinu! Wake!"

He was still shouting as he charged into the cell.

Questioning voices rose behind Tron. Bare feet slapped stone. The grunts of struggle rose from the cell of the One of Sinu, and then Tron found himself carried forward by a rush of bodies to the cell door. Two men in nightshifts pushed past him and joined the dim-seen struggle. A heavy, dazing odor drifted out of the room. Then the strugglers convulsed and fell apart, the three priests of Sinu backing against the bed as if to defend their master, and the black-robed priest standing by the window, outlined against the last light of Aa. He pulled the cowl back from his face and took from the pouch of his robe a small object whose lid he carefully prized up.

"Breathe shallow, my brothers," he said in a gentle voice, then lowered his head, sniffed deeply and closed the lid. Turning to the desert he began to chant.

> "Mistress of dark,
> Mother of Gods,
> Aa never born,
> Ruler of birth,
> Aa never dying,
> Ruler of death,
> A man's . . ."

He choked, staggered and collapsed to the floor. Voices muttered. One of the men by the bed swung round to Tron.

"You!" he snapped. "Explain! A servant of Aa comes, takes our master, takes himself, you are here watching. Explain!"

Men seized Tron by the elbows and pushed him forward. He gathered his tattered wits. What would the King want? What would he need to tell them to achieve that?

"The General of the Southern Levies has come," he said. "He has brought an Ambassador from Falathi, carrying the Red Spear. The King suspects that the Major Priests will try to prevent the Red Spear from reaching him. He sent me by secret ways to fetch the One of Sinu. When I came I saw this priest of Aa kneeling by the bed. I ran to wake you."

A wavelike mutter of anger and astonishment rose and stilled. A lamp was brought. Its sickly light made masks of the priests' faces as they gathered round the bed. Outside the circle the dead priest of Aa lay in a sprawl of black robes beneath the window as his Goddess sank out of the sky. Nobody seemed to know what to do. Suddenly Tron remembered a line of the little hymn that deals with the drugs used in surgery.

The scent of honey, the stink of decay.

"Revered Lords," he said. "Perhaps the One of Sinu is not dead. I think the smell in the room is the juice of the root of leopard-flower. You drip it onto a cloth held by a man's nose and it causes a deep sleep."

Somebody knelt by the bed.

"He breathes," he whispered. "Heavy and slow. What now, Tanta, my brother?"

"Now," barked the man who had first spoken, "we dress in our day-robes. We light torches. We march to these priests and demand by what right a servant of Aa is sent to drug our master? By what right is he prevented from playing his part in the rituals of the Red Spear Treaty? Where are they, boy? Where is the King?"

"In a secret room above the Gate of Saba," said Tron. "Revered Lord, if your master is forced to stand and walk, he will wake sooner."

"Good," snapped Tanta, too angry to question how Tron should know this. "We will take him with us. And let those to whom the duty falls prepare the Horn of War."

the door stopped their tug-of-war to stare at him. The
women put their hands ... eyes and turned away.
Tron paid no attention ... them as he settled the
...

XIII

HUDDLED BESIDE THE DOOR OF THE WISE, TRON LIS-
TENED to the tramping rhythm of the Great Hymn of
Sinu echoing across the starlit courtyard.

> Man-harvester,
>   Sinu!
> Town-plougher,
>   Sinu!
> You fill the canals
> With reeking blood
> To water fields
> From which will grow
> Fresh crops of Man
> For your blade to harvest,
>   Sinu!

An orange spark pricked the night where the first torch
of the procession showed near the middle of the western
halls. Governed by the staggering paces of the One of
Sinu as he was dragged between two priests, it would
take a long time to cross the Courtyard. Tron sucked at
his lips, hesitating.

He longed for the comfort and company of his own
hawk, asleep in the King's mews, like a priest in its cell.
Always when he had carried it on his wrist it had
seemed a living sign that what he did had the blessing of
the Lord Gdu. But now events seemed suddenly to have
rushed beyond anyone's control, and there were no
Gods here to guide them back into their proper channels. He did not feel that he could achieve anything, but

was ashamed to stay there, crouching by the door, doing nothing. This shame forced him across the threshold and sent him groping up the stairs. At least he could check whether the way to the secret room was clear on this side.

Aa had set now, and the Room of Days and Years was a cavern of dark, given shape only by the starlit rectangles of the windows. Tron felt for the rack of rods and, guided by the rail along its lower edge, stole down the room. It seemed endless, but just as he reached the last window he heard the slide and thud of a bolt being drawn. Tron crouched. The dimmest of lights showed as the door into the Keeper's cell opened. A man strode through, as calmly as if he had been walking about in broad daylight, and crossed to the other wall of the room. Tron saw his outline against a small window that opened onto the Courtyard, and realized that he had come to see who was singing a Great Hymn in the silent hours that belong to Aa. An indecipherable voice came through the open door.

Tron's whole impulse now was to reach the King, and the King had said he would go to the priest's council room. Almost without a thought Tron slipped through the door and crouched in the corner of the Keeper's cell. The inner door was slightly ajar, and Onu Ovalaku's voice was clear now, talking in his own purring, guttural language, some appeal, passionate and frustrated.

"Perhaps the Lord General can interpret for us," said the calm voice of the One of O.

"Not in so many words," snapped the General's voice. "This much I know. Falathi has been attacked and almost overwhelmed by a horde of savages called Mohirrim. They ride horses, fight with war dogs, paint themselves blue and take their women everywhere they go, almost into the very battles they fight. They are like locusts, eating a country bare and then moving on. They live by war. The Princes of Falathi sent us Ambassadors to invoke the Red Spear Treaty, of whom only Onu Ovalaku came alive across the Peaks of Alaan. My

Lords, I tell you this in some impatience, because it is no concern of yours. It is a matter for the King, who has an Obligation to Falathi under the Red Spear Treaty. You have kept us here since before O's going, and . . ."

"My Lord General," said the One of O coldly now, "we are not concerned with these so-called Obligations. Our task is to see that everything is done in the Kingdom in accordance with the will of the Gods, and that can only be known through the hymns. I have never heard any hymn mentioning this Red Spear Treaty."

"Of course you haven't," snapped the General. "There's only . . ."

But at that moment the Keeper of the Rods came striding into his cell from the Room of Days and Years. He slid the bolt shut, and went on through the inner door, still leaving it slightly ajar. The argument seemed to stop at his entrance, but Tron realized from the General's words that the King had not yet come there. There was no point in staying huddled in this trap, then. He tiptoed to the outer door, eased the bolt open, and slid out.

The procession of the Order of Sinu was a caterpillar of men crawling with extraordinary slowness across the paving, their scarlet robes catching the torchlight and looking from a distance as though the great gawky beast were gashed with wounds. The beast's head staggered and weaved where the One of Sinu, with his arms around the necks of two of his priests, took a half-step, fell asleep where he stood, was dragged out of the pit of dreams and took another half-step. His head lolled, a dribble of saliva glistened down his chin, and his eyelids sucked slowly open to show the sightless eyes before drifting shut once more. Tron flitted into the gap behind him where his deputy, Tanta, walked and led the baying hymn.

> Over your helmet,
> Sinu!

Poised the scorpion's tail,
  Sinu!
"Ho, little God,
I have come to suck
The sap of the world.
Your sword shall not stop me.
Out of my path,
  Sinu!"

Priests learn how to listen to a whisper while they themselves are singing at full voice. Tanta nodded when he heard what Tron had seen and done. He was a stocky, taut man to whom anger came easily. He took two more slow paces, stopped singing, and said, "Go back, boy. Keep that door open if you can. Three of us will bring my master to these priests. The rest will finish our hymn at the Gate of Saba."

Tron slid away. Since he knew his path now, the pools of total dark seemed easier to pass. No one challenged him in the Room of Days and Years, and the door into the Keeper's cell was still unbarred. The clear voice of the One of O was speaking from the council room beyond.

". . . for those who claim without authority from any hymn to interpret the will of the Gods."

The General's answer came like the snarl of a trapped animal, so weary and desperate that it is prepared to slash out at anything.

"The Red Spear Treaty is an Obligation, I tell you! It has nothing to do with your Gods!"

The priests allowed the silence to last for several breaths. There was a shudder of triumph in the voice of the One of O when he replied.

"There, my brothers, we have it at last, though it is as we suspected from the first, when the Gods rejected the stranger's offering. My lord General is claiming freedom to act without the blessing of the Gods."

This time the silence seemed endless. The Great Hymn of Sinu came less faintly now as the procession

moved into the Inner Courtyard below the Gate of
Saba. Tron crept to the stone door and peered through
the slit, but all he could see by the steady, yellow-
greenish glow of the oil lamp the priests had lit was the
white fold of one edge of the robe of the Keeper of the
Rods and a stretch of carved wall at the back of the
room. He wondered what would happen now. The
hymns were full of tales of men who had acted without
the blessing of the Gods, and the hideous penalties they
had paid.

"I didn't mean . . ." the General suddenly blurted,
then fell silent. It was too late. Whatever he had meant,
it was clear what he had said.

Suddenly Onu Ovalaku's voice burst out into the one
sentence he was sure of.

"By ancient treaty and by der Red Spear I call der
King to aid us."

Tron heard a click and a stir of movement as the
Keeper took a pace forward and out of Tron's sight-
line. A carved slab of the rear wall vanished, becoming
a slot of dark, out of which stepped the King, with the
Eye of Gdu gleaming on his forehead. The General
gave a yap of surprise, but the priests seemed not even
to murmur.

"By ancient treaty and by the Red Spear I will come
to your aid," said the King slowly. He added a stum-
bling sentence in the language of Falathi, to which Onu
Ovalaku replied, then he too moved out of Tron's sight-
line. From the darkness of the Room of Days and Years
Tron heard a faint shuffling sound.

"Where is the Red Spear, my lord General?" said the
King's voice.

"Majesty, they burned it," the General burst out.

"The Gods rejected the stranger's sacrifice," said the
One of O. "He is accursed, and accursed too are all
who have helped him. The General has just said with
his own lips . . ."

"I heard what he said," snapped the King. "He said
that the Red Spear Treaty had nothing to do with *your*
Gods. And he was right. It is a treaty under the shield

of the Lord Sinu. It is a matter for the One of Sinu. Why is he not here? Where is he?"

In the silence Tron heard again the noise of the blind old man being dragged forward through the Room of Days and Years. Now he could see an orange crack down the outer door of the cell, where torchlight struck. He felt the urgency of keeping up the momentum of the King's attack, of not giving the priests time to consult or to argue. Quickly he crossed the cell, opened the outer door, recrossed the room, and threw his weight against the slab of stone. It gave more easily than he was prepared for, so that he almost fell sprawling as he stumbled through. For an instant the whole room stared at him, and then their eyes switched away beyond.

They looked from light through darkness and into light where, under one flaring torch, four red-robed men came slowly down the Room of Days and Years. The priests supporting the One of Sinu tried to hurry his pace, so that his bald yellow head flopped heavily from side to side as he came. His mouth opened and shut ceaselessly like the beak of a sick hawk. His eyes blinked stickily, and when the weary lids were raised the film of gray across the eyeballs reflected lamplight and torchlight, so that they gleamed like a jackal's in the dark. The lion-headed staff of his office had been lashed to his left hand and its end scraped uselessly along the floor. While the others in the room stared, Tron slipped unnoticed to the King's side.

"He's been drugged," he whispered. "Leopard-flower. They sent a priest of Aa, but we caught him. He hadn't finished. He killed himself. I don't know how long the drug will last."

The King nodded, frowning. The priests' faces showed no sign of surprise or doubt. There were only four of them in the room—the Ones of O and Aa, the Mouth of Silence, and the Keeper of the Rods. They waited in calm patience until the shuffling procession reached the lamplight, and then the One of O stepped blandly forward.

"Welcome, my brother," he said to the blind, stupefied old man. "The Gods have brought you in a good hour, as we have need of your knowledge. Send your helpers away. This room is for the Major Priests alone."

The blue lips of the One of Sinu continued their meaningless gaping. Tanta stepped forward.

"My lords," he said harshly. "The Order of Sinu comes to demand by what right . . ."

"We do not hear you," said the One of O coldly. "Only Major Priests have a voice in this room."

". . . by what right," shouted Tanta, heedless, "you had my master drugged so that the King should not hear the hymn of the Red Spear Treaty?"

"Now it's out!" said the King eagerly. "How does the hymn go, Revered Lord?"

> "Let them send from the south
> From beyond . . ."

Tanta stopped short, staring at the One of Aa, who with three dancelike strides had moved to face him. As the swirl of black robes settled, the pearl-pale hands floated upward.

"Shall my master curse you with his lips, then?" whispered the Mouth of Silence.

Chill seemed to seep out of the stonework, up from the earth, down from the dark of Aa, filling the lamplit room. Tanta hesitated, licked his lips, and took a pace backward. Slowly, with the wavering movement of dead things sinking through water, the hands of the One of Aa sank back to his sides.

"Now," said the One of O, "you will settle your master in that chair and leave."

"One moment," said the King, moving forward. "Or will you curse a King rather than let him speak to a Major Priest? I fear that kind woman, but I am not afraid of you, Revered Lords."

They all waited until he was standing face to face with the blind priest.

"Sinu," he said gently. "The Red Spear Treaty. Let them send from the south."

The old man's filmed eyes blinked slowly, and his mouth stopped its yawning for a moment and shut tight.

"My brother of Sinu knows of no such hymn," said the One of O. "Therefore this Red Spear Treaty is nothing more than a stratagem to allow the King to raise his levies against the will of the Gods. It is as we thought from the first, my brothers."

Tron stared at the old man, hopeless and despairing. Only the Lord Gdu could break the chain of the drug and free the imprisoned will, and He was far away. Shadowy in his mind Tron formed a picture of the Blue Hawk, his contact with the God, as he had first seen it, drowsy like the One of Sinu, sick and bedraggled. The picture became firmer, became like a living bird in the dark room.

"Let them send from the south, Sinu," said the King. "Let them send from the south."

The One of Sinu swayed and tried to draw his arms free from his supporters. His head jerked erect, lolled, and straightened again. The spittle down his chin became a steady stream. His lips began to move. The words were slurred into a dull mumble, only just interpretable.

> "Let them send from the south,
> From beyond the peaks,
> A rider with a spear
> Strung like a bow—
> One string for each people
> Bound at the tip
> With flamingo feathers,
> Tan's holy bird.
> Then, then must the Horn
> Of War be sounded.
> The breath of Sinu
> Must fill the Kingdom
> That the King may call
> His levies to muster
> And ride to war
> Through the Pass of Gebindrath."

As he ended, one bony old hand rose and feebly tried to wipe the saliva from his chin.

"How deep the hymns root," said the Mouth of Silence in an awed mutter.

"So, Revered Lords!" cried the King. "There is no Red Spear Treaty? There is no hymn? And you have taken it on yourselves to reject and burn the symbol of friendship between two nations!"

The One of O said nothing, but glanced at the Keeper of the Rods, who nodded calmly, just as though he had been giving the signal for the start of a new phase of a ritual in the House of O and Aa.

"Let us all sit down," he said. "The lesser priests of Sinu may wait in my room beyond. The boy too."

His glance at Tron caught, held, and became a thoughtful gaze. Then he nodded again. His face showed no sign of surprise, only a look of satisfaction, as though a rod lost from his rack had been found and settled into place again.

"No," he said. "The boy must return to the Halls of Gdu. By O and Aa I hereby vow that he will not be harmed."

"The boy you are talking about went on a journey to that kind woman," said the King. "How can this be the same boy? He stays with me."

"Perhaps he is still on his journey," said the Mouth of Silence in a trancelike voice. Tron shivered. He knew by now how often the Gods put truth into the mouths of the priests, even when they themselves might think they were lying. Instinctively he moved to behind the King's shoulder, as if into the sphere of his protection, but standing a little sideways so that he could watch the door through which the King had entered. What mustering of silent priests, each gripping a leaf-shaped sacrificial knife, was waiting in that dark cranny, ready to burst into the lamplit room? Tron wasn't afraid of them now, only wary. As far as the human actors went he was beginning to feel a sort of exhilaration in the King's success, a sense of being part of a controlled onrush. A sudden thud in the room made him start, but it was only the One of Sinu collapsing forward across the table. The old man sprawled now with his yellow skull stark on the black wood, mouth half open, lids closed over the sightless eyes. Tron stared at him without pity or horror, but with a sort of awe at the way the Gods contrived to squeeze Their purposes through such a narrow and fragile channel.

This room was full of purposes, layers under layers— the General's to fulfill his Obligation to the Falathi; Onu Ovalaku's to bring help to his country; the King's to provide that help and thus to reassert his own power, and in the end to break the power of the priests; the priests' to retain that power; and so on. But under all these lay the invisible purposes of the Gods, Who had willed this meeting, Who had used the One of Sinu and now were letting him sleep, Who had used Tron and now . . .

Tron shivered again. This was what he was afraid of. Glad and happy though he'd been to serve the Lord Gdu always in dance and prayer, he did not feel that he could endure again adventures such as those that had taken him to Kalakal, to serve Their purposes. And yet the Mouth of Silence had said that he was still on that journey.

"Well, Revered Lord?" said the King as the lesser priests of Sinu withdrew. His voice sounded light and careless, but his right hand was taut around the hilt of his dagger, below the table, out of sight of all but Tron.

"Majesty," said the Keeper in a flat and passionless voice, "ask yourself why we were so certain that this treaty was a lie. The answer is that we already knew that the Gods had rejected the Red Spear which this stranger brought, and thus shown him to be accursed. And we knew why. You have now shown that the treaty is true, but it would have been better to have left it as a lie. Because, treaty or no treaty, you can never lead your army through the Pass of Gebindrath. The Great Curse of Aa is on that place."

He turned to the Mouth of Silence, whose dry, painful voice took up the story.

"That curse is the greatest of our Great Rituals," he said. "It is performed by twelve twelves of priests, led by the One of Aa, chanting with his own lips. It has been heard only twice in three hundred floods. Each new generation of priests learns it in a whisper. Majesty, do you think your levies will follow you through a place where such a curse is laid?"

"And there is no other road through the Peaks of Alaan," said the Keeper. "The stranger must have come that way. That is why the Red Spear was rejected by the Gods. That is why he is accursed."

"Majesty . . ." began the General, but the King held up a hand.

"Keeper," he said. "You count the days and years. Can you tell me why the Pass of Gebindrath was closed with a curse? And why the paths through the northern marshes which used to be known are now lost? And why the desert wells which were built by the Wise are now poisoned, so that no merchants can cross the sands? Why?"

"It was the will of the Gods," said the Keeper. "There are no hymns about the closing of the Kingdom. The Gods said, 'Let it be done,' and it was done."

"That is all?" said the King in a slightly mocking voice, and then with sudden urgency added, "Mouth of Silence, is that all?"

Tron saw how well he had chosen his man and his moment. The One of O might have ducked the question, and the Keeper would have blandly lied. But the Mouth of Silence served the Gods in a simpler manner.

"The passes and the marsh roads and the desert are all closed," he said, "for one great purpose. We must keep the Kingdom holy, serving the Gods. There was a certain King, Dathardan the Ninth, who fought a war against a people on the far side of the desert and returned with many captives, one of them a woman for whom he became mad with love. And because of this love he built her a Temple for the God she worshipped, a snake god, false and abominable. And Dathardan made for the woman a jeweled image of the snake god, and for her sake on a certain day he fell at its feet and worshipped it. That night, as he and the woman slept, Aa took them. And next day Sinu raised up a holy madness in the people, priests, nobles, and peasants, so that they hunted down and killed all the strangers. Then Dathardan the Tenth reigned, and he was a child, so there was a Council of Regency, and the Gods made known their will to the Council, that the Kingdom must be closed thenceforth and for ever. . . ."

The tired voice droned on, hypnotic. This was not a hymn, true, but Tron could tell from the stiff turns of phrase that it was something learned and passed down through generations of priests, a secret knowledge that threaded through all the unchanging rituals of the Kingdom just as the secret ways threaded in darkness through the Temple. In a half-trance he saw the green-robed priests of Tan supervising the demolition of the canals that drained the barrier of marshes to the north; he saw the small party of priests of Gdu making every ten years the appalling journey to add more poison to the desert wells; he saw an army of laborers breaking down the wonderful road cut by Gebindrath, and leaving sheer cliff; he saw the slow dunes beginning to creep across that other road, built by the Wise, that led to it. He felt, across the stretching years, the power of the Gods drawing the Kingdom close around Them, just as a hunter draws his cloak around him against the chill of the desert night.

". . . and finally," said the Mouth of Silence, "the One of Aa with twelve twelves of his priests journeyed to the pass and made the Great Ritual, calling down the power of Aa upon that place, to hold it closed against man and beast until the Gods unmake what They made."

"So the pass is sealed and the road is broken," said the Keeper of the Rods. "And with good reason. Majesty, you cannot and you must not cross the peaks."

"What men have broken men can mend," said the King. "What priests have done priests can undo. I have an Obligation to Falathi."

"But the Gods have already rejected your Obligation," said the One of O impatiently. "They made that clear when they rejected the stranger's offering, brought here by him through the Curse of Aa."

"But he didn't come that way!" burst in the General. Every head turned toward him.

"There is no other way," said the Keeper. "The hymns of Alaan are clear."

"He climbed," said the General. "He has drawn pictures to show me. At one point he fell three hundred feet down an ice-scree. Both his guides died. And six other Ambassadors set out, of whom only he has come through. But still he didn't use the Pass of Gebindrath, so the curse is not on him. That's clear."

"It's also clear I cannot take an army the way he came," said the King. "Revered Lords, the curse must be lifted from the pass."

They looked at him in silence, their faces unreadable. Tron realized that the muffled, repetitive chant from the courtyard had ceased and was being replaced by a new sound, or rather a shuddering of air, a note so deep that it seemed to quiver along the bones rather than be heard through the ears. It lasted through twenty heartbeats, and as it faded the voices of the priests of Sinu came in with a harsh, unmusical yell.

"Sinu! War! Sinu! War!"

The shudder of air began once more.

"What is that?" asked the One of O, sounding mere mortal and nervous.

"That is the breath of Sinu. That is the Horn of War," said the King. "You heard the One of Sinu give the order to sound it. Now it is done, and all according to ritual. Now, until the peace offerings are laid on His table, Sinu is supreme in the Kingdom. At dawn tomorrow my messengers must ride to my Generals of Levies, carrying the war tokens so that the army can begin to gather. You cannot stop me now."

"We cannot stop you," said the One of O heavily. "The Gods can. You will never lead your army through the Pass of Gebindrath. It takes priests of three orders to lift such a curse as lies on that place. It takes a ritual known only to the servants of Aa. No servant of Aa will tell you the ritual. No priest of any other order than Sinu's will help you. Do you think one man of all your soldiers will follow you through the pass, with the curse unlifted? King, you are doomed."

"Doomed," said the Keeper.

The One of Aa's pale hands swept through a slow arc.

"Doomed," croaked the Mouth of Silence.

In the courtyard below, the long note of the Horn of War began again, making it seem as though the whole world shuddered.

XIV

EVEN THAT END HAD BEEN ONLY ANOTHER BEGINNING. Twelve days later Tron stood with his hawk in the shade of a creeper-tangled cliff and remembered his last conversation with the King. It had taken place two days after the confrontation in the room above the Gate of Saba.

"Yes," Tron had said doubtfully, "if a lost ritual has to be found again, then I think Odah, servant of O, might do it."

"And perform the ritual too?" the King had asked.

"Yes, I think so. But he's very crippled. He'll have to be carried to the pass."

"So will the One of Sinu. If you take him to Kalakal, Tron, you can talk to this Odah, can't you? You can persuade him?"

Tron shrugged. He felt sick and uneasy. The King turned on the balcony, where they'd been watching the parade of one of the first levies to arrive at the Temple.

"We must be quick, you see, Tron," he had said. "In about fifteen days I'll be able to get the first war party up to the pass, to hold it and start to repair the road. The longer I leave that, the more chance there is of these Mohirrim reaching the pass first. And the longer I sit idle here the more time it gives the priests to start working against me. There's nothing like an army for rumors. They're saying that this very dawn a priest of O, singing the Welcome on the tower, saw the face of the God as He rose, all streaked with blood. They say the vision was so powerful that two other priests were needed to stop him throwing himself off the tower."

"It may be true," Tron had said.

"Perhaps. It's a sign you could read several ways. But Tron, have you asked yourself why the God guided you to Kalakal? Why, if not so that you should find not just the Ambassador but also this priest, Odah? Listen. . . ."

But at that point a horn had sounded in the courtyard and the King had been forced to turn and salute the parade of gaudy banners passing below. While the fretted colonnades had echoed to the rhythmic clash of sword blades on shields, while cascades of petals had streamed down from the screened balconies of the women's rooms, Tron had seen and heard nothing. *He will ask me to travel with Odah and the One of Sinu to the pass. The One of O said it takes priests of three orders to lift the Great Curse of Aa. . . . Lord Gdu, is this what you ask?*

Nothing whispered in Tron's heart. The soldiers tramped about below, raising the dust in heavy duncolored swirls. Tron glanced at the King and saw that the confident smile on his face was meaningless, a mask. He felt cold, as though in the aching heat Aa had breathed on his spine. *Twelve twelves of Her priests called Her power down—will She remove it for a blind man and a crippled outcast and a boy? Will She not rather . . . But who else can the King ask?*

Tron looked at the fierce brown profile below the Eye of Gdu. He remembered a day's hawking above the Temple of Tan, a marigold scorpion, a glaring salt-flat. *The Gods have sent me no sign. Perhaps they mean that our friendship should be enough of a sign. I must offer to go, so that he does not have to ask.*

Now, Tron stood in a ravine far to the south and watched the meeting ceremony of two clans of the wild hunters who had captured Onu Ovalaku. The warriors of each clan rushed at each other with the usual silent grimaces, then pranced face to face with fierce spearthrusts, cunningly parried, until a warrior received a minute wound and cried aloud. Then the mock fight stilled, the chiefs of the two clans inspected the injury, and the man who had caused it was wounded to exactly the same extent. After that everyone sat down and began the weary process of bartering girl brides. Odah, hunched on his litter, watched this performance with a strange eagerness.

"It is a ritual," he'd said to Tron after they'd first seen it four days ago.

"It's not a real ritual," Tron had answered. "It's got nothing to do with the Gods."

"Who knows? But it is a true ritual in this—that the men who perform it do not know its inner meaning. To the chiefs they are bargaining for the necklace that the child wears. Each girl child wears an ancient and famous necklace. You can see how often it has been repaired, and how reverently they handled it. The child merely happens to have the right to wear it. But by this means, you see, women not yet ready for marriage are exchanged from clan to clan, so that the blood is mixed and the breed remains strong. The chiefs do not think of that. They are concerned only with the necklaces. In the same way we think only of the rituals we perform as they appear to us—how should we know what they mean to the Gods themselves?"

Tron had shrugged, uninterested. In the past six days five separate clans had passed them on from territory to territory, always working along the ravines, in which the hunters lived like scorpions in the cracks of an old wall. At each meeting the same dance and bargaining had taken place (though at one there had been no girls to exchange, and the ritual had been performed with two dolls made of dry grass, wearing necklaces of leaves). Each time Tron had moved well away from the group, using the excuse that his hawk disliked company, but really because he needed to be alone to brood and dream, and to try to master his dread of the task they had come to perform.

Now O pressed with harsh heat on the tableland; even in the cooler ravines any rock on which He had leaned for an hour gave back His heat like a blow; along between the cliffs the air shimmered, distorting vision. The Gods are here, Tron suddenly knew. They have come back. The hot, still air prickled with Their presences. For a moment, as though from an enormous distance, he saw the circle of hunters where they sat in the shade of an old holm oak that clung to the cliff with half its roots scrubbed clean by sudden floods. Their figures, and the two bright litters and the red-robed priests who carried them, were tiny but like jewels, and moved with impossible slowness. Then the hawk beside Tron rattled a wing as it tore at the green finch that one of the hunters had snared for it, and Tron was looking at his friends with ordinary eyes again. Odah, he could see, had stopped peering at the hunters and was praying with closed eyes and moving lips. Tron whispered a hymn of welcome. The fear slid from his mind and he was glad to be doing what the Gods seemed to demand.

There were, he had come to realize, two Trons. There was a boy born to walk alone through wild country with a hawk on his wrist; there was a boy born and trained to serve the Gods. There were two hawks—a bird born to hover free between the roaring cliffs of the Jaws of Alaan, and a bird born and trained to come without resentment to swung lure, and to submit to long hours of hooded darkness. So Tron now welcomed the Gods and allowed himself to sink into stillness, neither praising nor asking, an empty bowl that They might fill if They chose. They sent him no sign of approval or disapproval, though he could feel Them filling the hot air with their presence as vividly as he could smell the sweetly peppery scent of the little white flowers that frothed all over the tangled creeper above him.

After a while the bargaining session became the midday meal, and when that was over the women wrapped their few utensils in twists of grass and packed them away in leather sacks so that nothing could clink or rattle, and then the rock-owl clan, after a final blessing from Odah, drifted away down the ravine with their usual silence, daytime ghosts; not even the boisterous little children seemed to click one pebble or crackle one twig.

The black lizard clan were now the priests' guides, first a group of hunters scouting ahead, then a wizened chief, then the priests, then the women and children, and finally a rearguard of more hunters. The stifling afternoon seemed much as other afternoons; one side of a ravine was usually in shadow, so it was possible to travel despite the heat of O: there was sometimes water in pools among the rocks; twice they had crossed roaring snow-fed torrents; but though all was much as before, all was changed for Tron by the invisible presence of the Gods. So it was no surprise when the chief halted his clan and explained in the smattered dialect of the Kingdom that he could go with them no further.

"Ntree mans ntake," he said several times.

After some talk among themselves the hunters chose a mark on the floor of the ravine and threw their spears at it. The chief studied the fallen spears and from their position selected three hunters to continue with the priests. Gifts of farewell were exchanged, blessings given, and the black lizard clan stole back the way they had come.

When the priests moved on, the three guides seemed to have lost all confidence. They peered about them as if they were in strange territory, frowning and muttering, and scouted in scuttling dashes from cover to cover, but as soon as something rattled in the bushes on a ledge of cliff they threw down their spears and came rushing back to cower among the priests.

"What do you fear, my sons?" asked Odah, who had developed a marvelous bond of trust with the clans, so that they instinctively chose him as the one to obey. "No beast could frighten such hunters, I think. Is it demons or ghosts?"

"Ngoat! Ngoat!" moaned the leader.

Tron stared at Odah, suddenly reminded how their separate stories had begun with the Goat-Stone in the Temple. Odah stared calmy back, nodded as if accepting the sign and raised his right arm in invocation.

"Outcast spirits
O walks among you.
Beware, you dead!

To your black crannies
His light pierces.
In your cold caves
His fire burns.
Beware!"

The light and fire in his voice seemed to vibrate along
the cliffs like the last shimmery notes of a gong. The
hunters looked at one another, muttered in a more confident manner and moved on. Thus they covered another slow mile before the leading hunter stopped,
pointed ahead, and beckoned to Tron to come up beside him.

The bridge ahead leaped the ravine in one clean arc
from cliff to cliff. Only the Wise could have built it.

"What is the matter?" called the One of Sinu in his
impatient, grating voice.

"I think we have reached the road to the pass," answered Tron. "There is a great bridge across the ravine."

"I praise O that I have seen such a thing," said Odah
a few minutes later. "Talatatalatatehalatena, my son,
how are we to climb the cliffs? Can you find us a
path?"

(It was part of Odah's nature that he should so easily
have mastered the strings of syllables that made up the
hunters' short-names. Their long-names consisted of the
short-names of all their male ancestors back to the day
when Gdaal had cut off the tails of nine black lizards,
stuck them into the ground, and created the clan.)

The hunters halted and gazed about them, pulling
nervously at their lips or scratching their ribs. One of
them pointed to a great beard of creeper that flowed
down a cliff, and at once the other two ran to it and
began to swarm up the vines, shaking out a flock of

gold and scarlet finches, which twittered away along the cleft.

"There is no path for me there, my brothers," said Odah without bitterness. But when the hunters reached the top they took little flint hatchets from their belts and began to work along the cliff, hacking at the vines until a whole tangle of vine and leaf and flower flowed suddenly down onto the washed boulders below. At once the remaining hunter ran to the spot and began to sort out and test the thickest strands of vine.

"What do they do?" snapped the One of Sinu.

"They are making ropes to haul the litters out, my father, my brother," replied Tron.

But it was a slow process, choosing and joining lengths of creeper. As usual when there was a halt, Tron moved away from the rest of the group, so that he could unhood the hawk in something like solitariness. He chose a place where another, smaller cataract of creeper flung itself down the opposite cliff, and as he stood in that pepper-scented shade the other Tron, the one who had been sleeping for so many days, suddenly took hold. There was time to spare, there was empty wilderness above, there was a creeper to reach it by. Why wasn't he up there, hawking?

Without thought he loosed the leg thongs and held his gauntleted hand above his head. The hawk opened and closed its wings twice, in a puzzled way, as though it too had forgotten its true nature; but then the whim took it and it shrugged itself into the air and started to circle upwards. Tron watched it with gladdened heart. It was in glorious condition, despite its lack of proper exercise during the journey. It found an updraft near the heated cliff and seemed to float into the sky like a child's kite.

Tron gripped two vines and began his climb; it turned out harder than the hunters had made it look, because of the way the vines swung to and fro, or slid beneath his weight, but the tangle was so interwoven that when he seemed sure to slither ridiculously down, something would hold and he could clamber on in a

shower of insects and petals and bits of dead bark.
After moving for so many days at the tedious pace of
the litters, his muscles seemed to rejoice with the effort.
He reached the top sweating but grinning and at once
gazed upward to see the hawk poised a hundred feet
above him, black against the heavy blue of the sky.

Though O was now well down toward the west, His
heat still beat back off rock and gravel. He would have
to shine only a little more fiercely, Tron felt, for the
patches of wizened scrub around him to burst crackling
into invisible flames. Nothing stirred in that heat. Pulling the lure out of his pouch, Tron began to walk away
from the cliff edge. Suddenly, with a thump like one
huge heartbeat, a covey of kingfowl exploded around
his feet and curved clackering away, only three feet
above the ground. The hawk flung itself out of the sky,
the plunge of its path curving slightly to intercept the
racing kingfowl. It came so fast that it seemed certain to
shatter itself on the rocks, but there was no hesitation,
no slowing. Its wings were half-folded, its whole body a
shaped missile. At the last whistling instant its taloned
legs jerked forward. Tron saw the puff of loosened
feathers, then heard the double thump of the hawk hitting the kingfowl and the pair of them hitting the
ground. In his excitement he longed to shout aloud, to
run forward, but he controlled himself to a gentle pace.
As he stood looking down at the hawk, so live and
clean, perched on the mottled plumage of the kingfowl,
it struck him for the first time how strange it was that
the perfection of the moment had to end in a death. It
was as though he were a God who needed the sacrifice
of the kingfowl to fulfill His nature. Were the Gods indeed like that? No. It was the Blue Hawk that needed
the death, to fulfill *its* nature. It was priests and Kings
who needed the sacrifices. The Gods were quite otherwise.

"I shall never do this again," Tron said, aloud, in a
voice that sounded quite unlike his own, but which he
knew still spoke the truth.

The hawk looked up and hissed at the sound, but

skipped willingly to his gauntlet and gazed about it in a puzzled way, as though it had made its kill in a fit of absentmindedness. Whispering his praise to Gdu for all the happiness he knew he must now forsake, Tron carried the living bird and the dead toward the bridge.

The road speared toward the mountain, now very near and steep. Looking at the ground, one could not see, even on the bridge, that here was a man-made surface; the small stuff of the desert, sand and pebbles and even a few dry tussocks had drifted all across it. But the line of it through the rocks and scrub was still clear. Tron scuffed at the surface with his toe and uncovered the edge of a flagstone. Then he bent and stared, not at the place he had cleared but at a patch of half-firm sand beside it. On the bridge itself, where the covering was pure sand, the marks seemed clearer. He walked quickly back along the north side of the ravine and beckoned to Talatatalatatehalatena, who was supervising the process of hauling the first litter out from the depths.

The hunter grinned and rubbed his stomach when he saw the kingfowl.

"Will you come with me?" said Tron. "I want to show you something."

On the road by the bridge Talatatalatatehalatena knelt and peered at the ground. He sniffed at one or two of the indentations, moved on to examine some invisible signs on harder ground, cast back a little way up the road and returned frowning.

"Mans!" he whispered. "Mans!"

He spread his hands in front of Tron's face, opening and closing his fingers a dozen times. Then he pointed dramatically toward the soaring peaks.

"Mans here, ndere," he muttered. "Two nday. Tree."

So there was no more hawking, only waiting with as much patience as possible for the second litter to come creaking up. While the last four litter-bearers followed, Tron told Odah and the One of Sinu what he had found.

"There are footprints on the road," he said. "Talata

thinks that a large group of men went toward the pass two or three days ago."

"Temple guards, of course," said the One of Sinu. "A Major Priest to give them their orders. They will stop us performing the ritual. Twelve litter-bearers and three hunters cannot fight armed men."

"What should we do, my brother?" asked Odah.

"Find a safe place to camp tonight. Tomorrow let the hunters scout well ahead of us as we move, and in this way come as close as we are able to the pass and wait there for the King's first war party to clear a path for us. *Then* I will show these dogs what it means when Sinu rules in the Kingdom!"

"In two days comes the night of Aa's Most Brightness," said Odah.

"And in thirty days another such night," snapped the One of Sinu. "One moon is not a long time to wait in a war."

The peaks were now pinky-gold with O's going. About a mile beyond the bridge and a few hundred yards from the road one of the hunters found a small crater among the rocks which would do for a camp. The hunters built a fire of smokeless dry wood and were already roasting the kingfowl when Odah hobbled painfully up the slope of the hollow to sing his Farewell hymn. He did not vary words or notes in any way from those that the listening priests had heard every evening since their first year. In this place, barren, savage and haunted, he seemed to build a canopy of ordered safety over himself and his companions.

"How did we let such a voice leave the Temple?" asked one of the litter-bearers when the last note had followed the fallen God.

"If you had asked me a month ago," said Odah, "I would have told you a story of foolish pride and foolish pain. But now it seems to me that long ago the Gods chose that I should be ready at Kalakal, unused and forgotten by men, waiting for these few days. And my brother of Sinu and my brother of Gdu, we have all three been chosen to perform this ritual—not by the

King, not by ourselves, but by the Gods. They are already gathered here to accept or reject. They will not let a party of Temple guards prevent us. Can you not feel them all about us, waiting?"

Next morning Odah sang his Welcome. The hunters covered the ashes of the fire with sand, and with twigs brushed out all trace of human presence. The bearers lifted the litters. Tron set the hawk on his wrist. Without a word they were on the march again, brisk with the strength of that first hour when the shadows stretch in spindly bars across the night-cooled sand.

"My brothers," said Odah quietly. "We must talk. I have made this journey, until last night, with a feeling of emptiness and dread. When we agreed on the ritual we would perform I thought it acceptable, but I thought so only with my mind. My heart did not speak. And the Gods were far off and sent us no sign. Yesterday I felt Them return."

"Yes," said Tron, "so did I, when you were eating under the holm oak."

The One of Sinu grunted, expressionless.

"Last night," said Odah, "I did not sleep. I emptied my mind of thought and fear. I emptied my body of pain. I waited for the Gods, but still They did not speak, either to say yes or no. Then, at the noon of Aa, She came. She filled the emptiness of my soul, but not with dread. I knew the depth and the weight and the power of Her dark that lies behind the stars. Odah, servant of O, ceased to exist though his body lay openeyed under the night. I became a part of Aa. Then, gently, after an enduring time, She sent me back into this crooked body, and I found it was still the noon of Aa. The shadows had not moved. Then until dawn I worked to unravel and make sure of the ritual She had shown me. Listen. This is what She demands if She is to lift Her curse from the pass."

The road reached on. The peaks changed outline and color as O rose through the sky. His beams became burning swords, piercing the feeble flesh. The rocks and bushes lost shape behind the layers of heated air. Tron did not notice. He felt neither heat nor thirst. When the hawk fidgeted, longing for shade, he soothed it without thinking. All that long march he walked beside Odah's litter, repeating with his lips the words he must say and in his mind the movements he must make. Neither he nor the One of Sinu asked any questions or made any suggestions. From the moment Odah began to speak they were absorbed into the preparation for the ritual, and in the idea of the ritual itself, a perfectly shaped, growing, branching, blossoming structure of word and chant and dance, a Great Ritual to be made for the service of a God, made not to be repeated again and again unchanging through the centuries, but this once, on the night of Aa's Most Brightness, on Her dark altar on the knees of Alaan.

When it became too hot for walking the hunters led them off the road to a place where a number of gawky, branching cacti, twice the height of a man, made little patches of shade in which it was possible for one or two people to hide from O's heat. Tron and Odah and the One of Sinu would not be separated, so the priests rigged the scarlet canopies of the litters to make a wider square of shade and the hunters covered them with brushwood. Even then each breath burned in the nostrils, and all the time the sweat streamed down their flesh. But Tron and Odah and the One of Sinu might have been sitting in a cool stone cell in the Temple, as they rehearsed in quiet voices the ritual which, in two days and a night, they must perform.

It was long past noon before they had finished. One of the priests brought them bread and water and despite the heat they ate heavily, knowing that from now until the night of Aa's Most Brightness nothing but water must pass their lips. Suddenly the One of Sinu spoke.

"I have served the Gods for sixty-two floods," he said in his angry-sounding voice. "I have always been impatient when my brothers spoke, as you did this morning, of feeling the presence of the Gods, or of a God speaking in their hearts, or such things. Never once have They spoken to me. But now I have heard Them in my old age, speaking through you, Odah, my brother, my father."

It seemed to Tron perfectly proper that the One of Sinu should use the formula by which the boys in the Temple were supposed to address priests confirmed in the service of a God, though he was a Major Priest and Odah only the priest of two shepherd hamlets, forgotten in the hills.

"My brothers," said Odah in a voice that was almost a whisper, "Aa showed me two more things: first, that the coming night of Her Most Brightness is the night on which the ritual be performed, and that no guards, priests, or other dangers must make us turn aside or wait; and second, that we shall know that what we do we do with Her goodwill, because close by the place where we must perform the ritual we shall find waiting for us a terrible sign."

XV

THEY HAD PICKED THEMSELVES UP OUT OF THE SHADE and were trudging wearily back toward the road when the leading hunter suddenly flung himself to the ground and lay as still as a dead man. Everybody stopped and waited. Tron saw that the fallen man held one ear to the ground, as if listening to the heartbeat of the world. Then he rose frowning to his knees.

"Mans!" he said. "Mans ncome!"

He made his finger-signs to show a multitude, then pattered his hands on the earth in the exact rhythm of hoofbeats. The other hunters peered anxiously round. One of them pointed at a large patch of scrub and they all raced toward it. It seemed an impenetrable thicket, but working like demons they hacked a path toward its center and made a small clearing into which the priests dragged the dismantled litters. Two of the hunters were already sweeping away their tracks, and now Tron could hear a distant bass mutter, like the far boom of the falls at Kalakal. Once inside the clearing he found that the central bushes mostly lacked lower branches and that it was possible to worm his way outward under their cover. The hunters dragged the bushes they had cut back into the path and the clearing. The whole party lay there in silence, still as a hare crouched beneath the hovering wings of a hawk.

Tron had lost any sense of direction. The hoofbeats seemed to fill the desert air, coming from all round him. He could not think who or what the approaching horsemen might be—all the cavalry of the Kingdom were with the King's army, now making its slow way to reach the road farther north. The marks he had earlier seen on the road had been of human feet, not hooves. He was just deciding that the Falathi must have given up hope of their messengers and sent a party of horsemen over the Pass of Gebindrath to seek help, when through a small opening among the twigs he saw a man.

Two hundred yards away the rider reined his horse to a halt and gazed back over his shoulder. He was naked, except for a short leather kilt. His scalp had been shaved smooth on both sides, leaving a bristling hedge of hair down the middle, like the cropped mane of a horse. His skin was dyed bright blue all over. He rode without a saddle or stirrups, but his horse, despite the heat, seemed carefully groomed. It was taller and gaunter than the ponies of the Kingdom. The man rode with a lance across his thighs and a short bow slung from his back. He carried a small oval shield, black leather decorated with brass studs, on his left arm. He was so lean that all his ribs showed, but his arms were well muscled.

He shouted an order, and a huge gray dog loped into sight, a creature with scooped flanks, deep chest and long yellow-fanged muzzle. The dog's head turned toward Tron. It lowered its muzzle, sniffed the ground, and with half-raised hackles began to work along a trail of scent—human scent. Until this moment Tron had seen and done everything as if in a slow dream. His real world was the coming ritual. Now, suddenly, just as a dream becomes nightmare, ordinary fear broke through. This dog was to the hunter what the hawk was to Tron: a companion, an extra limb, a finder of prey. The prey, now, was Tron.

All the time the drumming hooves came nearer. The patch of thicket would burn like a torch. Tron's mind slid to the hawk, hooded and tied to a litter pole; that at least could fly free, if he moved fast enough when the flames began to crackle. . . .

The blue-dyed rider yelled harshly at the dog, which instantly turned and trotted back to its master. Another rider swept up and shouted to the first, who snatched his lance from his thighs, waved it above his head, and with an answering shout cantered on. Almost at once the whole cavalcade came by, moving in a cloud of dust stirred up by their own march. There were horsemen on the skirts of the cloud, many of them with similar dogs; in the middle of the obscure and swirling mass moved about forty light wicker wagons, two-wheeled, each pulled by a pair of horses and driven by a fair-haired woman. These women wore many-stranded necklaces and huge earrings, but were otherwise as naked as their men; their skin was not dyed, but tattooed in curling patterns, and where the skin was unmarked it was of a clear, coppery orange color. They held themselves with the poise of queens and looked as wild and dangerous as the men.

After the troop had passed—about two hundred riders, Tron thought—the priests and hunters lay still until the hoofbeats could be no longer heard, even along the far-sounding veins of the earth. At last they crept out of hiding and looked about them.

"What were they?" said one of the litter-bearers. "Were they *men?*"

"I think they are called the Mohirrim," said Tron. "It was because of them that the Princes of Falathi sent to the King for help."

"And now they have found the pass and mended the broken road," said the One of Sinu. "My brothers, see how the Gods have taken care for the Kingdom, that the King had already called his army together when they came. Think of the Kingdom, basking in peace, unready. If it had happened like that . . ."

"We must send the news of them to the King," said one of the litter-bearers. Being a priest of Sinu, he had been trained to think of such things.

"They were traveling faster than any of us could," said another.

"Our place is in the hills," snapped the One of Sinu. "Let them be their own news."

"They have come through the pass," said Odah sadly. "The curse of Aa is on them."

The hunters spread out as before. The bearers shoul-

dered the litters. They turned once more toward the
peaks. Despite what they had seen, there was no question of their stopping or going back. They were sucked
toward the ritual, just as the river in the Jaws of Alaan
was sucked toward the roaring falls; hiding from the
Mohirrim had been like an eddy in the river, a short
delay. Now Aa called them on.

Vultures flapped away as they came to the place
where the Mohirrim had made their midday halt; they
passed as if it had been unholy, and found a camping
place almost among the abrupt foothills, where a torrent
from the snows, dry at this season, had cut another ravine. The hunters scuttled into it like cockroaches rushing for shelter under a familiar stone. They found a trickle of water in its bed, but insisted on leading the party
half a mile from the road before they camped. Nothing
disturbed them all night.

Next morning the road lost its straightness and
wound into a steep, close valley formed by two spurs
from the main massif, a barren place all of whose soil
had been long washed away, leaving only scooped and
angular pillars of rock to give the sharp slopes a certain
strangeness. The road doubled back up the side of a
spur, turned as it reached the ridge, turned again and
ran sidelong, with innumerable bends, up an enormous
shoulder of mountain until all the fissured plateau could
be seen reaching away north, and beyond it, in mottled
yellow and faint blue, the desert and the plain.

It was nearly noon by the time they reached this part
of the road, but in the cooler air they found that they
needed to rest for less than an hour, and soon moved on
again. It was all steady marching, the road firm, the
gradients smooth and easy; in two places there had been
rockfalls, but the descending Mohirrim had cleared a
path over the worst of these. O swung to the west. The
litter-bearers changed places and changed again, trudging on up that incredible road. Now, once or twice, its
builders had needed to carve it out of a sheer wall of
cliff with overhanging crags above and a stupendous
drop below. Tron saw nothing of all this. He did not

taste the coolness of the water he drank at the halts, or feel the ache in his calves or the emptiness in his stomach. He did not hear the low-voiced discussion among the litterbearers about whether the men whose footprints Talatatalatatehalatena had seen on the bridge had met the party of raiding Mohirrim, and what had happened to them. Despite the effort of the climb Tron's pulse was very slow, and his breath too, like that of a sleeping man. All the energies of his mind and soul and body were being gathered into readiness for that night's ritual. He needed no willpower to achieve this. The Gods ordained it, and it happened.

O was far down toward His resting when Odah said, "This is the place, my brothers. You others, camp here. The Gods will not touch you, but keep watch against men."

He levered himself from the litter onto his crutches. The One of Sinu gripped Tron's shoulder for guidance and the three of them went on up the road at the creeping pace that was the fastest Odah could manage. They did not speak, but once the hawk, which had been motionless all day, opened its beak and gave the shrill scream of a nestling, something that Tron had never heard it do before.

The place where Odah had told the others to wait seemed like any other section of the long climb, with the road slanting on up the precipitous ribs of the mountain, but as they crawled painfully around the curve into the next fold Tron saw that there was no climbing scar of road on the rib beyond, and in a few more minutes he found that their path now drove into a cleft between two of the sail-like peaks, climbing only for a few hundred yards and then vanishing over a crest.

Where the shadow of the farther rib fell across the road Odah halted, turned, and chanted the Farewell to O, though the God still hung clear of the western horizon. The hymn came cold and sad, as though this were the last Farewell and there would never again be any

Welcome. Before it was over, the shadow of the cliff swung across them.

The crest proved not to be the top of the pass, and nor was the crest beyond it. But at last, where the slopes on either side swooped down in a line that would have blocked the road if they had not been cut away to let it through, Tron discovered that they were climbing no more. For barely a hundred yards they walked on, awkward with the sudden disappearance of the gradient beneath their feet, and then they were looking down into a boat-shaped valley, some half a mile long and two hundred yards broad.

"This is the place," said Odah. "She is here."

They stood, as it were, at the stern of the boat. The bottom of the valley was almost flat and then the cliffs curved in to make the prow, where the road vanished along a ravine. The snow-streaked sides plunged down so steeply that O could only have warmed the place for a few hours at midday. Now, though the peaks above them still glittered with the God's life-making fire, Aa seemed to have taken hold of the valley before Her hour. It was already as cold as midnight, and the downdrafts off the snow eddied about in sudden shuffling breezes that stirred and stilled without reason. Halfway across the valley, close by the road, was a small cairn, around which lay what seemed to be patches of midnight shadow not cast by any object from any light source but simply there, tatters of night.

"Now we begin," said Odah quietly.

They had halted when he had spoken before. As they began to move down into the valley, fear rose through Tron's body and soul like mist rising from a flooded field. For a moment he rejected his part and became mere human, in a human world, longing to speak, to reach for a warm hand, to fondle the plumage of the still bird on his wrist. Perhaps the One of Sinu felt the same, for his grip on Tron's shoulder tightened savagely. But the discipline of the Temple kept them both steady to the slow, gliding pace they knew so well, though the breath of Aa seemed to float round their shoulders.

Odah's crutches clicked and scraped, the only sound in that icy bowl. Slowly they crept nearer to the strange patches of shadow and the conical pile of stones in the middle of them. Tron found his eyes drawn to this cairn as though it held a secret that was the key to the strangeness of the whole valley. The stones were all the same size, roundish, pale, mottled, fuzzed with dark moss. No, not stones . . .

"Do not look, child," whispered Odah's voice.

But at that moment Tron had seen a pallid thing glimmer at the edge of one of the black patches, a foot, protruding from a black robe. By the next patch a spread hand clawed into gravel. The bodies were not whole. A flick of vision transformed the stones of the cairn into heads, the severed heads of the slaughtered priests of Aa, piled together into a careful pyramid. At the apex of the pile the sulky face of the One of Aa stared open-eyed across the valley.

So this was the sign that Aa had promised to Odah. The One of Sinu could not see it, and his hard grip on Tron's shoulder saved him when he swayed and all but fell. For two paces the blind man held him upright and forced him onward. The click of Odah's crutches did not hesitate. Tron found the rhythm of the priest-pace again and, staring only at the road, marched on across one of the larger patches of black, the cover of a canopy that the priests of Aa had brought with them to shield them from the sight of O. The bodies lay close beside each other, as though they had been killed in the ranks where they stood. That was proper.

As the fog of horror cleared from his soul Tron did not begin to ask or wonder who had killed the priests, or why the cairn had been piled. To him it was simply a sign that Aa had accepted into the ritual, and that he and the other two must therefore accept, just as priests in the Temple accepted the sacrifice of victims. It did not matter whether Aa had caused these deaths, or merely allowed them to happen. What mattered was the ritual.

About fifty yards beyond the last of the sprawled bodies Odah halted, leaned on his crutch, and raised one twisted arm in a gesture of supplication. Tron led the One of Sinu ten paces farther on, then moved to become the third point of a triangle. Close by the place where he must begin his part he found a low rock, onto which he settled the hawk. A whisper in his heart told him to let the servant of Gdu witness the ritual, so he slid the hood off and weighted the leg thongs down by tying them to a smaller stone. Slowly he turned, dragging himself free from this last familiar creature, and raised both arms to salute the invisible Goddess Whose presence filled the bowl between the hills. Odah started the ritual in a quiet voice that was nearer speaking than chant.

> "Mother of night
> Mother of birth
> Mother of death
> To Your dark altar
> The Gods have sent
> Three gifts.

> "Your son of blood
> Gives a man in old age
> Who has offered to Sinu
> A whole life's service.
> The Gods have taken
> Above that service
> Sight and light
> And all that O gives
> To the eyes of man.
> Accept him.

> "Your brother of day
> Gives a man in his prime
> Who has offered to O
> A whole life's service.

The Gods have taken
Above that service
Ease and strength
And all the Gods give
To the body of man.
Accept him.

"Your son of the air
Sends a man half-grown
Who has offered to Gdu
A whole life's service.
The Gods have taken
Above that service
Home and love
And all the Gods give
To the heart of man.
Accept him."

The One of Sinu answered at full chant, his harsh
and bloodless voice falling into place beneath the life
and warmth of Odah's. Tron moved without hesitation
into the first slow dance of supplication, steps he knew
well, in a sequence he had never practiced but which his
limbs seemed to perform of their own will, unfaltering.
The fire-tinged glitter of the eastern peak dwindled to
the summit. In the quick-darkening sky the stars
blinked into being. At the tip of the western peak a silver spark grew, became a silver spear-point, a silver sail
of moonlit snow as Aa rose at Her Most Bright, though
still for a long while hidden from the valley.

The ritual flowed on, inevitable as Her climb up the
sky. Tron never needed to pause or wonder what his
part next demanded of him, because the logic of every
pace and word was so strong that at any given moment
there seemed to be only one possible set of steps to
move through, one possible phrase to chant. Teamed
with a blind man and a cripple, he had to perform all
the dances alone, while the other two sang most of the
words, but his in itself was something that the ritual allowed for, a part of its completeness, and he wasn't

aware of any unbalance, or indeed of anything but the flow of the ritual and the presence of the Goddess all around him, accepting without sign or comment his worship and his offered soul. The first part of the night was the darkest, when the last of daylight had been absorbed down into the west; then, gradually, as Aa climbed, Her rays lit more and more of the snow peaks, a light that glimmered directionless and shadowless into the depths below, making it possibly for Tron once more to place his footsteps other than by feel and to take his cue from the gestures of his companions.

Now the brightness advanced down the mountainside, seeming to move without hurry but still to come at the pace of a marching army. It reached the last of the snows and swept on across the black rocks, picking out tussock and boulder and the bodies of the murdered priests. The impetus of the ritual slowed, reaching a moment of stillness in which Tron found himself standing back by the rock where he had begun. He waited, motionless as the hawk beside him. Odah and the One of Sinu waited also. The light reached them in a blaze like O's rising as the rim of Aa floated above the suddenly glittering drifts of the eastern skyline. All three voices rang out to welcome Her with the same throb of gladness as that with which the priests on the tower of the Temple had for centuries greeted O's daily return.

She floated dispassionate above the snows. But She was here also, filling the valley from brim to brim as water fills a bowl of offering, Herself now part of the ritual. Odah and the One of Sinu answered each other in echoing praise as Tron swept into the central dance. He seemed to himself bodiless, with limbs of air, a creature formed to do this thing alone, as effortlessly as a hawk hovers above its hunting ground. It was a long dance, full of difficult sequences and sudden transitions from swift to slow and back, but when it was over he felt no tiredness in his limbs and continued his part of the ritual without a backward thought of what he had just achieved.

It was in his soul that the strain lay. As the silver

hours marched by he began to feel something in the ritual which he had not understood when they had rehearsed it. It was as though he and the other two were between them beginning to lift from the earth an enormous, sluggish weight of spirit, to wake into motion a force that had lain inert through the centuries, to use all the small strength of their three souls to heave it free from the clogging earth, up into a region where its own energies could begin to move it. It was a task that was just within the limit of their strengths, and the power of the ritual lay in the manner in which it concentrated their souls into that one task alone, so that they could perform what they had come to do.

At that moment called the noon of Aa, when a standing man casts no shadow, the last note of the last hymn floated away among the snows and boulders. Tron felt the Goddess withdraw Her presence. He felt the valley become vacant, and She was gone. As though She had been water around him, buoying him up, when She left his limps were suddenly heavy, almost too heavy to lift, and his mouth and stomach longed for food, and every nerve vibrated with weariness. With a sigh he bent to pick up the hawk; it was awake, perhaps to watch the ritual, perhaps merely deceived by Aa's brightness into thinking this was daytime. Tron was too tired to be careful, and it never entered his head that a hawk might fly in the noon of Aa, but when he untied the leg thongs from the stone, the hawk, instead of hopping to his gauntlet, sprang into the air.

For a moment he saw it start its habitual spiral climb, then he lost it against the black of the sky. He heard its wingbeat whisper in the silence and he picked it up again, curving away in flight along the whiteness of the castern snow peak. Once more it vanished into sky, this time for an aching minute. Then Odah pointed and there it was, sharp-shaped against the brightness of the other peak, farther off now, skimming round the rim of the bowl.

When it vanished again Tron walked a little further along the road and whistled for it. Because of the pollu-

tion of raw meat, he had left the lure and his other
hawking gear with the priests on the road, but he didn't
think it would have been able to see a lure anyway, gazing down out of that brightness into the dark below. He
whistled several times. Nothing happened.

Suddenly he felt the searing pang of loss, of emptiness,
of all the pleasure of life gone with those blue wings. He
flung his arms wide and stared up at the icy circle of
Aa.

"Mother," he whispered, "I offered you all. If You
take all, that is good."

Her shape changed. The hawk hung there, hovering,
every pinion sharp as metal against the brilliant circle.
He whistled once more, softly, and it plunged to his
wrist. He gripped the thongs, slipped the hood on, and
walked back to his companions.

"The servant of Gdu flew in a wide circle around the
valley," Odah was explaining to his blind companion.
"It was as if to assure us that the Goddess has really
departed."

"She is gone," said Tron.

"Yes," muttered the One of Sinu like a man in a
dream. "Even I felt Her all around us. Ah, but the
cold!"

He swayed, and when Tron moved to steady him the
hand that gripped his shoulder was frail but icy. Tron
realized that though he himself had been moving
through most of the ritual, the other two had simply
stood through the chilling midnight hours. The One of
Sinu sounded very old and sick—unable, even if he had
wished, to move any faster than Odah as the three of
them crept toward the mouth of the pass. When they
reached the obscene cairn it glittered with specks of
faint light where the beams of Aa were reflected from
still-open eyes, but Tron felt neither fear nor horror.
Nor did his heart vary its pace when, thirty yards farther on, a tall shadow floated out from the rocks beside
the road and a shivering voice whispered, "I will come
with you, O my brothers."

"Who's there?" said the One of Sinu.

"A priest of Aa," said Odah. "Come with us, my brother. Help the One of Sinu or he will fall."

In a silence broken only by the click of Odah's crutches the four of them crept out of the valley.

XVI

IN THE MORNING BRIGHTNESS THEY HURRIED DOWN THE mountain road as fast as the litter-bearers could travel. Now they were afraid with ordinary human fears, of being trapped in that hopeless place by the murderous blue horsemen, coming from either behind or in front. Tron was dizzy and aching, but the priest of Aa who had spoken to them in the valley took his turn at the litter poles. The One of Sinu looked as he had when Tron had first met him, blue-lipped and feverish, though his followers had taken turns to rub his icy limbs all night. Odah had a different sickness; his Welcome to O had come with a leaden, apathetic note, and now his eyes were dull and his face for once showed the pain he had long lived with. He did not speak until after their noon rest, when the priest of Aa was walking beside his litter.

"Tell me your story, my brother. What have you seen, if it can be told?"

The priest of Aa walked with a young man's stride, and his voice had warmth and life in it.

"It began with the King's Going to War," he said. "After that there was said to be a quarrel among the Major Priests, and suddenly Aa, blessed be Her name, took the Mouth of Silence, and a new Mouth was chosen. That was four days after the Going to War. Immediately after the ritual of his choosing he summoned the whole order and told us that with him and the One of Aa twelve twelves of us must travel to the Peaks of Alaan to renew an ancient ritual. So we came, bringing no slaves, carrying our own bread and water. A Son of

178

the Wise guided us across the desert by night, and after three nights we reached a place where the sand ended and a great road began. There he left us. We were seven nights on the journey, marching with great haste. Two of my brothers died, but we made only the short ritual for them."

Tron heard a gasp and mutter among the litter-bearers. The short ritual was performed for peasants whose families could afford to pay for nothing better.

"At last we came to that place. I knew it to be a stronghold of Aa, heavy with Her presence. I was afraid, although I am Her servant. We arrived a little before dawn, but because O does not shine into the valley for a long time after His rising we were able to rehearse the ritual that the One of Aa had chosen. It was a ritual of power and fear, especially in that place. At the heart of the ritual he was to chant a hymn, aloud, with his own voice, not using the Mouth of Silence."

He paused for another murmur among his bearers.

"I have confessed that I was afraid. The Mouth of Silence told us that men might come to try to stop or interrupt the ritual, and that therefore one of us must stand sentry. I have keen sight, so I gladly offered myself, and was chosen. When O rose above the peaks my brothers went to rest under their canopies and I took up a post outside the valley where the shadow of a leaning rock shielded me from His rays. It was half a mile from the saddle of the pass, but from it I could see great stretches of the road where it climbed the mountains.

"I lay there through the noon of O. I was teased with strange notions, that I should be up there alone, seeing what no priest of Aa had ever seen, all the vastness and richness of the Kingdom under the rays of O. The mountains are very silent. In the middle of the afternoon I heard a cry, which I thought must be that of a mountain bird. Then I heard more cries and knew them for human. And then, far off, I heard a chant begin. It was not the ritual we had practiced, and it began raggedly, and still the cries continued. I ran toward the valley, but before I reached the top of the road I was afraid again and I left the road and climbed the flank of the mountain until I could see into the valley. Before I finished climbing I recognized the chant. My brothers, it was the Great Curse of Aa, which we learn in a whisper, leaving out certain names, knowing that we shall never need to chant it aloud. Now I heard it.

"I reached a place where I could see down into the valley. At first I did not understand what I saw. I thought my brothers were standing by the canopies where they had rested, chanting as if in the House of O and Aa, while a horde of blue demons on horses rode screaming round them, with strange gestures. Then I saw one of my brothers fall, and another, and I saw the demons were shooting at them with arrows, and huge dogs pranced beside the horses baying. So my brothers fell, one by one. I knew . . . I knew it was my work to stand and join in the chant. They had only reached the Third Naming, and already half my brothers had fallen to the ground. If I had taken up the chant I might have continued it to the Fifth Naming before the demons could reach me, and then perhaps Aa Herself . . . She was there, filling the valley. . . . She did nothing . . . and I was afraid. It was not my fear of the Goddess, but it was the ordinary fear of hurt and death, such as a peasant might feel. I lay down among the rocks and watched. The demons killed and killed, with terrible cries. I heard the chant dwindle, but I did not see any of my brothers move from his place or stop chanting until he died. The demons did not shoot the One of Aa, who stood in front of the front rank of my brothers, but when all the rest were killed one of them rode forward. There was a silence, in which I heard the voice of the One of Aa, still chanting. The demon took a sword and with careful aim hacked off his head.

"Then the other demons got down from their horses and moved among my brothers, cutting off all their heads. And women and children of the demons—they were not blue but orange—picked up the heads and piled them into a cairn, laughing while they did so. . . ."

He stopped. His black-gloved hand rose toward his

face, hesitated and withdrew. He walked on in silence.

"And then what?" said Odah in a tired voice.

"That is all," he whispered.

"No. You stayed in the valley two nights and two days after this slaughter?"

"Yes. . . . I was ashamed of my cowardice, my brothers. I knew that Aa was still in that place. I thought perhaps I had not been killed in order that I, alone, might perform the ritual we had rehearsed, so I decided to wait in that place until the night of Aa's Most Brightness. She did not tell me to do this, but I thought it best. When the demons had finished their work they gathered themselves together and rode out of the valley and down the great road. I waited. When Aa was bright I went into the valley and said the full ritual for my brothers. After that I slept and watched and said the hymns and did the dances as if I had been back in the Temple. On the third day I prepared myself for the Great Ritual. I fasted. Indeed, the demons had taken almost all our bread, so I was forced to fast. Toward evening I was saying the hymns of purification for my-self—who else was there to say them?—when I saw you three priests come into the pass. I hid. You did not see me. The One of Sinu I knew by sight, and the boy with the hawk I remembered from the Renewal, but my brother of O was a stranger. My ritual was prepared to begin at the noon of Aa. But as I listened to your ritual I began to perceive that I should never perform it. And when you finished I knew that the Goddess was gone."

Tron walked on in a daze, remembering the lively look of the One of Aa as he chomped his bread in the secret room, or sulked over his colleagues' refusal to let him sacrifice a convenient boy. Below them the coloring of the plateau changed as the shadows shortened. The heat of O became a blessing, and later a burden.

They camped in the ravine they had found on their way to the mountain, and there, quietly, the One of Sinu died. Tron knew from the little hymns of Gdu that the night chill in the pass had got into the old man's lungs; but he also knew there was an illness mentioned in no hymns, an exhaustion of the soul after that ritual. He could feel it in himself. He could see it in the dullness of Odah's eye. Since the night of Aa's Most Brightness they had all three been, so to speak, half-loosed from their moorings in the living earth, ready at the snap of one more strand to drift down the river to Her kingdom. They said the full ritual for the harsh old hero and buried him among the rocks.

Now at least Tron was able to ride in the second litter—with the mountain fever in him he could never have managed the trek across the blistering desert to the ravine from which they had first climbed. He lay all day under the canopy, dry-mouthed. If he opened his eyes the glare of O seemed to pierce to his brain like heated needles. If he closed them he found himself roaming dizzily through the darkness inside himself, searching for a way . . . a way into what deeper dark? He was not aware of the moment, toward evening, when the litters were at last lowered into the ravine.

Next day he was better in his body but worse in his mind. He rode in the litter again. The priests of Sinu were anxious to return to the King with the news that the task was performed and the One of Sinu dead, and were impatient at having to carry the litters across the difficult paths in the beds of the ravines. The black-lizard clan had moved camp and so, to their guides' surprise, had the rock-owl clan. The ravines seemed empty. The hunters became almost distraught with worry.

Next morning as they ate their priest-bread Odah said, "My brothers, we have done what we came to do. Tron and I are ill, and this hurrying does us no good. If two of the hunters will stay with us to look after us until we are well, the other can guide you back to your war."

Tron was too dismal in his soul to notice how faint were the murmurs of dissent, but despite his illness Odah enforced his will. Hymns of farewell were said, and so they parted.

The first thing the two hunters did was to find hiding places for the four of them, and to make sure that Tron and Odah understood the signal to hide—a series of clicks at the back of the tongue which sounded like a few pebbles falling, accompanied by a sharp outward movement of the arm, palm down. Then they dismantled the litters and carried the poles and the betraying red canopies and cushions half a mile back up the ravine, where they piled scrub and boulders over them. All this was mere habit—from birth the hunters had been trained to see to it that a stranger coming to any ravine should find it apparently empty—but as the day wore on Tron realized that his two guardians were extra nervous.

He himself sat with his back against a rock, heavy-eyed, dull-minded, and drowsy with the scent from the white-flowered creeper that foamed down the cliff behind him. The strip of shade at the foot of the cliff narrowed as O rose. Soon he would have to stand up and cross the scorching boulders to shelter beneath the other cliff. It seemed a long journey. The two hunters were out on the tableland, looking for nuts and roots, termites, lizards, fat thorn beetles, and anything else they or the priests could eat.

"How are you?" said Odah suddenly. "How is your soul, Tron?"

"Empty," said Tron. "Everything seems to have gone."

"The Gods have left the world, I think," said Odah. "I have had strange . . . I do not know what to call them . . . not thoughts, not dreams, not visions . . . it is as if everything that has happened was an answer to a *need* of the Gods. We believed that we performed the ritual because the King needed the Pass of Gebindrath to be opened, but the King's need was only part of a long plan, and so was everything else. The closing of the Kingdom, the struggle between priests and Kings, my going to Kalakal, your taking of the Blue Hawk, the coming of the Mohirrim to Falathi—all these things happened in order that such-and-such a ritual should be performed on such-and-such a night, because the Gods required it for quite other purposes."

"What?"

"I do not know. I do not know that what I have just said is true. But the Gods have gone, and I think They have taken something out of us, because They needed that also. Sinu is dead. You say your soul is empty. So is mine."

"Have they gone forever?"

Before Odah could answer there was a sudden urgent rustling above their heads. The creepers swayed wildly and the two hunters came almost falling down into the floor of the ravine. One made the clicking noise and the gesture, then they both bent and lifted Odah and carried him bodily to his hiding place. By the time Tron had crawled behind the scented vines and found a nook for his hawk the hunters were scuttling like disturbed spiders among the boulders, picking up nut kernels and other traces of their presence, and scattering handfuls of gravel over footprints. Then they too darted into hiding.

Out of the noon silence Tron heard a noise begin to swell, at first no louder than the movement of his own blood, then seeming to drum through the rock against which he huddled. When at last he heard the sound waves directly though the air he recognized them for hoofbeats.

Close beside him the creepers rustled and he started, but it was only Talatatalatatehalatena joining him in the green and tangled shadows. They waited in silence. Tron could see the sharp rim of the opposite cliff through two or three places between the vine leaves, but he was not in fact watching when he sensed the hunter beside him stiffen into extra stillness. He looked up. There, appeared from nowhere, silhouetted against the glaring sky, was a blue horseman, motionless, with his rangy great dog beside him. The man peered down into the ravine, turned back and gestured. Then he jumped from his horse, lowered himself over the edge of the cliff and began to climb down. He was nothing like as skillful as the hunters, but soon he was out of Tron's sight.

Several more of the Mohirrim came into view with

the same startling suddenness, but simply sat there waiting. Through another gap in the leaves Tron saw the climber halfway down the cliff. All the time the hoofbeats came nearer, and above them Tron could hear cries, and very far off what seemed to be a trumpet. A few minutes later the creepers to his right shook and swayed as the man began to climb up. Soon Tron was covered in an itchy layer of falling debris. When the leaves were still again, he found that his viewpoints had changed and he could look at a place a little farther along the cliff where an archer was posed, all alone, aiming across the ravine. The bow snapped out of its arc and a fine cord floated across the gulf behind the arrow. Tron heard a cry above his head, and at once a heavier cord began to jerk its way over, in its turn pulling a good-sized rope, which was barely taut before two men came swarming across it with more cords trailing from their belts.

The Mohirrim worked at their bridge with controlled frenzy, despite the ferocious heat. There seemed to be very few shouts of command; each man knew what to do, and did it with the strenuous coordination of a gymnastic dance. As soon as the main bearer ropes were taut they were braced against swaying with angled ropes anchored up and down the clifftop, ready to take the wicker platforms—the bodies of the dismantled wagons—which formed the actual surface of the bridge. While lashing one of these fast, a man lost his hold and tumbled horribly to the boulders fifty feet below. He made no cry as he fell, and his companions above seemed not even to pause in their toil. Last of all, one stout rope was stretched from two structures out of sight behind the clifftops so that it ran six feet above the platforms; but before this was in place a fair-haired woman walked onto the bridge with an orange baby on one arm and a wagon wheel slung from the other shoulder. Two larger orange children followed her, carrying pots and furs.

Miraculously fast though the bridge seemed to spring into being, it must have taken a full two hours to build, and all this time Tron could hear, gradually seeping nearer from beyond the clifftop, the erratic pulse of hooves, harsh cries, and now trumpet calls. He could see no one until they came within two or three feet of the cliff edge, but soon he knew that more was happening than the arrival of these Mohirrim and their crossing the ravine by means of a rope bridge. Farther off men were fighting. The trumpets were the trumpets of the Kingdom. He guessed that the King's first war party must have met a band of the Mohirrim—the ones he had hidden from on his way to the Pass of Gebindrath—and had driven them back, somehow turning them off the road. Now the Mohirrim were in flight, but if they could cross the ravine while their rear guard protected them, they would be able to destroy the bridge and be, for the moment, safe. Hence the frenzy with which they had worked in the full heat of O. For them, all depended on how long their rear guard could hold out.

It was a slow process, crossing. They seemed to do it family by family, first the women and children, carrying everything they could, then the women returning to lead over the laden wagon horses. This was what delayed them, as each horse had to be lashed to the higher rope on a sort of traveling sling; it walked across, but if it missed its footing the rope above would save it. The bridge seemed only strong enough to take one horse at a time, and few of them crossed without at least once trying to back off again. When all of one family's goods and wagon horses were over, their war dog would tread delicately across, followed last of all by the warrior leading his own horse, unburdened, ready for instant battle.

Meanwhile the noise of fighting came steadily nearer, and Tron thought he heard once or twice a shout in a language he could understand. The hunter beside him hissed and turned his head; leaning carefully sideways Tron found a gap through which he could see a place two hundred yards down the opposite cliff where a man was advancing on foot toward the fight, a soldier of the

Kingdom with his pointed helmet and leather armor. Something about the way this man moved told Tron that he must be keeping rank with another man out of sight beyond him. He must be the very end of a line of men who were closing in on the Mohirrim. Now another man—the end of a second rank—was visible behind him. There was a cry, a trumpet call, and a clash of metal. The soldiers halted, tense, watching something that was happening farther away from the cliff. The front man raised his shield to cover his throat and lunged with his sword—Tron saw only the dog as it leaped. The man's thrust missed, but his shield caught the snap of the dog's fangs. The man behind him jumped forward to his help. An instant later the head and shoulders of a blue horseman showed, with one arm drawn back for a lance-thrust at someone out of sight. Then that tiny corner of the battle moved away behind the leaves. Tron saw the first soldier get groggily to his feet—the dog must almost have knocked him over the cliff—wipe his forehead with the back of his wrist, and walk on.

There was nothing Tron could do. Even to climb inside the creepers to a point from which he could have seen more of the battle would have been to risk betraying all four of them to the murderous horsemen. Then, as he watched the battle from below, seeing only a few sharp glimpses of fighting men and those distorted by the strange angle of his viewpoint, he realized that this was how he had seen almost all the King's struggle against the priests, a few snatched moments perceived from the quite different plane where Tron lived and moved in the service of the Gods. Though in the final clash with the priests in the Temple he had played his part like a warrior, though with his rational mind he was now anxious that the army of the Kingdom should defeat these raiders, in his soul he felt that it was proper that he should be seeing the fight in this remote manner, like a priest watching the rituals of some other God.

All the time the Mohirrim, children, women, and

men, were moving with hurried calm across the ravine. The warriors all looked exhausted, and one or two turned before they stepped onto the bridge and shook their weapons at the invisible enemy. The children were quick and obedient, the women more beautiful than any human Tron had ever seen, stepping with the confident pride of queens even when they were burdened with the belongings of their moving households. As the noose closed on the bridgehead, so its progress slowed. The Mohirrim seemed to know exactly what they were about. Tron thought that all but a very few would escape to safety.

But suddenly he heard cries of alarm and warning above his head, and shouts and trumpet calls from the far side of the battle. For once the woman who was at that moment on the bridge turned to look at what was happening farther up the ravine; when she tried to go on, the horse she was leading jibbed; she tugged once at its reins and it began to shy; the bridge bucketed about; the woman drew a knife, leaned past the whirling hooves and slashed through the sling that held it safe to the rope above; unbalanced, it slipped sideways, fell, and with a screaming neigh slithered off the bridge. The woman was already running to the near cliff, and another woman leading her horse onto the bucking platforms.

Beyond them Tron could now see the gleam of O's rays on serried lance-tips. A trumpet blew. The lances lowered out of sight and a cloud of dust surged along the clifftop. Tron saw the people at the cliff edge reel sideways, as if in a wind. The charge was halted, but another trumpet sounded, and there were more lances glittering above rocks, and the pounding of hooves, and the crash of the charge striking home, and once more the trapped Mohirrim were forced sideways along the top of the ravine. Now Tron could see the foremost lancers and the blue warriors struggling on the cliff edge, a jammed mass of men and horses, not ten yards from the bridge. One more charge like that, and the Mohirrim would be cut off from their escape route. The shouts above him rose to screams, then died to sudden silence as a man who had already crossed the bridge ran back almost to the far side, slashed through the top rope, and then, without taking any handhold, the main support ropes. He must have already cut the stay ropes, out of Tron's line of sight, for the bridge swayed wildly to and fro as he hacked at the gap between two wagon platforms, first cutting one side almost through, then turning to slash at the other with all his strength. The second rope parted. The bridge seemed to twitch, flinging the warrior clear, just before the first rope snapped where he had cut it. He was still falling as the bridge flopped back out of sight. Tron heard a shout from above his head, followed by a rhythmic chant as the warriors, safe this side of the ravine, began to haul up the wagon platforms they needed to continue their flight.

Tron turned his eyes to watch the end of the battle. Directly opposite him, framed in an oval of leaves, a fair-haired orange woman stood on the very edge of the cliff with a four-year-old boy in her arms. The slant rays of O flashed from her gold necklaces and the dust storm of the battle rose like a thundercloud behind her. Calmly as a priest performing a common ritual, she kissed the child on his forehead and tossed him over the cliff. He fell without a whimper. She picked up a baby from the ground beside her, kissed it also, took a pace back, then sprang out into the gulf. Her hair began to stream up behind her as she fell out of Tron's sight. A little to one side a half-grown girl put her hands over her eyes and leaped more awkwardly.

Gulping, Tron turned his head away and saw Talatatalatatehalatena peering goggle-eyed between the leaves.

"Ngdie! Ngdie!" whispered the hunter in an appalled voice.

Tron closed his eyes and watched no more. He was not outside this. Each leaping woman, each child tossed toward the flood-scoured boulders, falling and still trusting as it fell, died not only in the ravine but also in the dark cave of his soul. Long before the battle was

over he heard fresh shouts above his head, the squeak
of axles and the dwindling rumble of hooves. The Mohirrim who had reached safety could leave, but Tron
was forced to stay. It was as though he were needed,
somehow, to complete the ritual.

Up on the opposite cliff the noises diminished more
slowly. Not one warrior of the Mohirrim surrendered.
Those too wounded to fight were killed by their com-
rades. The woman leaped as their men died.

Dusk filled the ravine. Tron listened to the sound of
the soldiers moving away, calling as if to tell each other
that they at least were still alive. His whole instinct was
to stay where he was, to let time pass among the vines
while the appalling vision faded. He heard the click and
scrape of Odah's crutches.

"My brother," came the calm, sweet voice. "I must
perform the ritual for these dead. Will you help me?"

Tron felt his way hesitantly out into the open, looking deliberately away from the place where the blue and
orange bodies lay among the boulders. Soon they would
all be in the darkest shadows of the ravine. That would
be better.

"For the Mohirrim? A ritual?" he said.

"For them. For you. For me. For all who die."

"I will help, if you think it's right."

"Good. Will you do the answers?"

Tron nodded. Odah led the way to a flat rock in the
middle of the ravine. Tron settled his hawk, hooded,
onto a smaller boulder, helped Odah up to stand on the
rock he had chosen, and took his place beside him looking southwest into the gold leavings of O's departure.
The two hunters stared at them, made little mutters of
disapproval, and drifted away like shadows down the
ravine.

Odah raised his arms and began. Tron answered.
Their voices intertwined, lacing again into the echoes
from the cliffs.

Behind them a man heard the sound. His blue-dyed
body had been lying between two boulders, with both
legs broken, while he waited to go to the place which he

called Kwal-Vannor, where warriors who have never wept nor flinched spend their days in loot and slaughter and their evenings in feasting and their nights in the arms of faithful wives. He had been content to wait for death, but at the sound of human voices he raised his head and saw two Paharrim standing among the rocks, making an obscenity close to the dead bodies of the mothers of heroes. He still had two good arrows in his belt, and his bow lay a little way off, unbroken. With great care, completely oblivious of the tearing pain in his legs, he began to drag his body through the boulders.

Odah chanted:

> "Let the old man take to Aa
> The gift of wisdom
> Let the warrior take to Aa
> The gift of courage
> Let the woman take to Aa
> The gift of comfort
> Let the child take to Aa
> The small gifts of childhood."

Tron answered:

> "These they received from the Gods
> These they return."

Both chanted together:

> "These they will find twice over
> In the houses of happiness
> That Aa has prepared for them
> Beyond the dark archway."

As the last notes went twining away together Tron raised his arms and gazed toward the huge stars that were quickly being born in the black-purple sky. Behind and a little below him, the wounded archer tensed his back against a rock, with his useless legs sprawled anyhow beneath him. He saw the two Paharrim silhouetted against the last bars of daylight in the west, a good target, though the distance was difficult to judge. *Take the boy first, because the cripple will be slow to move away.* The archer drew back the string and aimed along the shaft. Alone, defeated, dying, he still did the deed he was made for.

Tron staggered. The fire seared along his spine from the small of his back. The stars went out.

"Lord Gdu!" he screamed.

He did not feel the shock of his own fall among the boulders.

XVII

In the darkness, falling.

A small child, tossed from the clifftop, helpless, falling and trusting.

A pool whose surface glistens blacker than darkness. Swim? I cannot swim. Spreading arms like a swimmer, into the pool. But that glinting surface covers more darkness too thin to carry down-dragging limbs, leaden with exhaustion.

In the darkness falling, falling and trusting.

A cliff of harsh rock. Stay still! Large as a gauntlet the marigold scorpion creeps from a cranny, tail tensed and pulsing. *Tro-ho-ho-ho-hoonn,* nearer, nearer along the ravine the whooping call of the jackal that can never die. Gripped hard, the scorpion is carved jade in the palm, twisting inward and upward to swing the rock open, a place of hiding while the jackal passes.

A slit of pure black. One blind pace. Another. Hands wavering ahead touch the loosely cloying flutter of cobwebs, touch cloth, touch robes, touch black-gloved fingers, reaching, groping. There's a niche two steps to your left. No. Only rough rock. A handhold, a cranny, a ledge. There is no path for me there, my brothers. Climbing. The cobwebs are creepers. Below, black-gloved fingers grope onward, cheated. Heavily up the unending stairs. The falls are silent, the canyon empty, Alaan speaks no more.

A knee and an elbow drag up the body to lie exhausted on cold, flat stone, stone vaguely lit, stone level and

stretching between vast pillars, a peopled cavern, the
Cave of Aa.

Ranked between pillars, each in his place the priests
stand watching a different entrance, so a boy can
creep unseen, unbreathing, to his proper place in the
foremost rank before the dark altar.

On the cupped slab one crippled body, gold-robed,
twisted. Its eyesockets are empty. The clay that covers the lips of the singer has dried into cracks.

Odah, my father!

The whisper echoes in the cave of whispers, grows and
becomes a cry, a full chant. Black cowls turn all with
one movement.

I am Goat!

On the end of the cord where the Goat-Stone should
hang, only the bleached skull of a hare.

The body of Odah smokes on the altar. The smoke
swirls, gathers, draws in on itself and becomes a hovering darkness.

Tron, says the woman, speaking from darkness, How
shall I judge you? Before I go, how shall I judge you?
You lied to the Gods, you murdered the King, you
spilt your sweetwater, you robbed the King's coffin.
Who gave you the right?

(One name. One known word. Gone from the tongue.
Gone from the mind. Gone from the world.)

Nearer hovers the darkness. Nearer. The Cave is empty.
Only the Gods, stone-faced, tunnel-eyed, watch un-
caring. The darkness knows all places of hiding.

(One name. One lost word. Gone from the world. Gone
beyond distance.)

Cupped in a crevice where two flagstones meet a slate-
blue feather, sharp as a jewel.

Blue feather. Blue Hawk.

　　　Lord of the falcons
　　　　Lord of healing
　　　　　"Gdu! Save me!"

The whisper echoes in the cave of whispers, grows and
becomes a cry, a summons, a full-chanted hymn.

Tiny with distance, sharp as a jewel, a boy, blue-robed,

lying among water-worn rocks. A feathered arrow-shaft juts from the center of a seeping circle of blood. Reluctance and weariness and something else unnam-able. The rush of coming, the hawk's plunge to the lure.

The darkness dwindles, puzzled among the echoes. A touch on the feather and it floats away, down, down into a ravine of harsh light as the crevice widens, light that is pain in the shadowed cavern.

Leaping after the feather, falling into light, falling and trusting.

Angry scrub-desert, thorned, rock-pillared, and the King striding through it. A pace to greet him, but he stalks by unfrowning, unsmiling, his brown, fierce eyes looking straight ahead and the jewel fallen from the gold circlet that binds his forehead.

A flat, bare plain, salt to the white horizon. Buried in salt a chariot wheel. The hawk on the wrist hooded in iron, and tied to the gauntlet with twenty thongs. The wheel is free. It begins to turn, to race through the plain. It bursts asunder like a storm-stripped flower. The spokes fly upward, grow, change, and become the flying statues of all the Gods. Huge, they darken the desert noon. They dwindle, dwindle, vanish in distance.

Now out of distance one God returns with the plunge of a hawk. Enormous, He settles on the empty white-ness, a crannied pillar, cool shade beside Him. Shade, dark shade, a hovering darkness. Out of the dark-ness, blue starlings, screaming. Blue horsemen, blue priests, blue ghosts in a circle, closing, closing. Two hoods, two curved beaks, two sets of fumbling fingers tugging at drenched knots. Ah, now, in the instant chosen and given, a sweep of one arm flings up the hawk to ride in the enormous freedom of air, seen there, poised as the blue cloud blots out the sky.

To float in a pool of light. Clutch at a spiky tussock, drag twisted body onto scouring gravel, stand heavy and bent. A scrape and a click as crutches swing that body through known paths among rustling thickets.

Not far now to the nibbled pastures, and beer brewing in Curil's hut, and the reek of fresh-woven blankets, and the long roar of the falls, and O's answer building itself in the fire of His going.

XVIII

TRON SHIFTED A NUMB ARM. INSTANTLY FIRE FLOWED from a point near his spine all down his right leg. He lay deathly still, while the sweat of pain sprang out over his body, and waited until the fire withdrew itself into its dully throbbing center. Only then did he dare to open his eyes.

He was lying on his side in a sort of tunnel of pale blue—no—under a long canopy of blue cloth with the sides let down. The hummocked shape only three feet away was a man lying under a coarse brown blanket. There seemed to be another man lying beyond him, and possibly more beyond that. Out of sight someone gave a long, fluttering groan. Tron's own blanket was of the fine Kalakal weave and pattern, and could well have been the one given him by the ghost's daughter-in-law.

He couldn't move his head without waking the fire again, and his body seemed to be strapped to the bed to prevent him from tossing about, so he shut his eyes again and lay still, listening. The canopy was full of little mutters and stirrings, and once or twice more the same groan of barely endured pain. From farther away came the occasional bleat of sheep, and from farther still, quite loud but so constant that the ears forgot to notice it, the ceaseless boom of the falls. So he was indeed back at Kalakal. He didn't remember crossing the ravine. The last thing he remembered was using Odah's crutches to hobble back . . . no, that had been part of the dream, surely. But the dream had been so real, so clear. Though it had been full of things he didn't understand, it still seemed as true as anything else in his life, as true as the moment when he had first lifted the hawk onto his wrist in the House of O and Aa, as true as the pain in his back.

For a long while he lay quiet, thinking his way through it, piecing the brilliant images into a meaning he could grasp. He didn't notice the stir of movement in the tent until a steady hand took him by the wrist and felt for his pulse. When he opened his eyes he saw the blue robe of a priest of Gdu six inches from his face. Pain warned him not to flinch.

"Awake, then?" said the priest. "Don't try to move. How's the back?

"It hurts. But it's not too bad if I lie still."

"Ugh. You've got to expect that. It's mending, so I've taken you off poppy-cake. You don't want to stay on that longer than you have to. I expect the Gods have sent you some pretty odd dreams, hey?"

"Yes. How long . . ."

"You've been six days in my care. For the first two I thought you were going to Aa, but then you began to mend. You won't be walking for a couple of months, mind you. All right? If you think you can't stand it I'll put you back on poppy-cake for a bit longer, but you're better without it."

"Yes. I know. Thank you, my brother, my father."

The priest grunted and moved away. Tron noticed that when he talked to the other patients he did so in the proper half-chant, and not in the brusque conversational tones he had used when talking between priests. It was strange that he didn't yet know that they were now living in an altered world, where none of that mattered any more. Strange, strange. And I have been in the Cave of Aa, and returned alive, as no man has done since Saba. Strange, strange.

The days passed with a slow, appalling pace. Men were carried out, half-healed to convalesce in other tents, or dead to be buried. More men were brought in, savagely wounded, to lie and groan and mutter. Tron shut his mind to all this, lying perfectly still through the creeping hours, summoning into himself the great invisible healing force that lay over the meadows. The pain steadily lessened.

On the fourth day he heard ceremonial horns sounding, and the clink of harness and the thud of horsehooves. Young priests of Gdu lifted the four beds nearest him and carried them elsewhere; in their place an ornate tapestry was raised to screen him, so that he lay gazing at a brilliant scene of Gdu flying above a plain where a group of nobles rode hawking. Then the tapestries parted and the King came in laughing.

He looked very tired. His face was drawn and crusted here and there with a mixture of sweat and dust, but the air around him seemed to tingle with his excitement and happiness. He stretched his arms down in a gesture that would have become a hug of joy in their meeting if Tron had not been wounded; life and warmth seemed to flow from his fingertips.

"Ah, Tron," he whispered, squatting onto a little stool beside the mattress, "I came as soon as I could—I've been riding since dawn. They told me three days ago that you'd woken—we've had a messenger ride each day from Kalakal with news of you—but we had to deal with another swarm of Mohirrim first."

"What's happening, Majesty?"

"Too early to say. They won't go on coming like this, a few hundred at a time. So far we've rounded most of them up—d'you know we've not taken a single prisoner, man, woman, or child?—but some of this last lot got back through the pass. So fairly soon I think we'll have a real horde to cope with. We'll manage provided we can keep them up on the tableland, because we know the ravine crossings and the watering places. If I get it right we won't have to do much real fighting. Thirst will do our work for us. But after that . . . Tron, what happened in the pass on the night of Her Most Brightness?"

"We performed a ritual and the Gods left."

"Left? You mean . . . that's not what I wanted. I need to know whether I can take an army through the

Pass Gebindrath without coming under the curse of that kind woman."

"Yes."

"Is that all? Yes, just like that? Listen, Tron, you've no idea what an army's like for rumors. The priests of Sinu who had carried your litter came back from the pass with the news that their One was dead, but that he had said that the curse was lifted. Then we got news that you were wounded and likely to die, and that the crippled priest of O . . ."

"He has died also."

"How did you know? I gave orders that you were not to be told."

"I saw his body in the Cave of Aa."

In the mid-rush of explanation the King stopped short, like a racing horse hauled back onto its haunches. His face wore its closed, armored look while he stared at Tron unblinking. At last he sighed.

"Yes," he said, "you were close to that place, I'm told. But I can't follow those paths. You see, Tron, what they're saying in the army is that the curse is still there. Half Her priests were slaughtered in the place, and of you three two died and one came near to dying. But if *you* will tell me plain that the curse is lifted, then I shall know it's true. And if I *know,* I can persuade the others to come with me."

Tron hesitated. Truth? All he knew was misty, half-glimpsed, ungraspable. All he had done had been for the sake of the Gods. He had been a tool in Their hands, and the finished work was Their affair. But now he remembered that there were really two Trons—not only this obedient and willing tool but also a boy who had met a King in the shadow of a desert outcrop, and who had discovered there the obligations of friendship.

"It's difficult to explain," he said. "Sometimes I think I understand, and sometimes I think I'm making it all up because I can't help looking for some sort of explanation. But I'm sure the pass is clear."

"The curse of that kind woman is lifted?" insisted the King.

"It wasn't Her curse, it was the priests'. Oh, she was there, but . . . She was there because the Gods needed the Kingdom to be closed off, I think. But now She's left. They've all left, all but . . ."

"They'll come back," said the King, almost flippantly. "But you are sure that I can come and go through the pass and She will not care?"

"Yes. The Kingdom is no longer closed."

"That's true. D'you know, I had news from the north only five days ago that a party of merchants from beyond the marshes had made their way through somehow and were asking permission to trade! And another thing—do you remember how I took you that first day to show you the salt valley? Apparently salt is a valuable stuff in Falathi! That'll be something to start on when this war's over. Lord Sinu, but the Mohirrim are warriors! I'm beginning to think that if only I could set up some sort of alliance with them, train them and control them—if you can tame a Blue Hawk, Tron, I can tame the Mohirrim—why! perhaps that was a sign! What do you think?"

"I don't know. A sign? Of what?"

"I've said this to no one else, Tron. Sometimes I dare not even say it to myself. But we've been cooped up too long between the marshes and the mountains, while outside there's a whole world to conquer. I'm beginning to think that with the Mohirrim on my side I could do just that!"

Sitting on the stool with his knees hunched under his chin, the King poured out plans and dreams. Tron was too tired now to listen in detail, but with a half-drowsing mind he saw that the King was, as it were, like the great river itself; even on the placid days when they had first met he had contained in himself energy and purpose, just as the calm reaches of the river contained their moving weight of water, building up the pressure that would roar in foam through the gorge and thunder over the falls. The struggle with the priests and this war were like that, but even in the flurry and hurl of them

the King's mind already sought the unknown lands beyond.

Tron now knew himself to be quite different, two-
natured, but beneath both natures something like a desert well, dug centuries ago, deep and still feeding on
streams that had never seen the light. He knew too that
if he was to answer his puzzle he must explore not only
outward, like the King, but inward into those depths.

"I'm tiring you," said the King, rising suddenly. "I'll
come again as soon as I can. And you've got to get well,
Tron, though the priest of Gdu who's been in charge of
you says that you're healing faster than he dared hope.
That's good. I want to go hawking with you again before too long."

"Where is my hawk, Majesty?"

"Here, and it's being looked after. But it won't let
anyone near it without a fight. It *is* like a Mohir, you
know."

"Majesty, there's a shepherd's shelter up above the
Jaws of Alaan. Will you give orders for the hawk to be
moved up there? And there's a girl in the village called
Taleel; she must feed it and keep the cave clean. It must
see no one else."

"It'll go quite wild again if you treat it like that,
Tron."

"It is wild, Majesty. It cannot be tamed."

The King laughed, once more not understanding. He
smiled his farewell, but Tron could see that as he vanished behind the tapestries he was already thinking of
the next things he must do. His voice dwindled down
the ward, a cheerful exchange of soldier-talk with the
wounded men.

For several days no new wounded came to Kalakal.
Muscle by muscle Tron recovered the use of his limbs.
Where he reached the fiery barrier of pain he found
that if he needed to he could, by the use of his own will
and the help of the power around him, roll the flames
aside and pass through without flinching. The pain was
there, but it was somehow outside him. But mostly there

was no need; he discovered calm and gentle movements, without waking the fires, to exercise his mending body as he lay there. He also rested, thought, and sang in his mind long hymns of praise to Gdu.

Ten days after the King's visit the priest of Gdu was accompanied on his rounds by a red-robed priest whom Tron recognized as Tanta, the deputy he had first awakened that night in the Temple. He now carried the lion-headed staff on the One of Sinu. As they straightened from beside a mattress a few places away, Tron heard Tanta say, "You are indeed a Lord of healing, my brother. There were men we sent back from the battles whom I thought it would have been kinder to kill, and here I find them well on the road to health."

"Praise the God, not me, my brother. And this mountain air. Now, take this boy here . . ."

The new One of Sinu stared down at Tron. It seemed somehow wrong that he was not also blind.

"We have met," he said drily. "The King sends you his good wishes, boy."

"What is happening, my brother, my father? Is he well?"

"He is well. Nothing else has happened. No more of the blue demons have come through the pass, but the Lord Kalavin led a scouting party up there and found a great rope bridge across the place where the road was broken, a bridge strongly guarded. That seems a sign that the demons intend to come back, and come in greater force, so we are preparing for them. I have come to warn my brother that soon there may be many more wounded needing his care, and to arrange for those who are fit to travel to be carried back to the plains. Can the boy go, my brother?"

"On a litter, certainly."

"No," said Tron, "I must stay here."

"Your place is needed, boy," snapped the One of Sinu.

"I have a hut in Upper Kalakal," said Tron. "It is mine. I built it. Let me be carried there."

"You may be the King's friend . . ." began the One of Sinu angrily.

"I remember this child, my brother," said the priest of Gdu in a curiously quiet voice. "It has been puzzling me since he came here, like a dream one cannot recapture, but when he spoke just now . . . He was the child who took the hawk at the ceremony of Renewal, half a year gone by. I think the hand of the Gods is on him. He must do what he must."

The One of Sinu snorted and turned away. He was a true priest of the old sort, Tron could see, living by ritual and precedent. Though he and Tron had been for a moment allies, in his heart he wanted nothing to do with a child who broke rituals, built huts in remote shepherd villages, struck up friendships with Kings, crept around the Temple at night disguised as a austringer, and told Major Priests outright what they must and must not do. Watching him stalk stiffly away down the ward, Tron felt a surge of pity for him. There would be many like him left in the Temple—what would they do, now that the world was so changed? How many generations would they spend performing meaningless rituals in front of empty altars? He sighed and withdrew again into his own depths.

Fifteen days later Tron was walking, with one arm around Curil's shoulders, in front of the huts at Kalakal. Under his free arm swung one of Odah's crutches, but he was standing straight and was now at last sure that in the end his back would heal completely, and that he would once again walk like a normal man. But it was a slow business. After even a few minutes he seemed to be very tired, and the ache in his back began to seep outward along his nerves.

"I must rest, Curil."

"That's right. Haste was what made the hut fall down, they say. Hello! What's that? News! Talk about haste!"

Following the line of Curil's arm, Tron could see the coming dust cloud, a puff of fawn smoke, narrow and glinting at its near end, several miles away through the mottled terrain of the scrubland beyond the ravine. To his eyes it seemed to be barely moving, but by the time he had rested and then made another feeble circuit he could just pick out the blue glimmer of the pennon on the rider's lance. He allowed Curil to help him onto his cot in front of his hut, and lay there on his side, watching. At last a horn rang out and another answered it, and then the messenger led his horse between the sentries at the edge of the ravine. The animal looked near foundering. Tron saw the glint of brandished swords and a second later heard the sound of men shouting. A soldier ran off toward the spread of tents along the lower slopes. Curil was already striding down the hill when the uneven, wavering note of cheers began to spread through the wards of wounded men.

Toward evening next day, long caterpillars of dust began to rise in the scrubland, where the first trains of litters and stretchers brought what seemed like an army of wounded soldiers toward Kalakal. By a promise of beer and roast mutton Curil coaxed one of them to come and sit with the villagers round their fire and tell them what had happened. This was a tough little man from the northern marshlands who'd had his shield arm horribly mangled by one of the Mohirrim war hounds. His twanging northern accent was made harder to understand by the slur from the poppy-cake he'd been given to dull the pain, but he repeated himself so often that at length his hearers puzzled his story out.

"Sinu! But that was a fight! They'd left their women an' wagons behind this time, an' I don't wonder. So many of 'em! An' I'd thought we was a big army! Huh! They could've eaten us for breakfast if we'd let 'em! But we knew what we was doing. First we let one of their scouting parties get right along the road to where it ends in the big sands—y'know, it looks as if it's not going anywhere from there, and you've only got to ride a mile into them dunes and you're lost. That was while the main body of their army was still coming through the pass. And before that we'd spent a lot of time making two or three trails up toward the place where we wanted to lead 'em. We'd even built a couple of villages and made 'em look as if they'd just been abandoned—you know, just to make the savages feel they was getting somewhere at last. And we'd left other bits of signs along the way—a smashed chariot, a bit of dropped baggage with jewels and silk in it, campfires, that sort of thing. An' we let 'em see our patrols, always from that direction.

"They didn't stop to think. They came after us like a dog after an otter. Sinu! they was quick. A couple of our patrols got caught and they wiped 'em clean out. But you see they got to be quick. Army like that can't hang around in desert country—they got to get to where there's water for their horses and food for themselves. We put up a bit of a fight at a couple of ravines, but then we let 'em bust through. We even let 'em capture our main camp—tents, bedding, hangings, clothes, wine—lashings of wine—a bit of food. But no water. Not one drop.

"So we sat around that night among the thorn bushes and listened to twenty thousand men getting blind drunk. Noise! I daresay they thought it was music. Next morning they woke up (them as *did* wake up, 'cause there'd been something in some of that wine) and found themselves sitting in a flat desert bit between three ravines with us all around, grinning at 'em from the far sides. There was a narrow way out at one end, and that was where most of the fighting happened to begin with. I saw it like watching a hunting, because my Lord's household was guarding the ravine to the right. The savages came swarming down, all disorderly, and our front rank gave a bit and gave a bit, slowing 'em down, and then the second ranks came through and punched 'em back into the mess of their own second ranks. Then they'd draw off and come again, just the same way, not learning anything.

"Them dogs is a terror—*I* should know—till you work out how to deal with 'em. One man takes the dog and the other takes the savage, that's the way. But the horses was pitiful. One charge, I saw a savage riding full tilt and before he reached our lines his horse dropped dead, just like that, died of thirst at full gallop! Y'see, that made a difference too, their horses not being fresh. They was a handful enough as it was.

"Then, after quite a bit of that, they went back to the middle of their plain and thought about it, and then they did the sensible thing—nah, not *sensible*—sensible thing would have been to surrender—but at least they decided to try to break out all round at the same time. Not as difficult as it sounds, 'cause we couldn't guard every yard of it. The bit they was on was, oh, couple of miles and almost twice that long. Our orders was to push 'em back where we could, but soon as they got across in any numbers to let 'em join up and send a runner back to the cavalry, lying in reserve behind us, and they'd come up in force and punch 'em back over the cliff. It worked a treat, far as anything works a treat in a battle. Quite a long while they was losing ten, twenty men for every one of ours. Y'see, in a lot of places they couldn't get the dogs across, let alone the horses. Even so they kept on coming at us like madmen, never gave us a rest, an' by the middle of the afternoon they'd got a couple of those bridges of theirs across farther up the ravine from us—don't know how we let that happen—and then everything was a real mess for a bit. I expect it was really all under control if you'd been looking at it from the outside, but it didn't feel like that from the inside, just dust, and yells, an' a blue savage coming at you round a thorn bush an' you've only got half a second to get your guard up, an' you can't relax even in the middle of your own troop, 'cause one savage will fling himself at half a dozen armed men soon as he sees 'em, an' then there's dogs whose masters have been killed racing up and down through the mess biting anything that isn't blue—that's how I got mine—things seemed to be calming down a bit by then, but he came at me from behind, an' . . . well, that's about all I saw with my own eyes, 'cause though I still had my good sword-arm my Lord sent me back to the rear saying it was as good as over anyway.

"Our real camp was tucked away in another ravine, so I reported there. But there was wounded men coming in most of the night, so I heard what was going on. It finished up with the King taking his troops out of the place they'd first attacked an' letting what was left of the savages get away that way while he cleaned up the ones who'd made it over the ravines—drove 'em back an' let 'em straggle away up farther into the desert, fewer than us now, more than half of 'em on foot, no food, not much water up that way. There won't be many of 'em left in a day or two, I shouldn't think. An' then when the army's had a bit of rest he's going to see if he can force the pass."

That night Tron dreamed a dream he'd had once before in Kalakal, about the great rock plain full of statues of the Gods, and his search for the Lord Gdu, and his finding a sand heap on which lay the Blue Hawk, dead, being eaten by ants. This time the dream continued. When he gazed round the plain he saw that all the statues had turned into ordinary pillars of rock, such as dotted the desert above the Temple of Tan. But there was still one statue of Gdu, smaller than the others, and becoming steadily less before his eyes. This remorseless dwindling seemed more horrible than anything else in the dream. He woke when the statue was no larger than a man.

It was very early dawn. Carefully he rolled himself out of his bed, picked up the crutches, and laboriously swung himself away from the huts and along the hillside path. The green world was drenched with spray. He seemed to breathe strength from its sappy freshness, but even so he needed to rest every thirty yards. The sun rose with blazing suddenness and twinkled into its seven colors off a million grass-poised droplets. Below him horn answered horn as the sentries changed posts. Sheep bleated, but he was over the round of the spur before the village truly woke.

The hawk was in the cave, stiff on its perch and glowering at the morning brilliance. The moment it saw him it flung itself back with wildly beating wings, but the tug of its leg thongs threw it off balance so that it tumbled clumsily to the ground, still in a frenzy of pinions, too crazed with fear of his approach even to strike at him when he bent down to loose the thongs. Even in the worst days at the Temple of Tan it had never seemed so wild as this.

White fire burned down his spine as he lifted the bird by the thongs, a blur of slate-blue wings. Unwincing, he gripped the legs above the talons with his left hand and moved the right to grip one wing close to the joint and force it back against the body. Another quick change of grip and he had the hawk the right way up, both wings held firmly folded. Blood oozed from a gash in the back of his left hand, in just the same place as that where the hawk had once struck the One of Gdu in the Temple. But apart from a few galvanic jerks the bird lay still between his hands, glaring furiously about it. He waited in stillness and let the pain in his back die away. Then he caught it unaware and managed to slip the hood over its head.

With only one crutch, because he needed an arm to carry the hawk, the walk across the hillside was slow and painful. He found Taleel sitting on an antheap and winding wool into thread. He put the bird down on another hillock and hobbled toward her. She looked up and jumped to her feet.

"Tron! You look awful. You oughtn't to have come so far. Are you all right?"

"Yes. I had to come."

He eased himself onto the grass and lay there for a while, letting the pain-sweat dry and watching her quick fingers, clever and thoughtless on the thread, and the hypnotic dance of her bobbin.

"You've not changed," he said at last.

"You have."

"Most things have changed, but you haven't. That's good."

"Oh, I've changed. Didn't you know? The King was so pleased with Curil that he gave him all sorts of rights and titles and a gold necklace, just for looking after you, and then Curil was so pleased with me that he gave me nine sheep of my own, so now I only need twenty-two more and I can marry anybody I like and not just who Curil tells me!"

She pointed out her possessions, grazing among the flock and indistinguishable to Tron's eye from all the others. She told him their names and pedigrees and asked him to bless them for her.

"Not yet," he said. "I want to tell you something— it's a story about the Gods."

"Like the one you told me about the jackal who can never die?"

"It's not that kind of story, really. I don't even know if it's true. I've pieced it together out of some dreams I had, but they may only have been poppy-cake dreams; and a few things that Odah said; and everything that's happened; and what I found inside my soul. But I don't think there's any point in telling the King, or one of the priests, or Curil, because their minds are all fixed and busy with what's happening on the surface of things . . . you remember the Wise, who come in so many of the hymns and stories?"

She nodded.

"Well, suppose they were ordinary men and women, just like us. They weren't any wiser than we are, but they were cleverer. I mean they had found out how to do extraordinary things, like building an enormous dam across the Jaws of Alaan, to . . . I don't know why they did it . . . it doesn't matter. I used to think that the hymns contained all the knowledge there was, but now I think it's only a tiny amount compared with what the Wise might have known. And suppose even then they were always looking for new knowledge, that's how they might have found the Gods."

Taleel's bobbin stopped as if stuck in the instant.

"But the Gods were there before the Wise," she said.

"That doesn't mean that men always knew about

Them. Taleel, this is only a story. It's a might-have-been. It's a way of explaining to myself what's happened to me, and a feeling about what I've got to do next. But suppose . . . Yes, the Gods were always there. They have no beginning and They don't die. But They don't belong in this world. The Wise found Them somewhere else, outside, among the stars somehow. And because there was so much power in the Gods, the Wise thought they could use it, so somehow they managed to trap Them down into this world. . . ."

"That wasn't right," said Taleel, frowning. It was hard for her to understand—Tron wasn't sure how much he understood himself and how much was only the aftereffects of poppy dreams, but he was glad that she grasped what mattered to him.

"No," he said. "And it wasn't wise either, but it was clever. Suppose the Gods aren't clever, not even as clever as you and me. But They're strong, stronger even than the Wise understood. So just by being here, and living for ever, slowly They would make the world quite different. Listen, when I trained the Blue Hawk I was much cleverer than it was, but even so it made me different. It didn't *plan* to change me, but I was changed. The way I lived, the way I thought, the kind of person I was—all different. It might have been the same when the Wise captured the Gods. You see, the Gods would have been like the hawk, and the Wise like me, and so the world became different. The Wise slowly became less clever, became like we are now, and when they remembered the things that had happened in the old days they talked about them like something in a dream, and in the end they turned them into hymns. . . ."

"But the hymns are true! They've got to be!"

"Perhaps they're as true as we can understand now. I mean when the hymn says that Saba murdered his father and the Lord Gdu made him alive again perhaps that's just a sort of picture of what really happened, something that won't go into pictures, but something with the same sort of rightness and wrongness in it. I don't know. . . . But listen. I think the Gods have

been working for ages to escape from the trap—which
is what our world is for Them. I can't explain how except by making a picture. It's like a great weight of water held up behind an irrigation dam. If there's a small
hole in the dam, the water can burst out and smash the
dam down and roar away down the valley, but it can't
make the hole by itself. It needs something—oh, a little
burrowing rat, or something like that. Compared with
the water the rat is completely feeble, and of course it
isn't burrowing on purpose to let the water out—it's
making a nest-hole, or digging for worms or something,
but then . . . Do you understand?"

"I've seen sheep break out of a pen. Often it's a stupid little lamb that finds the first hole, and then the
mother gets frantic to follow it and barges a way
through, and then suddenly they all come tumbling
out."

"Yes, that's right. Now, suppose the Gods are a bit
like that. Then They'd need two things. First They'd
have to build up the pressure—like the weight of water,
or your mother sheep becoming frantic. So They'd close
off a bit of the world and concentrate all Their power
there. They'd need a place that *could* be closed, with
barriers all around it—deserts, marshes, mountains.
The Kingdom's like that. Even then it would take Them
thousands of flood-times, but when it was done there'd
come a special season when the trap was weakest at one
particular place—the Pass of Gebindrath that night of
Aa's Most Brightness. Then They'd need men to make
the first small break in the trap. I don't know why, but I
suppose if men made it in the first place . . . I sometimes think that even the rituals we used to perform at
the Great Temple might have been part of the trap. We
were always summoning the Gods down, binding Them
into the lives of men, holding Them to us. I even felt,
last time we were going to the Temple, that the Gods
didn't want to get too close. But suppose everything
that's happened—not just to me but to you and the
King and Onu Ovalaku and the Mohirrim—was all
brought about so that Odah and the One of Sinu and I

should journey to the pass and there make a new ritual, doing exactly the opposite, asking a God to leave. . . ."

"How did you know what to do?"

"At first I thought it was simply that Aa came in the night and told Odah, and that everything we did was absolutely necessary, even our being a blind old man and a cripple and a boy. Now I don't think it was like that. The Gods aren't like that. They couldn't tell Odah exactly what to do. But really it didn't matter what we did—I mean it didn't matter what words we chanted and what steps we danced. What mattered was that we three should believe with all our souls that what we were doing was what the Gods wanted, because then we would be putting all the strength that was in us into asking one of the Gods to leave that place. It had to be a great ritual, but only so that *we* could believe in it. What the Gods needed was the strength of our souls, all aimed at one point, at the full moon, in that narrow place, to cause the first minute crack in the trap. After that They could burst through. And we did it. We all three felt afterward . . . you know that sometimes a man can make his body find more strength than he knew was in it, and afterward the body will lie in a sort of coma for several days? It was like that with our souls. We gave the whole strength of them to the Gods. So the One of Sinu died next day, and Odah and I felt as though we had no life in us—he spoke as if he didn't expect to live many more days. . . ."

"But you're not going to die! I won't let you! You're much better."

"Yes. But I would have died. Only when I felt the arrow I cried to my Lord Gdu. He made me live."

"You mean He hadn't gone yet?"

"He'd gone, but He came back."

"He must love you very much."

"Yes. No. The words are wrong. I think . . . Perhaps the Gods didn't only change us, we changed Them. He'd lived so long among us, and we'd called Him Lord of Healing all that time, so perhaps . . . You've seen how wild my hawk is, but if it were flying overhead and I swung my lure, perhaps it would still come down to it. Most of what I've been telling you is just guesses. Perhaps it isn't any truer than the hymns. But I *know* my Lord Gdu, somehow, in some way, came back to heal me because I cried to Him."

"Where is He now?"

"Here."

"Oh! . . . Tron, you remember that day we first met, and I screamed because I was so frightened. I was frightened before you came. I felt there was someone watching me. Was He here then?"

"Yes."

"But I can't feel Him now."

"He's here and not here. He came back no more than He needed to, or He would have been trapped in the world for another age. Even now He is like . . . like a hawk, freed from its master but tangled into a bush by the leg thongs it still wears. Now we must free Him."

"Now at once?"

"At the sun's noon."

"The sun? And just now you said 'the full moon'! They really are gone—O and that kind woman and the rest?"

"I don't know. I've been delirious, and eating poppy-cake. All the little hymns say that poppy-cake visions can't be trusted."

"But still you do think there aren't any Gods any more," she insisted, her voice hushed as she began to grasp the hugeness of the change.

"Oh, there are Gods," he said. "There must be. Look, you've got hands—you wouldn't have them if there were nothing to grasp. You've got eyes—you wouldn't have them if there were nothing to see. Just like that I've got something in my soul which is there to love and serve the Gods. So even if all my supposings are right there must still be the true Gods of the world to love and serve."

"But where are They?"

"I don't know. Do you ever hear the noise from the falls?"

"Only sometimes when I wake up in the middle of the night. We're so used to it here."

"Perhaps the true Gods are like that—inside us, all round us, like the air we breathe without noticing. The noise these other Gods made meant we could never hear Them."

"What are you going to *do,* though?" said Taleel in a down-to-earth, almost nagging tone. "You can't just build a shrine and see Who comes."

"I could," said Tron. "But first . . . you know, I've sometimes felt that I was becoming two different people. There's a me to serve the Gods and do whatever They want without choice or question, and a me to choose and be free. But then I remember that I first really began to know the Gods when I *was* free, alone at the Temple of Tan, training my hawk. So there aren't really two of me, only two halves which come together when I'm free to choose and then choose to serve."

"What are you going to *do,* though?" she said again.

"Go with the King, if he'll let me. He's going to conquer the world with the help of the Mohirrim—though it won't end like that—nothing ever does. He understands about choosing. He didn't order me to help him—he asked me."

"And you'll find these new Gods of yours somewhere out there?" she said, waving her brown, square hand toward the mountains.

"I don't think They're like that," said Tron. "If there's an answer, part of it is deep inside me and part of it out among people. It's two halves again, which only become true if you put them together."

"Well, good luck," she said. "I'm staying here. Kalakal's a good place. Only . . ."

"Yes?"

"If you find a strong young man with brown eyes and twenty-two sheep, you'll tell him about me, won't you?"

Tron laughed. With great care he turned himself over and lay face down on the grass, silent, letting the energies above the gorge gather and tighten round him. Even the steady drumming of the falls seemed to be softened as if by an invisible barrier. He did not feel time passing but knew the moment without looking to see how the shadows of the grass blades had shortened. Using the crutch, he hauled himself to his feet and hobbled to the hawk. Hooded though it was, it fought against his touch.

"Come and help me," he called. "Good. Now, I need both my hands to hold its wings. Can you untie the leg thongs—you'll see the long bit beyond the knot slips through a slit and then . . . that's right. No, go right round to the other side in case it strikes at you with its free foot. Good. Now the hood. Slip it off forward and down. Don't snatch, but get your hand out of the way as quick as you can. Well done. Now I can't use even one crutch like this, so you'll have to help me down to the cliff edge. Put your arm round my waist. All right? Let's try a few steps. . . . Yes, that'll do. Stop. Now listen, Taleel. This is a ritual. All you need to do is to help me move slowly and evenly. Don't say anything. We begin."

The need to move in step turned their pace into an almost dancelike rhythm. Taleel's arm, used to manhandling sheep, was tough and steady. Nothing else moved, and the hills waited in silence. Even the prisoned hawk stopped struggling as they came nearer and nearer to the green lip of the gorge. There Tron stopped and held the bird forward like an offering held up toward an altar. He shut his eyes and concentrated his soul into the ideas of release, of going, of freedom. He knew it did not matter what words he chanted, so he let them come to his lips without thought.

> "Lord of healing
> Lord of the air
> Lord of my life
> Be wounded no more.
> Fly beyond air
> Fly beyond my prison
> Be free from my service

Free from my worship
Free from my love."

His voice sounded weak and almost bloodless, but that didn't matter. At the last quiet note he opened his eyes and with a smooth movement tossed the hawk outward and upward. The wings opened so swiftly that he felt the brush of the spread primaries against his palms, and then the bird was whirling away with swift, pulsing wingbeats, dwindling fast but clear against the white pillar of spray above the falls. Suddenly the pulse of wings stopped and it curved out of its path in a smooth glide, slowed, and hung hovering.

All around him Tron sensed the world poised and still. He felt the forces of the God contract and contract, moving away from him, gathering into a cone of energies above the hovering bird, and at last in one clean instant withdraw from the world.

He looked up, almost expecting to see the sky open to let the traveler through and close again behind Him, but there was only the glaring disc of the sun, hazed with the mist from the falls but still too bright to stare at.

He looked back to the hawk. For a few heartbeats it hung, sharp-seen against the white spray. Then its wings swung back and it was hurtling in that familiar dive, down into the gulf, down out of sight, into the life it was made for.

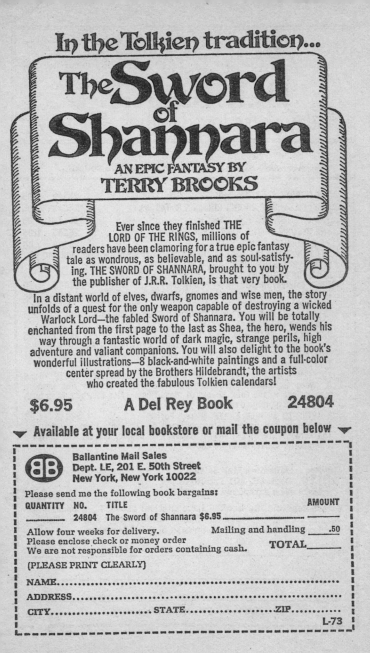